T0356324

THE LIVES AND DEATHS
OF VÉRONIQUE BANGOURA

THE LIVES AND DEATHS OF VÉRONIQUE BANGOURA
by Tierno Monénembo

Translation by Ryan Chamberlain
Copyright © 2025 by Ryan Chamberlain

This is the first English translation of the work originally published by
Editions du Seuil under the title SAHARIENNE INDIGO.
Copyright © 2022, Editions du Seuil. All Rights Reserved.

Published by Schaffner Press

Cover and interior book design by Evan Johnston.

*This work received support for excellence in publication and
translation from Albertine Translation, a program created by
Villa Albertine and funded by FACE Foundation.*

Library of Congress Control Number: 2024950605

ISBN 978-1-63964-059-1
EPUB 978-1-63964-060-7
EPDF 978-1-63964-061-4

Manufactured in the United States of America.

THE LIVES
AND DEATHS OF
VÉRONIQUE
BANGOURA

TIERNO MONÉNEMBO
TRANSLATED BY RYAN CHAMBERLAIN

SCHAFFNER PRESS
TUCSON, ARIZONA

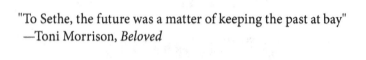

"To Sethe, the future was a matter of keeping the past at bay"
—Toni Morrison, *Beloved*

YOU'RE FORCING MY HAND, Madame Corre. Could you imagine me, Véronique Bangoura, writing a book? Belting out my life on the plaza like a convict or diva? With whose breath, exactly? What pen? Of course not. There's nothing special about my life, I promise. I only have this handful of events to my name because they happened to other people as I passed by. Do I look like a Carmen or Lolita to you? I'm just me, your neighbor: the simple woman in apartment 43. The one whose personality pairs so well with anonymity and quiet.

And what would be the point? Mine or someone else's, they're all the same shocks, the same endless hurricanes. Better to keep quiet, clamp down around it, take things as they come. That's what I think, anyway. Grit your teeth and bear it. Then, soon as you can, forget—forget everything. That's all I'm interested in. I'm not here to tell a story: what I want to do is turn the page, empty the memory. Dump my grief and regrets down the drain.

Do we understand each other?

As a girl I used to dream I turned into a sheep—that noble

creature—happy to graze and let time drift on without worrying about some appointment made the day before or tomorrow's forecast. And it suited me, my ewe nature, until I crossed paths with a certain Madame Corre. So I'm finally giving in. Because you are a dogged, tyrannical snoop.

It's been barely a year since we met. How did you manage in so little time to fold yourself into the faithful dumb shadow that's walked behind me since my mother bounced me on her knee? How'd you do it? Here I am standing on Rue Mouffetard, nose pressed to a pastry shop window, trembling, shaken less by the cold than solitude and worry, hands locked in fists so the cart wouldn't take off. You come up to me like a ghost. Slide into my life easy as an eel. That's right, I can't escape you. It took you all but three days to bury me in criticism.

"It has little to do with wheelchairs," you said, "the job of a personal care assistant. Often it's the ones who still have their legs that are sickly—just look at the miscreants and psychopaths! You're not even listening to me, Countess. Oh, you've got an Ottobock! My cousin is in the same line of work as you—I lent her a hand a time or two. They aren't the best, Ottobocks. What you want is a Küschall. Küschalls are the Rolls-Royce of wheelchairs, especially the upholstery—armrests and so forth. Incidentally, why do they call you 'Countess'? Why would they be so cruel? No one's ever seen a countess who looks like that."

I was just starting. I had everything to learn. Like what was meant, first of all, by "personal care assistant." A personal care assistant just pushes a chair with a half-dead man in it. I was expecting something a little more expressive, something magnanimous and dazzling. "Third Kidney," for example. "Extra Heart" or "Backup Soul." But that was it: "personal care assistant." The choice is limited for people like me: nanny or personal care assistant. I escaped the first, but I couldn't avoid the second.

"The florist," Rue Cardinal-Lemoine! "The baker," Rue Monge! "The haberdasher," La Clef Ave! And me, "the personal care assistant," only everywhere: from the Jardin des Plantes to Cluny, from the Sorbonne to the Panthéon, Austerlitz to Notre-Dame, according to the weather's caprice and the mood of his eyes. Under the plane trees on the square, where I spend most of my time, the whispers are only for me—the "personal care" assistant. Winter and summer, I cart around this wheelchair from one street to another, one mood to the next. To give myself strength, I hang on to this morbid internal monologue, interrupted only when I buy bread or when the two of us talk at Vésuve or on the benches on the square.

No size, weight, age, or surname: "personal care assistant." My earthly presence is summed up by this one title. Only you, with your yellow cat curiosity, cared to know more.

But where to start, since now—willingly or unwillingly—I owe you a book?

AT THE VERY BEGINNING, it wasn't my name: Véronique Bangoura. I had another one altogether, a completely different look. A separate omen. I was of the age when the mind can't distinguish ash from flour, to borrow a phrase from the grannies back home. I couldn't hit as hard as my friends, but the gods watched over me. At my birth, the seer read from a fortunate mouth: I would mature easily, immune to fate, another Moses saved from the current—this time crowned with braids and in nothing but a loincloth. Then came the day I had to jump down from the balcony and run away. Since then a lethal, implacable hand has pushed me forward, amusing itself as I falter and collapse at every ditch and gust of wind.

As soon as I left the house I knew I'd never come back. The bronze chain, the precious and invisible chain binding me to my parents, just broke. The door all my childhood fantasies came and went through—in the absence of my parents—was forever barricaded. I had just thrown myself from the balcony into the world, a place I knew nothing about. My parents wouldn't let me go any farther than the zoo unless we were in the car, with tinted windows and the pedal to the floor. Outside was a shady universe: neighborhoods with bizarre names that reeked of depravity, murder, laziness, decay. An endless jumble of cinderblocks and rusted sheet metal where the unemployed were strung out on tambananya booze and girls in rags were surrounded by rat-bitten kids. Nothing interesting on that side of the world. I wasn't allowed over there. Papa was adamant about that, and Maman saw to it as long as her lovers left her the time. They were far from thinking about what the good Lord had in store for me—for me only—that wild night from among billions that make up the moment. That wild night my life toppled over far beyond the zoo, far beyond the bridge of the hanged, far beyond the stadium, far beyond reason.

It was early May, the time of the first rains in a city where Nialèyo, the goddess of lightning, could thunder and piss for days and weeks without stopping. Under a starless sky, Conakry looked like a deep cave dotted along the walls with a few fireflies. I guessed at where I was going by the glow of lights glimmering in the shops and display windows. When I jumped off the balcony, I could have exploded with rage. Five or six hours later, fear replaced rage, and then disgust. Fear of waking up transformed into an iguana or a snake, like you hear about in stories. Wicked Inna Bassal wastes no time. That devil! She turns thieves into iguanas and killers into rattlesnakes—or the opposite, according to her mood or fantasy. Unless her thunder blows the city up beforehand. Sweating, my heart almost surging out my nose, I ran, zigzagging between rockpiles and muddy alleyways, jumping over holes and hurdling fences. The police sirens quit shrieking once I reached a wetland whose water had risen above the mangrove and water lily leaves. Stalkers and stray dogs took over quickly. Just the place to get molested or have your kneecaps busted. I'd lost my shoes and needed several minutes to find my footing. I wound up falling into a creek that had a little bridge leading over it to a market alley with a smell that made me want to repeatedly throw up. I collapsed on a mound of rotten mangoes scattered across the sidewalk.

Like everyone else, I had heard of old Ténin but never seen her. Still, I recognized her the second she woke me up. Sleepy, or because of the drink she'd offered that my throat refused to swallow, I tried staggering through a few steps. She took me by the shoulders and patted my back to stop the coughing.

"Your name on the radio, the police on your trail? I don't know what you did, but it must have been serious."

She dumped another glassful of her mixture down my throat, not caring if I might die from the hacking it started, then dried my mouth with the bottom of her shirt before lifting her index finger to the dark lowland that opened up between an abandoned factory and the ocean.

"Go, my child. There, in the unfinished house, you'll find shelter from bad luck and thieves, you have Ténin Condé's word!"

I skinned my knees and elbows going down the embankment, chased by her gloomy voice:

"A genie is in love with you! He won't stand any man near you. He won't stand for it!"

The witch was right: an abandoned pit lined the lowlands where machines were rusting near a roofless, decrepit building with moss-covered walls. You couldn't hear anything out there, no sirens, no barking dogs, not even the apocalyptic clamor of basket cases and beggars. I was saved for a night or two, maybe more, waiting for someone to cinch a rope around my neck and haul me to the gallows. A room infested with spider webs that smelled like dead rats fully described the ground floor of my new home. The floor was littered with gravel, old syringes, and shards of glass. I felt my way around and miraculously found a gutted box that, in my tired state of confusion, was as good as a sultan's love seat. I had nothing left, no rage, fear, no regrets or sorrow. Only a starry void that numbing, restful sleep hurried to wrap around me.

■ ■ ■

But that wouldn't last long. One, two, maybe five days later, as the muezzin called for Isha prayer, the white beam of a flashlight flooded my face.

"You'll be safe from danger in my unfinished house."

Blinded, I couldn't tell who was—or were—behind that flashlight. Doesn't matter. Fair trial or not, my case had been heard: riddled with bullets, hung at the end of a rope, or, why not, trampled by livestock. I had nothing to lose. I used my rudest tone ("A dead goat fears not the knife," as they say in Abidjan).

"Get that light off me, you idiots!"

The light dimmed. It was a little girl. A young girl about my age who started yelling at me from above, probably to try to exorcize her own fear.

"What are you doing here? What the hell are you doing here?"

I didn't even startle. Surprise is a paralyzing force.

She turned around and yelled out:

"Ousmane! Where are you, Ousmane?"

She took a few steps forward and knelt down beside me.

"Looks like you haven't eaten in days."

She looked me over: my muddy hair, hollow cheeks, old lace undershirt and my indigo dress that went down to my knees.

"You stole. You . . . ran away? That's it, you ran away! Happens to us all, some day or another."

She unfolded some aluminum foil, took out a shawarma and handed it to me.

For the first time, propped up against a pile of rocks I was using as a pillow, I straightened my back and tried to follow the bright finger coming from her flashlight.

"Go ahead, eat! It's all yours, Ousmane's not here."

"A schoolgirl like me," I thought as I devoured the sha-

warma. I wanted to ask if she was also fifteen years old, but other words shot out of my mouth.

She took them calmly, which set me beside myself.

"Don't tell me you didn't understand?" I said.

"I prefer that."

"What? You're crazy!"

"That argument would do better than running away. It's more convincing, easier to explain. You haven't seen Ousmane have you?"

"So you didn't understand what I said?"

"That's no reason to writhe around in the frogs and snakes, even if you'd burned down the whole village. The thieves are right around here. Did they not see you come through? They don't suspect anything?"

"I snuck in through the mangroves and buried myself in mud. I could hear whispering in the brush. Then I met a crazy old woman … What about you?"

"Other side. The cliffs. You got a name? Hey! You hear me? Even trees have names. I promise there's no shame in saying what people call you."

"How did you know I was here?"

"I'll explain later."

"And who's Ousmane?"

She looked at her watch.

"Come on, we'll work our way out this way."

"To go where?"

"Don't complicate things, follow me and don't say a word."

It was harder to leave the quarry's filthy hollow than it was to enter: straight ahead was a shit-covered ridge planted like a hat on top of the ravine; to the right, the thieves' hideout; to the left, woods that ran along the main road; behind us was the silty gray ocean, with its ferruginous rocks and latrine-smelling odor.

We reached the top—after an hour of climbing and falling over crevices and jagged rocks, through clearings and barbed wire—covered in cuts and bruises. Sitting on a pile of deadwood, we were able to dry our foreheads, and cast incredulous looks at the depth beneath us, where we guessed in pitch dark the unfinished house and acres of jungle around it were. Only outlaws came here. Criminals or the insane.

She thought I was insane, of course, but said nothing. She was afraid to. Afraid I would vanish, afraid I would escape her watch and disappear into the smoke coming from the burning garbage or hazy splotches of the streetlights.

We'd stopped panting. Still on the pile of deadwood along the road, we looked at each other like twin pieces—two knights—on an unlikely chessboard. We stared on, our heads full of questions. Now that was possible, thanks to the streaks of light coming from the homes around us.

I was first to break the silence—the toads and odd warbles shaking the bushes made it unbearable.

"Let's get out of here."

"Looks like you're afraid," she said in a mocking tone. "It's just trees, toads, rats . . . Don't tell me you believe in ghosts."

"Is that a reason to drag this out?"

"No. Just a quick stop. Some time to catch our breath, maybe get to know each other."

She fixed her eyes on my face at these last words, which

had the effect of two smoldering augers. The pain made me answer right away.

"What's your name then!"

"Well look at this. It's rude to ask questions when you don't answer them yourself."

"Mine is Néné Fatou. Néné Fatou Oularé. But my friends call me Atou."

"'ll call you Atou then, even if I'm not your friend."

"How did you know I was here?"

"The winged angel! He came to me in my sleep, handed me this lantern, and said, 'Go find her! Take her out of there! Save a life, frightened child!' So I got up in the dark and just let myself be guided."

"And this winged angel didn't say anything about me, nothing about how I looked or what I'd done?"

"That's all he said. He's not the talking type... It's fine, Atou. It's time to go."

"Where exactly?"

"I live on the other side, between the market and the church, with an aunt who works at the harbor and prefers her old Honda to her delightful little niece—let's go."

"I'm not moving until I know your name."

"Diaraye. Diaraye Baldé. I just flunked out of school."

I followed her without saying a word, absorbed again by the torture I wound up forgetting about since I wallowed with the slugs and rats and that was again besieging my mind. I did have a diploma, but now this was worse than if I'd failed to graduate. Games, diplomas, plans, nothing made sense anymore. "I'll be recognized as soon as night fully fades away. I'll be found even if it's at the edge of a star. I'll be chained at the neck, hands, feet—and it will be a relief. Deep down, that's my wish: that they shake me, that my crime be put before their eyes, that I can stop lying to myself, stop denying. Be done with it! That they lock me up, behead me. That would be better for everyone. The misery was living without punishment, alone in the full world, alone under the weight of its awareness. Weighed down with remorse: with no judge, no jailer, no witness." A little earlier, opening up to this young stranger, I'd felt set free. For the first time, I was confessing not in front of Diaraye, but on top of the Himalayas, for all the world to hear.

A kilometer later, I sat in the middle of the path.

"What the hell, why don't we just take a taxi bus?"

"A taxi bus. With a fugitive. When it's almost midnight and Ousmane's nowhere to be found?"

She started walking again. All I could do was follow behind. She was shifting to an ease in this maze of dumps and hovels, knowing exactly where the path's bumps and ruts were. She led me to a market, split off to the left, abandoned the paved road for a red path spotted with crevices and rivets. Finally she stopped in front of a tiny villa and pushed a door open.

A woman was dozing off next to a bottle of beer, a shiny set of headphones splitting her hair. She jumped when she saw us and stuttered:

"You know what time it is, little Raye? They warned me about putting up homeless. . . Is this for the night or are we permanently hosting this kid?"

"Until the police show up. This girl has some trouble."

"Oh naturally! Let me guess: trouble with debt?"

"She just killed her father."

"**A**nd naturally Jesus has nothing planned for the miscreants and psychopaths: no Ottobock, no Küschall, no Rupiani."

You're always talking about Jesus, Madame Corre, even if no one's ever seen you in a church. But you don't just talk about Jesus. You also talk about Newton. "Newton missed his calling!" you shouted at me, sitting on the square lined with plane trees, near the cluster of homeless folks surrounded with canvas bags and dogs. "You don't have fun doing physics when an apple falls down on you, you write poems. He does nothing at random, Jesus. He'd have hurled a comet at Newton had he considered gravitation!"

You magpie! You rogue! Your confidence! You're good enough at getting under my skin that I've thought about killing you. But I won't act on it. I wouldn't have anyone to talk to. You consume my thoughts, you bother me, you push my nerves, but deep down I need you more than you need me. I only get the chance to open my mouth once or twice a day. My world is considerably smaller since I started following this dying man.

The nurse comes in the morning, Tuesdays we go to the doctor. She wipes his drool after giving him his drops as if she wormed her way through a wardrobe. The doctor could only mumble the two words I've ever heard from him: "torpid state." The rest of the time, after scouring the alleys and parks, I head for the counter at the bakery to trick someone into giving me a minute or two of conversation. Do you know what they whispered to me about you? Terrible, frightening things. I swear the florist couldn't mention you without widening her eyes. "Watch out. Seriously, watch out, Countess. That one, my goodness, I swear!" But at night, my morale's at half-mast, my muscles like jelly. I just have the strength to lie down, swallow some soup, and read my daughter's emails before I collapse.

After Rue Mouffetard, we moved on a few steps toward La Contrescarpe, so I asked you:

"Are you from the neighborhood?"

"Three doors down from you."

I shuddered. A burn would have had the same effect on me. And questions started multiplying in my petrified mind. "Three doors from me! Strange, strange... Me, a simple personal care assistant trailing a wheelchair, alone. Passersby and manholes in placid indifference. There was a person who could be interested in me? Who spied on me, maybe, who filed my address, my blood type, my tax ID number and everything? Who could that be? Tintin, Mata Hari, or Commissaire Adamsberg?"

I didn't realize you were leading me, with utmost authority, to a hot chocolate. After reading the lines on my hand, you touched my forehead and sighed.

"Twelve lives in one! I'd write a book if I were you."

The waiter leaned hurriedly down, giving you his worst smile.

"It's you, Madame Corre—it's been forever!"

Then, discretely, to me, "Oh no, I'm not going to miss her,

this one here—"

Look at that. "Mme. Corre," that's the name he used, the poltergeist.

"Tell me, Madame Corre, how many times did you follow me before—"

"You can't keep from crossing paths when you live on the same planet!"

You didn't even laugh after saying that. You had one aim in mind: to stop me from finishing my question. You'd followed it right away, with that signature twisted mind you have.

"It was a stroke, wasn't it?"

I leaned over the gentleman with limited mobility to rearrange his blanket. I intended this to mean I wouldn't answer.

"It was a stroke, I'm sure of it."

And I knew you were talking to yourself.

Then, again, you took my hand. Again, you let out a Pythian voice to spin your ridiculous yarn.

"I see a gun. A Beretta if my eye serves me right, and that's one big brute holding it. A handsome man. A handsome man with an ancient coin tattooed on his forehead. What is he doing here, this giant, in a city as puzzling as yours? Twelve lives in one! You'll tell me about them, won't you?"

Maybe you're not a journalist or a spy, but, my God, what a mysterious feeling. Tell me, Madame Corre, where did you learn to become so inscrutable? I never see you coming. I'm scanning the street and your mouth is at my ear before I realize you're there. And by the time I turn my head to the barren trees where pigeons bob around, you're gone.

They say some funny things about you. For starters, you weren't a cook, a haberdasher, not an all-season vendor or fortune teller, even. You were the wife of poor Farjanel. The old scholar who'd "bought" you through a Monegasque marriage broker. That's the story the florist on Rue du Cardinal-Lemoine told. It suits you, trying to pass for a cook: an incontinent non-agenarian's companion would have delighted the janitors a little too much. You shout at each other at night, apparently. The soup would be lumpy or, otherwise—and this seems more plausible—you were looking for what he'd laid out in his will, what he'd reluctantly do: "It's too soon, really too soon. I have to see it coming."

You know what Prospero, the waffle guy, calls you? Crotchety Anne. Where did he get that? Now that I'm getting to know you, there's nothing spontaneous to your name. You're constantly performing. You perform to push your true nature back. At heart you're reasonable. It's a comedy, the long green gowns, the neck rings, the bracelets, shimmering bands, forearms bedecked with pearls. You could never be a gypsy, Madame Corre, you don't have the amber skin, the long black hair, and the purple mantilla that contrasts just right with the somber face of cigar rollers from Seville or Marbella. Maybe a hippie, a long out-of-fashion 21st-century hippie. A 69-year-old hippie with no fear of being ridiculous. Yes, yes, you can see behind the curtain thick with years a young and pretty baroque girl, lanky, carefree, with no respect for decorum. The pretty kid of eighteen years, bust finely curved in the marble of her era. School year spent smoking joints and listening to Pink Floyd, then off to Kathmandu through summer, looking for nirvana—impossible to begin with. You stayed there, flowers in your hair, Bob Dylan and Pink Floyd in your ears. A hippie of your age inevitably gets people talking.

I know, you want to skin him, Prospero, when he gives you a waffle with his over-serious look: "Well, take one, Madame Corre, it goes so well with your rusty complexion—sorry, your rusty foundation." You shouldn't make that face when he induces you like that—"goad" isn't my word, Prospero talks like that. "I'll never speak French like the French do. I'm Italian, understand, Italian. *Italiano, primera lingua latina!...*" If he treats you that way, it's because you really deserved it.

Do you know what he says when you're not around? He says you'd have definitely tried, with your polished voice, your ballerina stride, and your cute little mug—reminiscent of Britt Ekland—but that just opening your mouth was enough to make it ugly. Prospero's right. You have a serious problem, Madame Corre: you love to please, yet, just the opposite, the second you open your mouth you're irritating. That's how it's been since you were young, I imagine. And since over time the worst outweighs the best... Please note, it matches your personality to ridicule others. You're the kind of person who loves to be surrounded by enemies. Faced with innumerable criminals and depraved people, it's you alone with your infallible rules and your sword of justice. People hear of you long before they get to know you. That's what happens with geniuses, bohemians, and nutjobs. Everyone knows Madame Corre, even if you've never seen her. I knew about you long before meeting on Rue Mouffetard.

One or two words to a stranger in a cold winter embrace and a whole life is turned around. I don't remember two words that upturned my own. But I remember the odd magnetism working on me that day, as if I had a piston in my back and inched forward despite my will on the slick sidewalk behind your little feline steps, fast and quiet, not knowing who I was behind, not knowing as I passed through the door if I'd encounter the fumes of a bistro or a shrine to Apollo.

After probing my hand for the umpteenth time, you straightened your back and your blue eyes started to glimmer.

"Well, well, well! And only now do our paths cross..."

I'd never before been groped by a fortune teller, but I knew they trotted out the same stunts to impress a customer. Grand gestures and cryptic declarations. To me, you were a stranger like any other. Nothing fated us to say hello, to drink a hot chocolate, dither over the thousand and one faces of the future. Exhausted from your weird mannerisms, I grabbed my purse and unlocked the wheels to the cart.

"Oh no, you can't leave, Countess! Don't think you can go so soon—we have a lot in common, you'll see."

Your natural authority was already having an effect on me.

"One hot chocolate how about."

"You're from Guinea, is that right?"

You raced to add, in a higher tone because of the bewildered look on my face, "Don't be angry! I haven't said anything bad, Countess! I heard you talking on the phone the other day, it was in their languages."

"So you followed me a long time before—"

"Not at all, Countess! Just the regular street scenes: a crying baby, an old woman hailing a cab, a bickering couple. I assure you, I barely even looked. Just heard. But those languages…"

It was "those languages," then, that earned me your relentless harassment. They were the root of my anguish and the reason behind this very book. But where? At the bank? The post office? Or under the plane trees on the square?

I'm guessing you spent a week or two spying before you accosted me in the icy wind on Rue Mouffetard. Evidently, I didn't notice: your presence has a gift for passing unnoticed. You haunt the sidewalks without a sound, without emitting one wave, like a ghost that slides through everything.

If only you were a real fortune teller! I'd have tossed you a coin after listening to your blah-blah-blah and we'd be quits for good. It wasn't my hands you wanted to read but my biography, my soul, my radiographs. But why me, Madame Corre? Do you also ask cops, doctors, Sunday strollers to leave their families and jobs behind so they can confide in you and turn it into a book so your morbid curiosity is satisfied? No. Just me, just mine. Those like me born and raised in the land of Sékou Touré.

"You must have lived through awful things there. It would do you well to tell your story."

Where did the idea come from that every person born there has a book where their larynx should be? Yes, things happened there. Does that allow you to think that my country is home to the one and only valley of tears on earth? What language did you hear me speaking on the phone? What do you know about Susu, Fula, or Maninka? And by what tip did you know they were my country's languages and not those of Togo, Malawi, or Mutapa?

"A lot of things in common." What do we have in common, Madame Corre? Just like me, you're a woman. And you know your way around a wheelchair like I do. That's the end of it.

Write a book! First of all, your bizarre proposition left me trembling, upset, my head full of difficult questions that pumped me with rage and helplessness. Yes that's correct, you pissed me off. Oh, your obsession with seeing, with knowing—deciding every single thing! I'd have gouged your eye out, I swear. But you know how I am... At the slightest opposition, I drool, stamp my feet. I seethe. Then some funny ideas pop into my head: an urge to burn down the city, reduce the earth to ashes, take the next person I see by the throat. But my internal fire doesn't spread to the outside. It only consumes my lungs, my guts and kidneys. Then I wind up reasoning with myself: "This Madame Corre, this monster who spends her time grilling you with her acerbic tone and her cop's bag of tricks, it's for your own good if that happens and not for the reasons you might think. Really, look: you exist in her eyes; that's the first time since you started following this dying man. She points at you and holds up a mirror. It's up to you to widen your eyes, hold your cheeks, sketch onto paper this face that no one names and that, to that end, even you will end up forgetting. Well, all the same now: if she hitches herself to me or merges with my shadow. Whether she rants, interrogates, or drains your life.

I'm done running away, done turning my back. I'm through pouting.

One day, biting into a vanilla tart, one eye on him, another on the hip-hop group performing on the square, an odd idea came to me. "I'll look Madame Corre in the face the next time we're on the square and I'll tell her in a firm voice, 'Tell me everything, Madame Corre. Are you a telegrapher, a psychic, pediatric nurse, or—? You know there's a funny rumor floating around about the crime on Rue de la Clef. I could call 911 if you don't stop bothering me . . . Hey, is it true you get paid to keep this dying M. Farjanel company? If so, what's your salary?'" But the next day, as you can imagine, I didn't dare open my mouth. It was actually you who opened your big mouth to douse me in criticism and bombard me with questions.

"You're hiding things, Countess. Am I a friend or not? How long have you been here, first of all? Who hired you? How much for? How long is the term? Is this your first job? It took a lot of trouble getting your residency card, didn't it?"

"Oh yes," I said, completely fed up with your interminable rambling.

"It seems to conjure up some bad memories, this residency card business. So let's talk about something else: are you going to watch the debate tonight? Who are you voting for? Sarkozy or Ségolène Royal?"

"I voted already. For him," I said, indicating the gentleman in the wheelchair.

I should say this didn't happen on the square, in front of the bums and the birds, but in the deli section of the grocery store. I was looking for a cut of veal when you materialized before my eyes. You took me by the hand first thing as a means of offering a chocolate at Vésuve.

We had our routines at The Antidote, on the other side of the Montagne Sainte-Geneviève, when it stood on its own feet, spoke its own language, and had a vision all its own. We would go there every afternoon at the same time for strawberry-vanilla vacherin and a glass of rosé champagne. I continued taking him there. Then overnight, as you knew so well to do, you imposed the Vésuve on me, because of *The Last Days of Pompeii*—according to you, the "keenest", most exciting and poignant film.

"It had good cause, Vesuvius! All the boozing, all the sex, so many plots and conspiracies! The orgy followed by the penalty! Jesus punished quickly in those days. And the people in Hollywood know how to sniff out a good story... No one would dream of directing a film called *Antidote*."

After the chocolate, you proposed a glass of Sancerre. You wanted to be able to take your time, study me for hours and hours in hopes that a pore might end up opening, wide enough to become a slit, then a rift, through which you might scurry into me with a microscope, examining every single thing, from soul to intestines.

DIARAYE MADE ME SIT on a rattan sofa after a short exchange with her aunt. My head was still ringing, and that demonic carillon continued to hammer my ears. But I was also beginning to sense that my anguish was loosening its grip and that things would make some kind of sense again. From the mouth of Raye, as her aunt called her, the word *kill* worked on me like shock therapy: the healthy swipe of a scalpel under an old boil. Yes, there had been a murder, and I was the one who'd committed it. It was time I faced the facts, reconstruct the events the way detective novels do. At root, what exhausted me so much was the fervor with which my conscience denied my actions. But now, in this house I had just set foot in for the first time—in front of two strangers—the word *kill* echoed in my head with the inarguable violence of courtroom evidence. I couldn't deny it anymore...Yes, yes, impossible to deny... This thing in that hand...That never-heard-before sound... This body collapsing....That young girl who soared, jumping off the balcony...Those memories aren't easy to carry and the chaos with which they burst into my memory made them even more unbearable. "She just killed her father." I thought I sensed cynicism in Raye's voice, a reinvigorating cynicism though, the famous jar of cold water that brings a drunk to his feet.

I could tell them apart now: Raye, ravishing in her olive-green suit despite traces of mud in her hair and bruises; Yâyé Bamby, regal as a pharaoh in her leppi robe, her long legs stretched out, feet on the coffee table beside a glass of beer. She was looking at me as if I'd fallen from the sky. I realized Raye was seeing me for the first time, too. Under the lamplight, that is, and not in the interstices of night. But I was tired and didn't care what they thought. The next few minutes, like a broken record all I heard was that stupid question in the least hidden corner of my mind: "What was keeping them from calling the police? Good God, what were they waiting for?" Then Yâyé Bamby's voice echoed with the grating tone of an alarm clock:

"So, what do we call our cute little murderer?"

"Atou!"

"Ever try alcohol, Atou? Now's good a time as any. That's how it goes with the first glass: you've either lost someone or your head's on the chopping block."

Raye lifted her glass with a half-smile, as if there were nothing more natural than toasting the crime I'd just committed.

"Come on, Atou, cheers! You can tell us about it first thing after we eat."

Yâyé Bamby looked at me pensively and sighed after what felt like permanent silence:

"An assassin under our roof... Just what I was missing!"

She put her headphones back on without taking her eyes off me. Her body moved to the beat of the music, which she was the only one listening to, while running her beer glass in zigzags across the wet table.

Diaraye led me to the shower and offered me some clean clothes. She slipped out into the kitchen to make something to eat. Yâyé Bamby meticulously took off her headphones humming an Afro-Cuban tune. After that, she turned toward me, her eyes wide.

"So. Now that we're alone: why did you kill your father?"

"He raped me."

"That's a good reason there! It's funny, you said it like he'd always done it."

"I would have killed him already."

Diaraye reappeared with the plates and rice. After eating, Yâyé Bamby did the dishes and offered us a basket of fruits.

"The girl has a serious justification: he raped her, her father did... Can you tell us, Atou, did you regret what you did these last five days?"

"No!"

Shocked, Raye started her moralizing commentary.

"We are always remorseful when we kill."

"I'm not bothered with any remorse."

"People in your situation always lie, you know that."

"Why would I lie to you? I'm not in court yet."

"Why the wax face, then?"

"It's not so much I don't feel remorse as it is I refuse to condemn myself. Plus, of all the punishments, the ones we inflict on ourselves are cruelest."

"So you recognize you've committed a serious act!"

"I killed my father, what's more serious than that?"

I felt tears running down my cheeks, the first since the crime. It was my body that needed to cry, not my mind. I made no effort to dry them. They traded a look that made me uneasy. It felt like they were pitying me. I pushed back at the Kleenex Raye was offering me.

Yâyé Bamby widened her eyes again and leaned toward

me to scour my face for signs of lying, weakness, or annoyance.

"Where was your mother?"

"In the village, for Tabaski Feast... I would always take kinkéliba tea at night to her bed. This time, he jumped on top of me. I didn't understand at first... Then, I saw my blood and grabbed the pistol sitting on the headboard. So?"

"So what?"

"You aren't calling the police?"

"See how she is, your new roommate? She's just now thinking about the police, now that her belly's full."

"Maybe we should, don't you think, Raye? It's true she's in trouble—we are too by extension."

"I'll go to the police myself tomorrow."

When I woke the next day, I wasn't in handcuffs, and it didn't occur to Inna Bassa to morph me into an iguana. I managed to avoid a lizard's state, but I wouldn't get away from the justice of men. In my head was the image of a creature without claws or scales, though equally disconcerting, whose look suggested killing, remorse, panic. Mirrors don't lie. I saw myself for the first time, and I was certainly a criminal—a gentle criminal—of fifteen years. From this moment on, the eye turned from Cain to look down at me.

When I got up, no one was home. On the coffee table, they'd left me a note next to a delightful breakfast:

Dear prisoner, don't try to force the door open, it's locked. Here's the only tip we could think of:

–first, you won't be able to get away and take refuge in Sierra Leone, for example

–second, you won't do the police's job for them (we're

giving them a spare key). It's up to them to come find
you (that's what they're paid for)

Some advice: don't open the window. Watch TV on
mute. Pointless in your case to attract attention. More
than anything, do not scream. You're in a neighbor-
hood that's never seen a murder

I took my time eating my breakfast and made myself a
little bag of clothes and toiletries that Raye left me while I waited for my visitors. I didn't need to mute the sound on the TV.
Outside, there was so much noise that at the start of the day I
watched five Brazilian soap operas and didn't miss a thing, not
even the rustling of a dress. Besides the breakfast, there was
still some of the old woman's rice I could reheat in case I got the
munchies.

Finally, the sound of keys at the stroke of 6:00 PM.

"What! They didn't come?"

Raye seemed disappointed saying this. She acknowledged
me with a short hello, threw her bag on the couch, and ran to
the kitchen to make a plate of fried yams.

No, they hadn't come. Nobody had come. One more day
of freedom, or rather a brief eternity of jitters and doubt.

"Does it scare you—prison?"

"You know well and good it does."

"You committed a crime, Atou. Sooner or later you're going to pay, OK?"

"How about as soon as possible—let's get it over with."

"Tell me, Atou, if I opened this door, would you turn
yourself in?"

"I don't know."

"You know you wouldn't do it. We're all the same: heroism is a fiction of the mind."

She left to take a shower and came back in oversized pajamas.

"I'll put some rap on for us before Lady of the Honda comes back with her Afro-Cuban CDs. That's the only thing she says is worthy of being called music. It's all she listens to, morning, noon, and night. Have you heard of Johnny Pacheco? He's like her Mozart. Tonight I'll see if she can take off her headphones and you'll see what kind of Mozart he is."

Entering a little later, Yâyé Bamby asked the same question as her niece.

"What! They didn't come?"

I sprang from my seat in such fury that Raye stepped back and Yâyé Bamby put her hands on her face as if to protect herself from a sharp object.

"What kind of game are you two playing? They would have come if you'd given them the key. But you didn't. You were scared! Scared, right? Scared for me or for you?"

"Scared for all of us! Ah! I wish we never met!"

"That's the dilemma for us all on this poor planet: we're all condemned one day or another to come across each other, whether we wish it or not," I said, as if I'd just read it in a book.

Yâyé Bamby didn't have the time to put on her headphones. She sipped her first beer, let out a satisfied *ahhh*, and, sinking into the couch, turned to Raye:

"What are we going to do?"

"It's up to me to answer that. Let me go!"

"Stop your nonsense, Atou. If they arrest you, they arrest us too. It's criminal accessory or worse if it ever happens."

"And if they don't arrest you, we'll be living the same hell as you: the sleeplessness of a suspect, hesitating at every door thinking it'll be broken down at the first light of day."

"You said it already, Atou. If we opened this door, you wouldn't have the courage to give yourself up. Let's go! Let's find something else to talk about and stop this huckster's back-and-forth."

"Yes, Raye. Murder stories are best told Saturday afternoons when the beer is cold and Johnny Pacheco kills you softly with his salsa. Ta-ta, girls! I'm catching a freighter to Valparaíso at nine o'clock!"

Saturday came. And Yâyé Bamby, who always seemed like she'd stepped out of a dream, was happy to trot out this riddling line:

"What do you call a policeman who rapes his daughter? …A policeman. Are you sure, Atou? Do you get it, Raye? Your friend was raped by her father and her father was a policeman. Interesting! Tell me, what was this policeman's name?"

"Colonel Oularé."

One or two Johnny Pacheco songs later, I overheard this exchange between the aunt and her niece:

"Colonel Oularé. That monster!"

"Don't say that. You might hurt her."

"The poor girl didn't just get hurt."

I was in the bathroom, but they didn't know I'd left the door cracked. I was noticeably upset walking back into the living room.

"See, Yâyé? She can hear everything!"

"My apologies to her, then. My mouth moves faster than my mind—I need to learn how to keep it shut."

I don't know what Raye said next. But their discussion picked up, darting to China's shores, then Chile's, and wherever else all night long while they nibbled on their beignets, drank their beers, ate their *bourakhé,* braided their hair, another Brazilian soap opera unfolding in front of them. I wasn't listening. I watched and let my thoughts stray to things that used to be mine and were no longer.

I was expecting handcuffs, a whip, a verdict, gallows. I thought my good luck had deserted me after what I'd done. Well, not exactly. I did think coming to this house was providential, to be in these people's arms. It meant another world existed, a carefree one. Of good taste, candor, and freedom. A world opposite the one I'd known.

At home, life unfolded under Papa's watch. Papa, strapped into his uniform. Papa, kepi screwed down on top of his head. Papa and the frightening pistol that never left his side. I ate with the housekeeper, played with the housekeeper, watched cartoons with the housekeeper. Mama spent her afternoons outside the house, buying clothes, getting her hair done, joking around with her lovers. Papa could be gone for days: it was work, work, work. Nothing more consuming than the job of a policeman! I remember asking him one day: "What does *policeman* mean, huh, Papa? What's it mean?"

"A policeman is he who puts an end to evildoers."

I didn't understand at first. But as I grew up I learned on the radio that the country was swarming with evildoers and that he needed to catch and exterminate them. It made me proud to have the father I did. I opened the dictionary for confirmation: it didn't say otherwise. This gave me free license to snub my friends. "Watch what you say. My papa's uniform has pounds of stripes, don't forget it." At home, there were no books, no board games, no checkers. My father never read, not even the army newspaper. And if I asked when I was going to have a little sister, he'd start grumbling and my mother would slip into the bathroom to hide her tears.

I didn't say a thing about all that. I wanted to put up a solid wall between my hosts and my past. Besides, there wasn't much to go back to (there was nothing new about my crime): it was an empty or—who knows?—crowded place, but still one covered in dust and deadly boredom.

I helped in the kitchen and around the house, doing dishes and laundry. When they left in the mornings, one for high school, the other for the harbor, I would lock myself in behind a double barricade and play board games or checkers while watching TV. Yâyé Bamby told me not to make a sound. "No one ever comes here besides people stirring up shit," but I had a hard time believing that. Plus, after a year living in reclusive solitude, no one came knocking at the door besides mango tree branches jostled by the wind. So I decided to open my cage and enjoy some freedom all the same, precaution outlined by the neighborhood's borders. I'd go out to get some air under the big trees and sometimes continued to the market to buy meat and seasoning.

No one thought to call the police. My crime had certainly not been pardoned but it seemed to be forgotten—except in Yâyé Bamby's esprit d'escalier. Always the same question when she got home from work:

"So, like that you killed your father? You're quite the precocious criminal... 14 years old? 15? 16?"

"I'm 15."

"Killing isn't typically done before 20!"

"I didn't want to."

"No one does. They kill, that's all there is to it. And let's stop the quibbling, it's not going to bring him back... Don't worry, go. There are plenty of criminals out there. No reason they'll arrest you, not you or anyone else."

After that, she emptied one or two bottles and replaced Johnny Pacheco with a Coupé-Cloué CD. She twirled around for at least a half hour, squeezing tight, her eyes hermetically shut, against an imaginary knight. Then she sat back down to drink another glass while, without a sound, tears inundated her face. She wiped her face with a Kleenex, drank down two beers, one after the other, and tried to make it back to her bed, clinging to the doorframe. "Don't worry about me, girls! These aren't my tears. Someone else's, no doubt."

Impossible Yâyé Bamby! One glance was enough to make you want to take up residence in her house, take advantage of her bathroom and her bed, gorge on beignets and homemade sauce. And yet it would have taken an expert burglar to break into the dark maze of her existence. I suppose she was born like anybody else, confident and available, then something locked her down between puberty and menopause. This made her into a fortress whose sole door wouldn't turn on its hinges or let anything out besides the sunshine of her heart and those few falling tears, almost without her knowing, as if there by mistake. As if they didn't come from her.

B.

That letter would often come back in her delirium. What could *B* refer to? A man? A country?

B as in Binlo, as in Balla, as in Boiro, as in Bernard, Barryor Bangoura? *B* for Belgium, Burundi, Brunei, Botswana?

Raye imagined it referred to the man she'd known when she was getting ready to leave for university in Washington. They met one 4th of July at a cocktail party at the American Embassy. When she had to decline her scholarship to Georgetown to care for the kid he'd impregnated her with. He may have been a foreigner, or diasporated—you know, those dirty Guineans from abroad who only come to the country to spit on it and knock girls up. Where was he now? Brunei, Belgium, or Botswana?

There's a topic no one dared to broach. She was shunned by her family and banished from the village as soon as news of her pregnancy got around. Even Oumar, her brother, crossed his adorable little sister off his list. Raye, who continued to visit him, despite everything, suffered the same treatment. So I kept my mouth shut whenever she'd get drunk on Guilix or red wine. Or when she'd burrow into that deep pit of silence from which she only ever surfaced to hammer out her litany.

"What did your father do, by the way, to deserve what you did? If you already told Raye, you don't have to repeat yourself—no need to double your effort. And the dead tend not to like it when you talk about them."

Especially the victims of patricide.

"**I** KNOW A LOT about you already, but the lines on a hand aren't enough for an oracle as unsure as this one. Want to know who taught me? Niharika, my 'grandmother' from Kathmandu. She knew everything. Your father's name, your mother's, your date of birth and the day you'd die, just by deciphering the lines on your hand."

A long time ago, someone else talked to me this way, Madame Corre, but I can't remember her face or voice now that all I have behind me are sunken bridges and huts gone up in smoke. Her name was Ténin. And like you, nobody knew anything about her. Where was she from? Did she sleep on a bed or on the pebbles of a beach somewhere? She was only seen at night, and only in winter. Since she spent her time lurking around mosques and markets singing songs that stoke fear, everyone was quick to wonder whether she was a crazy woman or just a lovable witch.

I very clearly remember our first encounter, that famous night I'd spent hours wandering down the city's muddy streets, cops and blaring sirens in pursuit. Early in the morning, I had collapsed, my throat dry and feet on fire, on one of those piles of rotting mangoes the market sidewalk is littered with. That's when she appeared to me, spectral and terrifying in the splendor of early morning. She leaned toward me with her corrosive smell and wetted my tongue with a few drops of a tasteless liquor from the gourd she venerably held in two hands. "Drink, my little Atou, and you will be sheltered from bad luck." How about that? She knew my name, like you did my apartment door. You'd have thought the city went silent to let her speak. Then the noise resumed: asthmatic muezzin, sputtering trucks, drunken skirmishes, the deadly sounds of maquis, toads, dogs, beggars. She cupped a hand around her ear as if the city were speaking to her, and then placed an icy hand on my forehead, where the good Lord lodged my soul. "It's vibrating, there inside. It's vibrating!" She muttered something else and turned toward the lowland brush. "Follow my finger, Atou. There at the bottom, in the abandoned mine, is an old unfinished house. No one will look for you there."

You and old Ténin, that everything keeps apart—the oceans, dunes, diet, faith—you still have something in common. You don't just read the lines on a hand. You have to rifle through the core of their being, where a stroke of luck has incited the least perceptible damages. We all have things to hide, some under the agreed-upon attire, others under a limpid veil of silence. Like old Ténin, you told yourself right away that my life was teeming with secrets, with atrocious and unspeakable things, so deeply buried that I'd lose my lungs the day I'd decide to cough them up. That's your way of thinking. Really, there's nothing more uninteresting than a life like mine. Nothing to say, nothing to hide, nothing to laugh or cry about. But you're hard-headed, you never admit defeat.

"I'm patient, you know that!"

The air was threatening (rain or snow through the night perhaps.) when we went our separate ways, and your usual somber look had a layer of rage and exasperation: like a cop when the suspect, in his bad faith, refuses to confess.

The next week, I ran into you on the Maubert-Mutualité square while talking leek prices with a vendor. You were grinning ear to ear and didn't bother with hellos.

"See, now, on the other side of the boulevard, just after the dry cleaner's? Well, that's Chez Ái Vân! They have the best phô in Paris. The prices are fair, the heat is perfect, and the owner's a friend. *And* there's enough space to park your wheelchair. Now does that sound tempting or what?"

Then after crab and a house aperitif, you waxed jovial.

"So, Countess? I'm sure you'll want to come back. He looks like he's just fine, your gentleman in his peaceful stroller. Have you noticed how his right eye twinkles when he's feeling good?"

"Fucking hell! Who do you think I am? You think I wouldn't have noticed that after all this time? You're always exaggerating, Madame Corre. Can you just be decent?"

I was ashamed. I got carried away, carried away for nothing, and I knew you were going to take advantage of it, perverse as you are. I lost my self-control. I was guilty and vulnerable. You, M. Farjanel's fiery furnace, have never been a gift giver. Especially not when it comes to a little creature as fragile as I am, right? Who's packed with complexes and dark thoughts?

"Calm down, child! We all get worked up. Me too—I have my own moments of weakness."

You looked at me with eyes of a hall monitor as you spoke. You'd won again. You could impose whatever you wanted on me now: appetizer, dessert, the subject of our conversation, wine. I had so much to learn about the balance of power.

"I know you'll be back. Ái Vân will welcome you with open arms. She does everything for her customers. Did you know she makes the ravioli étouffée herself? And you have to try this nice little wine. She has it shipped in from a winemaker in Burgundy who holds back half his production for her. This is his table, here, for the rare occasions M. Farjanel goes out. He's who introduced me to Ái Vân. His mother is Vietnamese. Born in Da Nang, M. Farjanel was. Pork ribs and sticky rice are his specialty."

Then, suddenly, your lovely reassurance vanished. I thought I noticed a cloud of remorse on your face.

"I have a confession to make."

Exactly as I thought. Meaning you had watched me a long time before accosting me in front of the pâtisserie on rue Mouffetard. You'd noticed me the first time on the Monge plaza because I was always sitting with my back resolutely turned away from all the bums—however well they imitated Quasimodo and Cyrano de Bergerac. I seemed odd to you because I wheeled my little buggy around with inexpert hands. Then one day you got close because I was talking on the phone. You'd heard those languages already: Fula, Manding, Susu, the languages of my home. That was the day you started to follow me, harass me. Piss me off.

"I owe you another confession: I have a great passion for Africa."

Then you went on again about Jesus and Newton while eating your phô. Then, I don't know why, you stopped abruptly to look at me with an abruptly inscrutable face.

"Tell me about Guinea."

It wasn't easy for you to say, I could tell. And since I didn't respond, you felt you should add:

"Sékou Touré's Guinea!"

"Amnesty International has said enough about it. What more do you want me to say?"

You were right. The phô was delicious. The rice wine, the sticky rice, and the pork ribs too. But, of course, we would end up at Vésuve. That's where you offered me coffee. And you looked like a wreck by the time we went our separate ways. A viper had bitten you, or else it was the word *Guinea* that had riddled you with bullets.

"I feel bad. I shouldn't have to talk about Guinea...But the damage is done. Please, Countess, no more mistrust. Nothing taboo between us from now on! I sense we'll come back often to Vân's. To eat phô and talk about everything, even Guinea."

The day after, you took the liberty to call me. Call me! I never gave you my number, Madame Corre. And I'm not in the phone book! You wanted us to meet on the plaza again— you had some secret to confide in me. But when I got there you didn't look like someone with a secret to reveal. You seemed distracted, absorbed by the homeless production of a Grand Guignol.

"I'll never understand why you turn your back to them, Countess."

"Please, Madame Corre. Your secret. That's the only reason I'm here."

"Um ... Well, I also know something about Guinea."

"You call that a secret?"

"Let me tell you everything...I didn't just visit. I lived there a long time."

And for the first time you caused me pain. Big, clay-colored tears started streaking down your cheeks. "Shit, Madame Corre's not so bad after all. She cries too!" Only you don't cry like other people. You don't put your head in your hands while your face stays completely still. It's like a faucet being turned on over the inert eyes of a wax statue. I was still bothered leaving the place, once I'd handed you a handkerchief. I hate tears, Madame Corre. Tears are the worst form of argument. We cry out of weakness, hypocrisy. I cry when I can't take it anymore. I cry so others can cry in my place.

See? What good could possibly come from stirring up the past, Madame Corre? What good?

The next day, walking out for my croissants, I almost fell backward: you were waiting for me on the sidewalk, lines on your face, eyes deep in their sockets, your voice nearly gone.

"I left my son there. In Guinea."

I turned on my heels and went straight for the bakery, not hiding my anger. I wanted you to know that I was about to shove you. You had no excuse to be there. I didn't think you were that crass. You had no right to stand there waiting like a crane in front of my house so you could hurl your trauma at me.

On my way back, bag of croissants in hand, I heard you shouting behind my back.

"Maybe you knew him! My son... Please, Countess, please. And maybe you've heard of Camp B? Please, Countess, please!"

I ran into my building, paying no attention to you.

Then came the two most painful weeks of my life.

The first two days, it's true, I had deliberately tried to erase you from my life: one fat line in red ink and no more Madame Corre ever again, no more Vésuve, no more Danton, no more nauseating subway entrances. Maybe you'd guessed my intentions: by the time I was feeling regretful and left to look for you, there was no Madame Corre to be found. Not at Vésuve or at Danton... The wildest ideas kicked around in my head. You had, of course, decided to forget me in return, cut ties for good. Or else you were dead. You'd killed yourself swallowing barbiturates, putting a bullet in your brain, or, more likely, throwing yourself off the top of Notre-Dame—the desperate person's pinnacle of romanticism. Then a panicked fear overtook me. I realized you were, despite everything, the only person left connecting me to the world.

So I quivered with an unusual joy the day that, on the corner of the Polytechnique et the Rue des Écoles, your biting voice again broke into my ears.

"You have an errand to run on this side of the planet?"

"Yes," I said, trying to hide my enthusiasm. "I'm haggling over a rocket ship on Rue Cujas."

It didn't make you laugh.

"You at least know what 'Ái Vân' means, right? 'She who loves clouds.' You don't give a shit, Countess. You don't give a shit."

Then it came back, that urge to kill you. My excitement about seeing you again never lasted long. You have a gift for subduing people's excitement, for erasing whatever nostalgic impulse your absence might have left them with. Maybe you did it on purpose, maybe just by reflex, because you loved it: to police and contradict, put off and nay-say.

Your dark voice, mixed with the grayness of the sky— which was raining down on his forehead and the armrests of his wheelchair—and the grandmas' sad headwear, the intermittent sounds of sirens, like chickweed, took over the landscape of my brain and sent shivers down my legs. If I had a gun, I'd have blown your abominable pumpkin head to bits. One hemisphere of my brain was thinking sincerely in that moment, and the other simply caved to the thousand questions tearing at it: "So who's going to watch him when you're on the shitter? Who's going to tell you hello? Who's going to rescue you from your Sunday soaps with a phone call? Who's going to talk to you over a glass of Sancerre in this drowsy city that fails to say hello?" That was the looser of the two. The right hemisphere. The most given to renunciation and compromise.

Well, I'm not going to blow your brain apart just because you smell like patchouli and annoy me with your piercing gaze and weird interrogations. To hell with your dated dresses and that bun you put your hair in for the satisfaction of looking ugly. That's one life saved! I've learned plenty of things since coming to Paris, most importantly this: when it comes to company, the devil's embrace is warmer than solitude.

An hour later, all was forgotten. You invited me on a tour of the Jardin des Plantes. Then we sat down at the Monge plaza in front of the plane trees, our backs to the homeless people. I'd gone into osmosis with this plaza. I read it like you would a book. I understood everything: the kids ribbing each other, the histrionic gestures of the homeless, the birdsongs and murmur of trees. I know the meaning of the bird that chants: "Don't be stupid, Pavlov! Pavlov! Don't be stupid!" We watched the pigeons flit from one plane tree to the next for a moment, then you helped me park the wheelchair and rearrange his blanket to shield him from winter's machinations.

"So, where were you?"

"Burgundy. My mother died. She loved him, that's why she passed. Her grandson was everything to her. And my late husband—she treated him like the son she never had. Maybe he's dead too—the kid. You see, Countess? I need your help."

I hesitated a moment. I didn't know for sure if I should believe you or not. Finally, I took you by the arm to lead you to the Vésuve myself.

"Look me in the eyes, Madame Corre... Is that true? All that, your son?"

"His name was Dian Diallo. Dian Charles-André Diallo."

"Why *was*?"

"You're right, maybe that's still his name."

My mind left me for a good while before I could hear you again:

"What are you thinking about, Countess? See, it touches you."

"You'd probably find him if you tried looking for him."

"I'll never set foot there again! But you, you could—"

"Me neither. I'll never set foot there again."

"But you're young, you didn't know those things."

"'Those things.' You don't have to witness them to live through them."

This time, you did go to the trouble of putting both hands over your face. Still, you left right away. You're well aware, Madame Corre, that tears horrify me. As I crossed the street, I heard your sobbing voice shaking behind my back.

"Come all the same on Saturday. We'll eat at Ái Vân's."

OK, Madame Corre, we'll eat at Ái Vân's. Empty our glasses at the Vésuve and I'll find an excuse to slip out the second you start to tear up. I'll wander like a sleepwalker down the evil streets, taken over with fog and acrid smoke, that passers-by joylessly roam with vacant faces, anxious to get home and drink their lives away in front of the TV. For the thousandth time, I caught a glimpse of the dome to the Panthéon and the Musée de Cluny, my full attention resting on his right eye, the one part of his body that still comes to life. It's been like this for a year. God only knows when it will end.

We can't tell who's pushing who anymore. Where is the mind? Where are the muscles? We're becoming one and the same person as the days pass. He crosses the boulevards and plazas with the strength of my biceps, and I see the city through his right eye. It's by emptying out that life makes its final palpitations known. That blue eye, that eye with an uncertain glow, the last vestige of a body in ruins. I learned to read its signs and follow its tyrannical demands. "A shepherd one day feels for his sheep," as they say where I come from. A nanny one day feels for her cherub and the paramedic his patient. Torment unites. Torment abolishes distance. We're no longer two distinct bodies separated by the absurd form of a seat on wheels. His life and my life, his body and my body, caught in the same stupefying vibration. I finally came to understand the meaning of Siamese twins. I feel his anger and his cheerfulness, I wake up the moment he wakes up. Every sudden glance gives me an electric shock. I know whether I did the right thing passing by the Seine or the Jardin des Plantes to get to Austerlitz. Austerlitz because it's the closest station, the most convenient, otherwise he'd love all of them, provided there are lots of trains arriving and lots of trains leaving. I know at Odéon I can never ignore the Danton monument on the left.

You accumulate some manias when you leave firm footing for a wheelchair. Once, not long ago, for a little change, I wanted to take in some air at the Jardin Médiéval instead of Monge plaza. The shock was so strong that I stood stock-still a full minute on the sidewalk before I managed to turn back. Still, Monge plaza didn't have much to do with the days when he could get up and sit down on his own. And now, thanks to the miracle of a wheelchair, it's become the funniest, most picturesque attraction in Paris. At first I would sit on the north side, back turned to the Garde Républicaine, to watch the students on roller skates and the bums clowning around. He liked facing the homeless folks, despite their dirty nails and elaborate piercings. In that position, he could get the most out of the pigeons on top of the trees and imagine, behind the houses dotting the slope, the bustling life of the Contrescarpe. But for me, it's decided, I won't face the bums ever again. Not for anything in the world.

Once we're set up on a bench, I have to open the newspaper right away. I go through the columns knowing he's going through them at the same time. I especially can't get the wrong paper. *Le Canard enchaîné* is his favorite. *Le Monde* or *Le Figaro* can pass sometimes, but definitely not *Libération*. That's Sartre's newspaper. Nothing's changed there. He's always been fanatically anti-Sartre, before and after his paralysis. He tried to explain himself, but I didn't understand much of it. He'd often talk about political engagement and would call Sartre a professional *engagiste*. "It's bullshit, engaging for ideas! You engage in the fire of action or not at all. On that count, I only see three people worth a damn: Che Guevara, Hemingway, and Malraux." I had a hard time following: he had several times attended the old egotist's conferences and talked with him.

Even when everything was going well, his curiosities were limited to the neighborhood: Les Arènes, the mosque, the forecourt of Notre-Dame, the Musée de Cluny, the Jardin des Plantes, the quays of the Seine and its charming booksellers. We'd go through these different places several times a week, wherever his whim and the weather took us.

At night, his eye lights up when I put on Ravel or when I change the channel from Planète to Arte. And, as much as I can, I dodge your efforts to get me out for lamb stew at the Antidote. In these moments he's in heaven, and the happiness that radiates through him warms me down to my toes.

One thing intrigues you: how could I know he loved wandering around in the train stations when he was still able-bodied? I must have told you between Sancerres without paying attention. A little nothing that poked through the sort of lady speak where, besides Sunday soaps, only desserts and clothing are discussed. The kind of thing everyone would have forgotten the second the TV went off and the wine was recorked. Everyone but you. And you imagined that you finally had it—better late than never!—the key that would let you into the secret, encoded world you worked up. This past sewn with enigmas I refuse to unveil for you.

"Let's be clear, Madame Corre. My past is no more enigmatic than anyone else's. It's in the words, 'a heavy past,' 'a past that doesn't pass.' It's not made of gold, the past. Everyone has one, even me. I have no glory riding on it, nor do I have any shame. I'll tell you about it one day maybe. Once the words are formed. Once my tongue is strong enough to hold it and spit it out."

"I'm not sure I have one. I've certainly dug around, but I've found nothing. Yesterday looks like tomorrow and tomorrow has the sad face of today."

"Find a mirror, Madame Corre, and you'll see your past in the condition of your skin. The color of your hair."

"Youth isn't a vocation, you know."

"I'm not making fun. I'd just like to make you aware that you can't live without the past."

"I don't have any bit of a past, and I'm not doing very well."

"Fine! But what's upsetting about people without a past is they're always trying to pry into others'."

"No—yours. Only yours. For starters, what's your name? I can't picture you, Countess. And 'Countess' doesn't mean anything. Do I go around calling myself 'Mathilde Countess'?"

We were at the Relais Odéon that day, somewhat far from our old haunts, but it didn't seem to bother him since he hadn't winked. Paris was aglow under a lovely winter sun. You would have thought it was spring. This whirling feeling of celebration festooned the air. Everything became unrecognizable, starting with you. Yes, we now had a good reason to meet each other. Although mistrustful, our relationship could only get better. Two solitary souls, lost in the coldness of Paris, living steps apart from one another: we were condemned to cross paths, to say hello, trade pepper for onions, and pontificate on Inspector Derrick. And that's how your son changed everything.

That day, you didn't talk about Newton, but you did go on about Puccini. And in the middle of your music-lover's ode, this sentence came out of your mouth like a hair in soup:

"Your French is very polished, Countess. No personal care assistant talks like that. That's what tipped me off to it."

And you grabbed me suddenly by the chin before I could show my shock.

"Are you a personal care assistant, yes or no?"

A long silence followed, then your hand came back down and you didn't answer anymore. We blended in with our neighbors' chatter at the table, outraged to see on TV the atrocities committed in Syria, El Salvador, Congo, Ivory Coast, and who knows where else. So you smiled at me and looked at your watch:

"Only eight! How is it just eight o'clock? They're so deceptive, these beautiful winter nights. Another glass of champagne! On me this time. Don't worry about him, he looks so happy over there."

"On one condition: that we eat at my place. His place, I should say."

"Is that allowed, do you think?"

"Right now, I'm the one who decides."

"If it's food from your home, a hundred times yes."

I didn't dare say you'd be eating basic scallops. Exotic food was for another time: it takes a long time to cook, plus you have to go all the way to the Saint-Quentin market to find any thiof, kobo-kobo, konkoyé, attiéke, etc.

We were in my building, downstairs, when you picked up from where you left off harassing me.

"When you're from a country like yours, you're bound to have stories. Perhaps without knowing it you crossed paths with my son one day. Someone going by the name Dian Charles-André Diallo would surely stand out in Conakry. A name like that!"

I offered you port as an aperitif. You complimented me on the dandelion salad. It was my understanding that the scallops with asparagus and julienned roasted vegetables also went over well. The highlight was the Cantal cheese plate with a *vin jaune* from Jura. The atmosphere was mellow, the conversation turned to subjects we'd never broached before. Giani Exposito, for example, as we drank our coffee. You closed your eyes, and a few moments later:

"Well how about that, I've never heard anything like that. Giani—who was it again, did you say?"

"Esposito. He was his favorite."

"I've never heard lyrics like that. And what a voice! '*Et pour tuer, il faut être calme and lucide...*' Killing is a form of love, don't you think?"

"That's a strange thought."

"Why 'strange'? You know what the Japanese say? 'If you hate a man, let him live.'"

"What if you love one?"

"Well, you have to help finish him off. The Japanese take things to their logical extreme!"

At your request, I played the record two or three more times. You smoked several cigarettes in a row, absorbed in obscure thoughts. You flinched when you heard me coughing.

"But tell me, if you were listening to the same record..."

I poured you a second coffee.

"You aren't a personal care provider, Countess. You don't know very much about wheelchairs, I only had to watch you awhile to realize it. What was he to you? A boss? A colleague? Lover? Those three are often the same, you'll note."

"He was—he's my husband."

You said nothing else. As if I'd less issued words than knocked you out with a club. You took up the Cantal and *vin jaune* again. Then you asked me to play Giani Esposito once more.

On your way out, you shot me a big smile.

"What a great night this was, Countess. We should do these more often. Here or my place—as long as there's Cantal, *vin jaune*, and Giani Esposito. Never have I seen your husband's eye shine in such a handsome way."

I WAS THROUGH HIDING MYSELF. It was pointless. The motorcycle taxis would tell me hello and the ginger juice vendors called me by name. The neighborhood thought I was a new maid. The old one had disappeared the night before my crime, taking with her the PC and 5,000 dollars that Yâyé Bamby had hidden in her dresser, wrapped up in an old bra. Raye told me how angry her aunt had been, so furious that day that the dogs ran off and the hard-of-hearing perked up. Just think: the money a lot attendant cousin from Philadelphia had sent so she could pay for the work on her house still under construction! So, when they saw me coming, they thought everything had gone back to normal, that she'd had the thief locked up and taken her money back. And since I was often crossing the courtyard to hang out the laundry and scour the pots and pans, I could only have been an employee of the house—certainly not a criminal. Tell me, Madame Corre, what better judge is there than the eye of a neighbor? No more worries, no hassles, no glitches. Like everybody else, I could come and go, shout and knock around, burn with desire, and sin.

One evening, coming back from school, Raye handed me a mirror, her face gleaming.

"Those eyes! That smile! That chest! Raise your little finger and every boy in this city is at your knees! Does it really still get your panties in a bunch that you're a criminal? Even the traffic cops think you're one of the good girls—they think you're the nicest one in the neighborhood. You see, you're absolved, forgiven, you're wiped clear. The city is waiting for you, with its wild nights and seduction. Friday after classes I'm taking you somewhere... On one condition, though: you have to do my trigonometry homework. Tri-go-no-metry! Obviously whoever invented it didn't have a brain in their skull... I'm offering you paradise and you're not even smiling."

Raye was like that, she'd harvest the millet too early, like everyone suffering from surplus optimism. We reached an agreement: I'd go to the market and buy fish, eggplant, and kobo-kobo to make us a nice konkoyé with palm oil. And, after treating ourselves, we'd put on our finest rags and party down.

When she came home Friday, she found the house in a grave silence, with no fetching aroma to delight her nose. She found me slumped on the couch, my face in my hands.

"What happened...? What are you trying to say? Enunciate, lady. Use your words. Did something happen to Yâyé Bamby?"

I was able to stand up and speak audibly.

"She still hasn't come back from work."

"What is it then? Did they rape you again?"

"They found me, Raye."

"Who's 'they'?"

"The cops."

"After all these years? Tell me you're joking! Please be a joke."

"Before it wouldn't have mattered, but I have a life again

now. Tell them I don't want to die."

She sat back down and in her most serious voice said, "OK, I'll tell them. In the meantime, try to calm yourself. What happened?"

"Well, I was by the yam vendors when I saw him. He was wearing an indigo bomber jacket and big sunglasses. He was standing like fifty meters from me... you know, at the corner where the butcher's and propane store are... and he looked at me like I reminded him of an old acquaintance. I acted like I didn't notice anything. He made no hesitation following me. Following me! Yeah, all the way to the new church, Raye! So my knees shot up to my neck running the whole way here."

"Come on, flirts are all over this city wearing indigo bombers. I told you, Atou, you have a way of attracting men. This dude didn't want to arrest you, he wanted to jump your bones. That's not necessarily unpleasant—saying from experience."

She couldn't make me laugh. Out of breath, my ears alert, I was on the lookout for signs of life outside. Kids' voices shook me with fear and moped motors made the same noise as certain kinds of sirens. "That devil Bassikolo cursed this country! And you, Atou: beware of any man who approaches you." Even the memory of old Ténin made me think of cops.

Yâyé Bamby, who got in a half-hour later, tried to reassure me.

"He'd have arrested you if he were a cop!"

Raye's invitation was still on later: nothing was stopping us from being careful.

We couldn't have made a better decision because Indigo Bomber showed up again. It was Raye who saw him this time, standing on the church steps. Two or three weeks later.

"I believe you now, Atou. There's nothing—not one thing—reassuring about this guy. He was looking at me from the side of our house. And he had in his left hand something that looked like binoculars," she stammered in an even more frantic voice than mine the day he followed me.

Yet everything was fine in the next season. At school, Raye didn't get one bad grade. Yâyé Bamby earned a raise. She celebrated her birthday at a restaurant and let us have avocado vinaigrette, pizza, and champagne. An odd idea dawned on her as she cut the cake.

"You know what we should do Sunday? Let's tour the city then go to the beach. We'll go dancing, just to egg on this indigo bomber scarecrow. Arrest us, if he's really a cop! Want to know what *I* think? He's no cop. He's a prankster. He's just trying to scare you."

These words had some sway. There was no more discussion of Indigo Bomber. He vanished from the market, the church steps, my thoughts and nightmares.

"Come on," Raye said one day after we finished cleaning out that mess of a shed. "I'm taking you somewhere! Don't bother with makeup: no one recognizes a criminal after they've been on the run for three years. Plus you're well aware Indigo Bomber's all but evaporated. He figured out we weren't afraid of him."

"Let's get going, girl! You're right, a real cop would have already shown up."

A half-hour later we were at the Oxygène, a hideout where my life was about to take a new, more surprising and gut-wrenching turn than the day I killed my father.

"It's as big and loud as a cruise ship!"

"Totally, Atou! You have to come a bunch of times to get used to it."

She took me by the hand, I noticed, the way moms do on

the first day of school.

"Check it out. This huge courtyard is called Bagataye: that's the maquis. They have the best aloko chicken in the city. In the middle is Folto-Falta, that nightclub I told you about. They have the best whisky, best DJ, prettiest girls, and so the best fights. On your right is Motel Ziama. That's where you'll rent a room the day you meet a guy. Come on… The path in front of you leads to the ocean. Watch it, though, there's sharp rocks and roots the whole way down."

We came out onto a pretty field of taro and palm trees a meter above the tide, after crossing through a slum occupied by squatters. Chairs and tables were set out in the middle of the grass and a rattan bar was jammed between the left side wall and the parapet. Jumping over the parapet, we landed on a little white sand beach surrounded by rocks. It was called Toes in the Water: the Oxygène's seaside feature.

"Pleasure and ecstasy! Sodom and Gomorrha! Free license and vice!" Raye laughed. "During the day, everyone's cool just kissing. The serious stuff goes down after dark."

My first night out. I told you, Madame Corre, I didn't know anything about life: not bars, not movies, street fairs, the zoo.

"Three years is the ideal interval: any earlier and you'd be recognized; later, you've missed the boat," Raye whispered as she led me back to the maquis, decorated like it was Christmas, with garlands and string lights. "Thus concludes our tour. Any time of day, you can drink here, dance, eat, and… he-he!"

She thought, and I still wonder why, that it was only at eighteen years old that the flame of desire hissed through your body. My stay with Yâyé Bamby had in some way prepared me for my new life. A gilded prison is happier and more instructive than school, and Raye ended up convincing me that any life without weed and cold beer lacked for taste. But I insisted on keeping my virginity. To be a virgin (even if your own father already soiled whatever little jar of honey the good Lord wedged between your thighs) is to cast an eager eye on the world. Reach out a restless hand to its fountains of youth and papaya orchards cinched with snakes.

We were served chicken and fish outside. Raye almost had to yell over the music and shouting. The air was thick with smoke from the grill and the beer flowed freely.

After the aloko chicken, we made our way to the club. Raye ordered some beers and went to find a seat. A young man walked with an unsure gait through the crowd and passed in front of us.

"If that one there cornered me in a bathroom stall, I wouldn't cry for help."

Raye followed me on the trail once she was able to stifle her crazy laugh. Our conversation kept on despite the decibel level.

"Does it really eat at you this much?"

"Hey, I've waited a long time!"

"You could wait a little longer."

"No longer than now."

"Why don't you jump the next guy you see?"

"I swear I wouldn't hesitate if I saw the guy in that mauve velvet hat again."

But I didn't see the guy in that mauve velvet hat just then: he'd left to go sleep off his hangover in one of the market warehouses or get picked up by the cops. Or, more likely, mortise and tenon with some girl on the beach or in that filthy bed in room 13, which everyone tried to avoid but recluses and gravediggers, drawn to the empty tombs and ruins.

The music was interrupted two more times due to fights. Then Raye, barely more drunk than me, dragged me down the trail because they'd put on Papa Wemba. Two or three guys circled around us to make fun of our self-conscious walk and fiendish shaking. But the event I was hoping—or waiting—for didn't come to fruition. In any case not right away.

Ten minutes later, sitting side by side, a Rasta man bent over toward me.

"Hello my same-mother, how are you?" (The Oxygène made me think of a far-away tribe, Madame Corre, with its own customs and argot. You didn't say *friend* or *brother* or *sister*, but *same-mother*. And the city? You know what they call the city? *The Other Tribe,* or sometimes *Babylon*.) "May I extend an invitation to this young and lovely woman who dances so fine to an Afro-Cuban beat?"

That's how I met Alfâdio. That's how my life became what it is today. A skinny boy with an athletic outline, chocolate complexion, a face like Mohamed Ali, the face of a playful kid who knew he'd only ever be liked by his mother. He danced the salsa like a god and that might be what drew me in. He wasn't wearing a mauve velvet hat but there was an aura of similarity with the young man I'd seen earlier. Maybe it was him.

"I saw you a while ago. With a mauve velvet hat, no?"

"You don't know all the things that happen to me! Two days ago, a lovely young woman like you saw me on Tayaki beach dressed like a cosmonaut."

"It was definitely you. This particular young man also had a scar over his left eyebrow."

"Maybe it was me, then, if he'd been staring at your pretty little tush."

"What?"

Out of his jacket pocket, not acknowledging my outrage, he produced a mauve velvet hat.

"Are you sure? I see you as more of a puncher. You don't look like Bob Marley, you look like Muhamad Ali."

"Still a compliment."

The Folto-Falta was crackling from the music. A wonderful world tour, from jazz to salsa, Congolese rumba to samba, hip-hop to raï. Each harbor had its own rhythm, every station its pulse. I laughed and turned around in the arms of this stranger, not paying too much attention to what he was saying: the words my body wanted to hear, of course, and that knew how to reach me without filtering through my ears. The truth is, I wasn't drunk, just a little tipsy. He was, but it kind of suited him. All around us, laughing—the same as ours—shoulders and hips and, no doubt, in their burning minds, the same feeling of innocence and freedom. Inside me was a feast; around me, the pulse of a youth bloated with optimism, drunk on carelessness. Everything was new, fascinating, unexpected. I felt feverish, transported, full of tonicity and an enchantment with life. I was wild, strong. I was free.

As my heart beat uncontrollably, as my mind wandered, his wandering hand came to life.

"No! Not that, not here."

"Don't be difficult. This is the Oxygène, look around!"

I wanted to, but not like that—even if it was at the Oxygène.

I ran to find Raye as soon as the song ended.

"You didn't like him?"

"Are they all like that here?"

"Oh, they're a little worked up but they're not all bad guys… People drink like fish out here, you have to realize."

"I wish it were just drinking! You haven't found your Ousmane?"

"No."

A chill of distress made her voice shake. I waited for her to recover a bit before continuing on.

"Are you going to introduce him to me one day?"

"It's complicated. It doesn't depend on me alone. Of

course I'll introduce you one day... Still want to dance?"

"I'm good for tonight. Freaking condoboye. That thug spoiled my appetite."

"Are you complaining? I was expecting you to jump him. Just earlier—"

"Forget what I said just earlier. Let's go."

In the taxi, she handed me a cig and asked what I thought of the Oxygène. I told her it was how I imagined El Dorado.

"We'll come back Sunday. Toes in the Water Beach is downright magical between four and seven on Sundays. And you'll like it at the Oxygène. You have a quality it requires: you never ask questions... And maybe he'll still be there, the Rasta in the mauve velvet hat."

"The Rasta in the mauve velvet hat! The Rasta in the mauve velvet hat! Ah, if I could only forget him, the Rasta in the mauve velvet hat."

A DAY OR TWO LATER, I invited you for tea out of the blue. A lovely opportunity to show you the whole apartment.

Your bewildered look scanned thoroughly around the rooms before returning to me.

"This luxury! These rugs! The gilding! So you really are a countess?"

"Don't talk about countesses: they all left their heads on the chopping block."

"Sure, but the title still sells. Tabloids and Saint-Germain-des-Prés rallies are full of countesses. I imagine you don't associate with tabloid readers or Saint-Germain rallies..."

"He hated his world. He was a soixante-huitard, you know. Those folks think they were born to roast their own class."

"And what's his title?"

"The Count of Monbazin. Philippe Claude Célestin, Count of Monbazin."

"How did that, you know, start?"

I just let out a long sigh.

"OK, OK, I'm not going to push. Later, later.... Let's say, 'once your tongue is strong enough to hold the words.' He-he-he! See? I remember everything. Nothing gets past me, not the smallest word."

"Words are hard to tame, especially when they're sour and especially when they've aged. How about this: the first book Philippe gave me was called *Mars*. It was about cancer."

"That would be too much for one home if you had cancer. Jesus wouldn't ask that much! Now that I've seen your home, it's time you come see mine. Saturday at seven work for you?"

You graced me with two heartfelt, audible kisses and waved goodbye before stepping into the elevator.

"I'm not actually M. Farjanel's cook. I'm his wife. Our lives have a few things in common, don't you think? Don't call me 'Madame Corre.' It's 'Mathilde.' Anyway, take care of yourself, Countess!"

Those words mark a step: the abandonment of mistrust and suspicion; the start of a more honest, more confident, and peaceful connection. It felt like a burn wound that day: the internal fire eating at you had, so to speak, licked my face. Impossible, however, that I call you "Mathilde." Madame Corre couldn't be erased. What difference did it make? You weren't alone anymore. You did what you could to hold on. As for me, I had gotten quietly back in touch with my contacts in Conakry. They were on the lookout for a Black man with blue eyes and a name as odd as your son's.

Saturday, over your fondue bourguignonne, I wanted to confide these things, but a piece as big as a stone was lodged in my throat, blocking the flow of words. I wanted to tell you I had a lead, a serious lead, but it was too early. I didn't want to give you illusions for nothing. I needed to be sure this Dian Charles-André Diallo was still alive and that there was no question he was your flesh-and-blood son.

During our aperitif, while the fireplace crackled and M. Farjanel played accordion, you offered it all up. You leaned in toward me, your face burning with curiosity. In a tone of voice that didn't allow for discussion, you egged me on.

"Go on, Countess, tell me everything! You'll feel better afterward. Poorly kept secrets always wind up mucking up someone's existence. And as you know, I get completely shaken up when someone refuses to confide in me. So, what's the latest you've learned?"

"Nothing at all, I mean it."

M. Farjanel wasn't paying attention to us. He was playing the accordion with a passion and precision that were strictly his, whether from his short life or his isotopes. Suddenly, he lifted his wrinkled chin from the keys and fixed his little glowing eyes on us as if noticing for the first time we were there.

"Continue on, ladies, please. Act like I'm not here. I'll only be here for eleven minutes and forty-two seconds. And since we'll spend thirty minutes on the fondue, if you add going pee and a mouthwash, I'll be in bed exactly forty-nine minutes and thirty-four seconds from now. I always go to bed at the same time, Countess, which leaves Suzanne to do as she pleases.... You're talking about golf, I imagine? At Poly, my colleagues were always talking about golf. Which made me distance myself from them at speed. Besides the accordion, I'm only interested in badminton. They thought it wasn't serious enough— badminton I mean—for someone working in isotopes."

He left with the frantic laugh of a slap-happy child.

It was my first time seeing a savant and I was almost disappointed. I imagined them having goatees with circular glasses, yet M. Farjanel made me think more along the lines of a retired actuary: graying temples, clean-shaven face, subtle balding, brown corduroy suit, turtleneck sweater, contacts maybe—in any case, no glasses. He looked nothing like the walking shambles I'd been told about. Ten years younger, maybe with a good cosmetologist to dye his hair and cover up his wrinkles, and he could be a young debutant on the red carpet. His slender body and chiseled complexion suggested he'd probably in his younger days held several movie stars in need, and not a few finely-dressed widows. "Hey, hey!" I thought to myself. "The ideal interracial man: no race won out over another. A perfect Eurasian!" I watched his fingers dance across the keys while making the bellows bigger or smaller as stupid questions bounced around in my head. "Does he really pee in bed? How much longer does he have to live? And when he does die, which part will decompose first? The top, bottom, or in the middle? What could *isotope* mean, this word with no known taste that's still able to conjure up my senses? A satellite, a new energy source, an aphrodisiac?" In that moment, my internal voice said, "Isotope or not, it's time to purge your memory, tell your full story, say every single thing. No cheating. You cheat by keeping everything bottled up inside. You're cutting yourself off from the world, you're drying yourself out!" You're right, Madame Corre, that's the point of life—telling its story. Mine, yours, the Buddha's and Jesus's, Pignouf's and Joe Blow's. Life wouldn't make sense otherwise.

Philippe knows everything: what little I revealed to him, what he found in the archives, what others have told him (the many others who knew more about me than my own little brain ever did).

After coffee came a little pear, then M. Farjanel recited a long poem in ancient Greek. Finished, he disappeared into the shower. We heard his voice, uncannily like Placido Domingo, surf the music of the water.

"You didn't ask me why I go by "Madame Corre" when I'm supposed to be the wife of Stéphane Farjanel."

"Your maiden name?"

"No. And you, besides the picturesque title of Countess?"

"Truth be told, I don't know. It depends on my age at the

time. There's no shortage on names, is there?"

She turned toward their speaker once the bottle was half-empty.

"I still haven't picked up any Giani Esposito. Do you like Anne Sylvestre?"

"I only know Giani Esposito. That's all he would listen to, that and opera."

"She's innovative and marginalized like him. Those two qualities go well together, innovative and marginalized. Listen to that phrasing, listen to that harmony, Countess, listen!"

"I came here with a bunch of tom-toms and balafons in my head. The music from back there."

"I don't want to hear about balafons!"

"To each their own. The good Lord put more barriers into music and food than in languages and skin color. It's just because of Philippe, all the Giani Esposito."

"Make no mistake, Countess, I'm completely in love with African music—Mandinka music especially. But balafons..."

You wouldn't stop smoking and drumming your feet that night. I could sense you were getting nervous. Your liver was acting up maybe, or water was getting into your house (water will eventually get into a canoe over time, same with houses), or else the sting of a bad memory just pierced your mind. You turned down Anne Sylvestre and smiled a tight smile.

"I'm horrified of balafons."

You almost flipped the table over saying that, as if you wanted to punch an invisible enemy. Then you crossed your legs on the sofa and your voice softened.

"Rest assured, Countess, you're not the only one with things to hide. I have them too and shouldn't harass you so much. Am I really Madame Mauricette Corre, Mathilde Farjanel? I could just as well be Amélie Beugras or Joëlle Pernet! You never know fully who you are."

You went back on your damn questions—which you have the insane habit of answering before I even open my mouth—the second you led me to the elevator.

"You didn't ask me what year it was when I discovered Guinea. It was 1961, the year of Sputnik! In my mind, my odyssey was as important as Yuri Gagarin's: I took a plane for the first time and I was only eighteen."

AT TOES IN THE WATER, a vague impression took hold of me, one that found me someplace other than the city I was born in. I had only seen the place at night. A row of kapok trees separated it from the squatters' slum and two tall sidewalls isolated it from the piles of trash and villas. Here, you had access to your own little piece of the ocean. Anywhere else, the sea was invisible, lost behind garbage heaps and whatever buildings. A paradox, Madame Corre, for a city built on one strip of land girded by the sea.

Oh, Madame Corre! The smell of the ocean, the taro fields, the coconut trees, that giant orange of a sun that was ready to fall on the crenelated roof of the islands, those beautiful kids, the cute girls lazing around, arm in arm. It all disturbed me and brought out of my body the fact that I was a novice with foolish emotions—to any new feeling. The place radiated poetry, inviting calm and sensuality. Once there, the overexcited gangs stopped squalling and motioning. You couldn't do anything but whisper in your friend's ear, and dream of travel looking out on the horizon.

"There are never fights over here. Come on, let's walk down the rocky side." Raye led the way.

On our way back, a young girl sprawled out on the sand waved me over. I hurried, my heart thrumming with curiosity.

"Excuse me, same-mother," she said, tugging mechanically at her sandal straps. "Uh...um, how can I put this? Let's go with: you're not a certain Véronique, are you?"

"Véronique? Me, Véronique?"

"OK, I bothered you for nothing then. I hope you'll forgive me. Maybe it was Dominique or Monique or Valérie, I don't really know anymore."

"No worries."

"I saw you the other day!" she yelled behind my back. "Salsa's your jam! The way you moved—who taught you that?"

"My aunt."

"She must be from Cuba."

"She just stayed there a while as a kid. A summer camp. She lived with some pioneers of the Party back in the Sékou Touré days. Honestly, it's more here that she learned it."

"And what's her name?"

"Yâyé Bamby."

"I'd love to have an aunt with that name who could dance the salsa so well. What if you taught me how to dance?"

The same night, I had her do some steps at Folto-Falta. Then, dripping with sweat, drunk on Fania All Stars, Los Van Van, and Roberto Barros, we joined the others at Bagataye around some moist aloko chicken. Her name was Mariam. A nice girl who, despite all these years of tumult, I still have a fondness for.

"And this Véronique, what did you want from her?"

"Not me, someone else is looking for her. Maybe it's not Véronique, but Monique or Dominique or Valérie or Virginie."

"And what's his name, this someone else?"

"I don't know, he didn't say his name."

"What neighborhood does he live in?"

"He's white. When you ask, he tells you so many countries that you have no idea where he's from. Could be France or Belgium or Cuba or Chile or Congo. Unless it was Burma?"

Raye's eyes lost the power of their curiosity. She leaned gently against my ear.

"Véronique, seriously Véronique? With these kids who self-medicate with cocaine? I'm glad we've never gone beyond grass. Off as we are, we'd already be dead."

Now we were sitting in the Bagataye courtyard to get a little air after the heated hour of salsa.

She could tell we were talking about her. She grabbed her bag and stood up.

"I have to go."

"You're not angry, are you?"

"Me, angry?"

She put a big wad of cash on the table.

"That's for the rest. And drink to my health, my same-mothers!"

Before disappearing, she took the time to walk over to me.

"Watch out for Indigo Bomber!"

By the time I realized what she just said, her car was already at the roundabout to downtown.

Raye was panic-stricken. The whole thing was getting serious, even in the eyes of Yâyé Bamby, with her irritating tendency to make light of everything. To start, we needed to definitively close the mystery: who was Indigo Bomber? A cop? A sadist? Con artist? After a long night of discussion, we agreed to see this mysterious Mariam despite the risks it posed to me. It was still out of the question that we go to Oxygène in broad daylight.

Mariam was nowhere to be found for several nights afterward. Surely this was intentional, just to blow out of proportion the already rampant anguish strangling us.

The week after, when I saw her at Toes in the Water, slumped at a corner of the refreshment stand, her head against the trunk of a coconut tree, legs stretched out on the low wall overlooking the ocean, I was overcome with an urgent desire to slap her. I almost screamed as I confronted her.

"You know him?"

"Who's that? Oh, it's you?" she said, taking off her sunglasses.

"Indigo Bomber!"

"I don't, but my dad does... He's dangerous, that guy. You should watch your back around him."

What she told me that night was so enthralling to Raye that she decided to get involved.

"Go ahead, cook it up! We're better off confiding in each other one-on-one. Other witnesses would just be an inconvenience."

Indigo Bomber was most definitely a cop, and her dad was too. They'd gone to the Police Academy in Prague, then to the one in Moscow. But her father, who hated Sékou Touré and anything that sounded like communism, had crossed the Berlin wall tucked in the trunk of a Volkswagen.

"The guy raged in Munich, Paris, Amsterdam, London. I saw the pictures, read his letters. What would you guess they ate up there? What do you think they drank? What'd they even wear? After Sékou Touré died, he came back here to marry women from the village, following village custom, with village clothes and an Islamic diet and everything."

"I'm not interested in your dad. Tell me about Indigo Bomber."

"He's a cop, I told you!"

"So why doesn't he arrest me? Do you know that I—"

"Everyone knows you killed your father. You father was a bastard. If you hadn't done it, someone else would have done it instead. So yeah, why doesn't he arrest you? He'll for sure arrest you one day. Cops are never in a rush."

"And what if I ran away?"

"To go where? You'd risk getting shot. In your position, I'd stay peacefully at home waiting to see what the good Lord has in store. After all, you murdered someone. When you kill, you pay. I'm not trying to be mean, it's just the truth."

"It hurts, that truth of yours."

"Plastic surgery, too."

It was crass, brutal, cynical, coming from a girl I liked just for her kindness and delicate appearance. Parting ways, I thought I'd see her again the next day because I had to see her, because I liked her. Because she had so many things to tell me.

At home, Mariam's words were met with great relief. She was smarter and more lucid than we were. It would be pointless to run away or hide: I was *jammed*, as they put it in their lingo, and had been since the beginning. They'd come find me that very night, or the next day, if not the one after that. I just needed to get ready to face my jury, my jailors and executioners. And since I didn't have long to live, well, I needed to live right now and right away. A hundred miles an hour.

The next afternoon, I left Raye at the counter of the Bagataye and ran to meet Mariam at Toes in the Water. She wasn't there. I was going to jump the low wall to look for her on the beach when I heard someone whistle at me. I headed to the spot where she was stretching out her legs.

"Is that you over there?"

"You having a hard time recognizing me too? I was hiding

it in my purse until I got far enough away from the house, till I was out of my dad's sight. Really, it's better to have it all the time."

"You're right, nothing more Muslim than a veiled woman with a glass of scotch! People make it into this huge thing—it's just a question of clothes."

"You should do the same. You could go anywhere, Indigo Bomber wouldn't recognize you."

"I've heard they quit pinching your ass in the streets when you wear one."

"Oh for sure, they think you're way more virtuous than you are."

"Men and their clothes—it's like a sorcerer and his spell book."

"Atou, please, can we not talk about Indigo Bomber anymore? I feel bad for bringing him up that first day we saw each other. And you too, don't think about him anymore, promise. It may be long or short, but you have a life to live. Don't waste your existence on that idiot. He had a reason not to arrest you—that was his way of torturing you."

From that day on, she wouldn't talk about anything but her father. He was drowning in money: a parking garage in Brussels, another in Philadelphia, a transportation company in Dubai. She could have toured the world and bought herself a lavish penthouse in Paris or New York, but her father saw things in his own peculiar way: for boys, sure, but girls should stay close to their mothers. He had three wives, Mariam's mother among them. The family home exuded the majesty and opulence of one of those seaside ministerial palaces on the coast of Koléa or Donka. She wanted to be a pilot like her grandfather who did his studies in Florida. At first, her father saw no inconvenience in what she chose to study. It wasn't until she was twelve years old that he started to twitch. And after she finished middle school he decided that was more than enough, that it was time she return to the home. Ever since, he'd watch her put on her veil when leaving, accompany her to the front gate, and follow her with a look until a bend in the road swallowed her shadow.

Suddenly, she cut herself off and took out an object that made a metallic sound against the table.

"I'll kill him one day. Why do you think I bought that revolver? It's his choice if he wants to live like that, but we're not from the same era, he has to realize that. Hang on, I'll be right back."

It was like that every time we met. She'd go downstairs to shoot up in the bathroom stalls and an entirely new person would come back, more radiant, friendlier, more relaxed. I pretended I didn't see anything. I didn't want to hurt her. She had the same complicated relationship with drugs that Yâyé Bamby did with alcohol.

She picked up her lofty monologue, but in a less biting tone.

"Know what he did after that? Well he took my kid sister out of school. He has no idea I'm already taking classes at the high school. When he took me out of Sainte-Marie, I enrolled in the Turkish school with Mom's help. He'll burn the house down the day he finds out. All I want is to go far, far, far way— there, way out there past the ocean."

Meanwhile, she'd downed her scotch before realizing she hadn't offered me anything.

"Have some, Atou. Hey! You there! Serve this young lady. I'm not the only one dying of thirst over here."

She pushed her empty glass away and moved in closer to me.

"I'm getting out! I'm going to rob him one day. I'll empty his safe and buy myself a one-way ticket. A pile of hot coals in hell is better than the buggy streets of this shitbag country."

We took a walk on the trail with Raye for her salsa lesson.

"You see, Atou, there's nothing shocking about a young veiled woman dancing the salsa. Everyone seems to appreciate it. But I have to go. You know what I'm waiting for. No use tempting the devil!"

Suddenly, it happened like a click. I tapped Raye on the shoulder.

"Look over there, on the end of the counter: the guy from the other night! The one with the mauve hat, with a scar on his left eyebrow."

"What are you waiting for? Get moving!"

"He's supposed to come to me!"

"You sound like a grandma sitting on her Fouta rug... There's nothing shameful about walking up to a guy. Come on!"

I made it seem like I was passing by him to get to the bathroom.

"Hey, it's you... What a surprise!"

"My lady," he shouted, "the one who ran off the other night! You're not getting away today."

"Just one second and I'm yours."

That's how it really started, my story with Alfâdio.

He followed me down the trail and got back to his scheme.

"You're not going to do the same thing as last time, are you?"

"Of course not. It'll do worse than that," he said, his arms around me.

With the flick of a wrist, he managed to make a bow tie out of my panties and drape it delicately around my neck with a boyish grin.

"Everybody's looking at us!"

"Don't worry about them, they're drunker than we are."

No one so much as flinched. He was right. They were drunker than we were.

"Next time, you will ask my permission."

"OK. As long as the young lady swears she'll allow it."

I wanted to say to him: "Ask whatever you want. Right now, I can't refuse you anything. Ask for more than that and you'll find out..." But I didn't have the courage, or maybe there wasn't enough time. Raye came to tell us someone just popped a bottle of champagne and that we needed to hurry if we wanted a glass. It was happening under the coconut trees. Someone was celebrating their birthday, I think.

I'd already met Saran, Battouly, and Penda. That was the night I was introduced to Yârie and Sény. Alfâdio was going from one guest to another, throwing an arm around them, making them laugh. I wasn't the only one who found him charming. My first thought was how hard a time I'd have keeping him to myself. But on that topic Raye's teaching had opened my eyes wide: "Why do you think it's going so well with Ousmane? Because he knows I'm ready to get my revenge the minute he cheats. When it comes to jealousy, they're more fragile than we are. Do what I do and your boo will keep his eyes on you...When you have one I mean."

Our champagne glasses empty, Raye pulled me into a corner.

"I got a message from Ousmane. He's in the neighborhood. He got us a room. You want in on one too?... Don't make that face, guys can't refuse a chick like you."

"And Yâyé Bamby?"

"Oh, she'll yell just for the hell of it. She's way more indulgent since you showed up."

Alfâdio, with his knack for provocation, asked for room 13, but it was taken.

Raye slipped out without saying goodbye to us. She always got that way when she was meeting Ousmane.

We went into the one vacant room, which had no closet, on the ground level adjoining the pantry that served as a reception desk.

He took my clothes off while licking my shoulders. Then he put his gun on the nightstand and started undressing himself, too.

"Don't be afraid. Just a little precaution: you never know who you're dealing with."

He lay down beside me and tried to squeeze me in his arms. I recoiled anxiously and hid in the sheets.

"I'm warning you, I'm not a virgin."

He got up, taken by an incredibly crazy laugh that made him stumble back and forth several times between the bed and bathroom doorway, doubled over, his knees knocked together.

"'Virgin!' That doesn't exist anymore, what a bunch of B.S.! Girls lose their pretty little whatever before they start junior high. And I don't like that, anyway. First off, it takes too much effort. Secondly, I don't like blood."

He caressed his gun and went on.

"At least not that way...You know anything about Hamburg, sweetheart?" he continued without transition. "Well I'll take you there one day."

We made love until morning. It was the first time and, in my mind, it meant for good. I hugged him tightly and said in a shaky voice:

"I love you."

"Oh yeah? And you want the same from me?"

"Yes, tell me you love me."

"Well..."

He took up his gun and started brushing my body with the end of the barrel.

"If that's how it is, I'm going to love you back with all my heart, all my strength, all my guts. But—"

"But?"

"If you cheat on me, I'll kill you."

"Me too!" I shouted, taking his gun away.

"OK, OK, OK! Let's make a deal, then. Cheat on me as much as you want, but if I catch you, I'll shoot you."

"Same for me. If I catch you, I'll shoot you."

He took a drag on his cigarette, blowing the smoke to the ceiling.

"So it's true? You killed your father?"

He added two or three more words and sank slowly into sleep, clinging to my chest like a newborn to its mother. Raye was worried for nothing: he wasn't the tough guy she thought he was. He was a baby, a beautiful, chubby-cheeked baby, fat with life and innocence. My own baby.

I sang him a lullaby.

'LL KILL YOU ONE DAY, Madame Corre. At the Vésuve, the Antidote, or—even better—Cérises de Lutèce. The perfect place to throttle your neck. In the basement's darkest corner. Boom, there go your brains! The thought of them across those rough walls makes me think of a watercolor done by the random hand of a drunk. There's your skeleton! A little pile of bones at the heart of a black puddle swarming with flies. On top of it, a sign brought by the server, or maybe a generous guest (a Norwegian tourist, for example): HERE LIES A CERTAIN MADAME CORRE, MODERNITY'S BIGGEST PAIN IN THE ASS. That's the kind of daydream I'd have mornings in the shower, the rare few moments I had time to think about something other than his pills and infusions.

I left with a firm desire not to say hello if I ran into you on the square. But, once there at the bakery level, it dawned on me that we'd eventually have appointments with the same physical therapist from Mary-sur-Marne who apparently worked miracles.

"He doesn't look happy," you said to me, rearranging his

hat as the train raced through the stops, even the most remote suburban stations. "Maybe you're better off sticking around the neighborhood."

But on the way back, his eye was glimmering again. Which presented the perfect opportunity for your big mouth to open and shower that voluble physical therapist with flowers.

"See? I wasn't lying! Arabian princes will call for him sometimes to treat arthritis or lumbago. You should do the same—you are a countess, after all. And you wouldn't have to charter a plane. A taxi would do the trick."

I don't like it when you're right about something, but still… Of course, I contacted him first thing the next week without resorting to your help (I have my dignity and, luckily, the phonebook is for everyone).

We didn't sign a contract, but I trust the man: he spends every Sunday afternoon—after visiting his aunt in chemo—at the Geoffroy-Saint-Hilaire clinic, two blocks down from us. No need to order a cab since for him it's just a detour, a simple little detour, a Sunday stroll! I should have thanked you, but I won't be doing that. It would just inflate your already insufferable ego. Still, it's a major service you provided me with. Yes, you said something true for once: he works miracles, your guy in Mary-sur-Marne. He's better than everyone I'd hired before. His hands aren't satisfied with massaging. They cajole, they inquire, they speak. Coming out from under their embrace, Philippe is able to breathe again. It's like he's going to burst out in praise of life, leap from his seat, stuff the city with his eloquence and zest for living. I think to myself sometimes that two or three months with this physical therapist would do more good than one of Necker Hospital's own surgeons. His visits have the effect on me of a party. He talks to him as if there was nothing but memories between them, and not the hard contour of a wheelchair. Like Philippe, he's attuned to the music of Giani Esposito, the works of Camus, Miró paintings. And to myself as well—he talks to me gesturing to the paintings hung on the wall. Philippe tried in vain to teach me the secrets of Chagall and Signac, Utrillo and Modigliani. Sometimes, I can tell from the glow in his eye that he wants to tell me what, when healthy, he never stopped repeating: "Véronique, you'll always be an incurable philistine." Only with the trainer from Mary-sur-Marne, I have the ability to cheat, to make him think I know more than it might seem. It's common practice, Madame Corre, to turn your nose up at everyone in art galleries. I never knew physical therapists could be so delicate, so gifted with sensitivity and compassion. Finally, a PT who's not only interested in bones but the soul, too! Anyway, I look forward to his visits like people do Christmas. It's a welcome counterpoint to your nonsense and bakery gossip.

But I won't. I won't kill you, at least not right now. I'll do it later. For the moment, you're the one thin thread connecting me to the world of the living. I still need you. But don't think for a second I find any pleasure in that. Fate didn't leave me a choice: you (your batty questions, your obnoxious tone, your spittle!), or else this awful solitude for two. A one-armed or one-eyed person has no alternative! I've long tolerated your presence like an inevitable chore, and now I catch myself calling you for our glass at the Vésuve, for our date on the square, our walk along the quays. At first, he was suspicious (you don't exactly inspire trust first thing), but now it's all right, this life for three suits him. He doesn't squint when you call.

No, I won't change doctors. I won't tint the windows either. What's wrong with you? He doesn't need anything new. No, no, what he needs is a routine. No one is more conservative than a disabled man. The bed sheets, socks, gloves of yesteryear, when all was well without a maid and a wheelchair, that's what reassured him.

How can I get away from you? I thought about pretending to run away or die. I sifted through epic travels and imaginary illnesses. I went as far as stockpiling food and barricading myself in with several locks. But I'm not one for the cloistered life.

Where I come from, it's in the shit outside that life grows tall, fed on dirt and noise. Silence, back home, is another word for death. Go one minute without laughing or singing and your neighbor sends your address to the gravedigger. I'd rather have your harassment than the TV or a crossword puzzle alone.

Like that, you let yourself back into my life, to spy, annoy, and prod all around like it was your closet or bathroom. Oh, what do you think? That I don't know a thing about you, your schemes and shenanigans, your weightiest secrets? If only you knew what I know! You'll see what's in store for you the day I decide to talk.

All in due time. For now, let's go out to Joinville-le-Pont, so I can see this famous guinguette you loved droning on about.

This time, his face was different leaving the city. He was easily dazzled by the 19th-century country atmosphere two or three leagues from Paris. A rejuvenation for him and a nice discovery for me. By his dilated pupil, you could tell the music had penetrated his soul. His hand got hot, as if the brass instruments injected him with a surplus of life. His face turned luminous, pure, almost transparent. I felt like he was describing the crazy feelings that arose from the sparkling reflections in the water, the trees' undulations, and the nestled couples in old-fashioned clothes who all seemed to have come out of a Manet painting. I didn't think you had anything picturesque left. France has a reputation for the gray, the serious, refined taste—in other words, boredom. Left out of its features are town dances and simple folks' way of speaking. How, Madame Corre, can you live without folklore? I swear to you, in Joinville-le-Pont I felt a little like I was in Africa. Food in the open air, lively music, and that joyous naïveté that makes up the souls of good people.

The physical therapist from Mary-sur-Marne, Saturdays in Joinville-le-Pont, Karima the sweet little maid, all thanks to you. I'd never have dreamed it up myself. Yes, OK! I admit it, our life is actually a lot better. I'll take you out for dinner one of these nights, M. Farjanel and you. No no, not at Ái Vân. The

Buisson Ardent, maybe, to change it up a little. Or Mavrommatis or, better yet, Bouillon Racine. That would be less painful for me than trying to give you a word of thanks.

The idea to hire Karima was great on all accounts. I should have thought of it myself, but how? You stop thinking about anything else when your husband ends up glued to a wheelchair. You sink along with him into such a black hole that the world loses its reality. Everything leaves you: ideas, dreams, your sense of pleasure and taste. Life only ever resumes at the dismal creak of a wheelchair. You don't have to try to imagine it, your Farjanel still has his two legs, even if on occasion he drools or wets the bed.

Little Karima brought back my appetite for pleasure. Tell me, where did you dig up such a treasure? She cooks like a fairy. And above all she's a fantastic storyteller. Her stories of the East are magical, they not only stun children—they resuscitate the half-dead. He seems to understand it all, interpret it all, savor it. The sparkle in his eye expresses the depth of his enjoyment better than some word.

Plus she's not like you, Karima. She's always smiling and is pleasant to live with. And our once-great maid chambers, which were starting to smell musty and fill up with cockroaches, could finally be used for something. No matter how much he insisted, I never wanted a maid. Out of jealousy, maybe. I wanted to keep him to myself. Cook for him myself, so he could be regaled with bourakhé and tartiflette while showering me with his brightest compliments. Hang our clothes to dry, make the vacuum sing while he lounged on the balcony listening to Mozart or Esposito. It was for him that I came here. Paris, the City of Light. Yes, Paris with its beautiful arrondissements and statues, yes, but only in his arms and in his bursts of laughter... *Et c'est Paris miroir...* No, Paris by wheelchair doesn't make anyone want to sing. We were going out for dinner often and sometimes we'd invite friends to the house. He wasn't a soixante-huitard for nothing. He loved a good meal, good wine, beautiful women, and good books... But it's as a couple that we savored our best moments, over a glass at the Antidote, on a bench in the Jardin du Luxembourg, or stuck right here on the couch while he talked about his travels and the books he'd left notes in. It was his first time living with a partner, and it made him laugh to realize it wasn't as bad as he thought. "What do you want? Nothing is disappointing at my age!... That's it, I know why we don't hurl plates at each other: it's our age gap. Thirty years older than you! Father and daughter—the ideal couple without the poison of incest." I regret not recording his laugh, not delivering that gem to the jewelers so they could make me a ring or a necklace for the rest of my days.

Apart from you, I don't know anyone in this city. I could have met plenty of people if I wanted to. Philippe wasn't opposed to it, and if I'd wanted I could have taken advantage of all his travels to get out and make friends. I never felt the need. I didn't realize I was setting a trap for myself: now that he has no tongue or ears, you're the only one to keep me company. You know why I have such a hard time confiding in you? You don't. I'll tell you one day if you give me the time for it. You're in such a hurry... Always rummaging around in the lives of others without suspecting that the others are just as interested in yours.

Oh, if you only knew what I know about you!

WAS AS TALL AS DICK in my earliest memories. I remember like it happened yesterday, the day he bit my thigh when we were playing under the lemon trees. Dad didn't like that I played with him because he would leave me with a bunch of hair in my mouth and his vicious barking disrupted our neighbors' siesta. But Dad wasn't around very often, so.

I wasn't allowed to go out, so it was Dick and Nantou, the maid, who guided my understanding of life. I suspected at a very young age we were forming a singular family. Mother would sometimes have kora and balafon players come over, but that wasn't enough to cheer up a kid who was just opening up to the world and expecting so much from it. My uncles, aunts, grandparents were never discussed with me. Why was there no friend who'd come visit us? Why were we the only ones in the neighborhood with a dog?

Often gone, especially at night, I missed him less than I was curious about him. Mom fascinated me with her beauty and her frivolous, libertine side. She would spend her days at the tailor's, playing Ludo, or in the nightclubs where she'd indulge her lovers. Dick and Nantou made up the only humanity I was really a part of. Jumping down from the balcony, that famous Tuesday night, I not only had to learn everything, but imagine it, too: father, mother, cousin, aunt, the color of angels, the breadth of a hemisphere.

I was feral and alone, desirous and impatient. But I was lucky to stumble on the only schools suitable for a wandering wild animal like me: Yâyé Bamby's home and the Oxygène. There, you get your education without a textbook or teacher. You learn open-book, life being the one book where everything is written. Yâyé Bamby was a book in her own way, too. A book I had to decipher the day she started in on her Byzantine hangover cure. She seemed so free, so full, with that glass in her hand. How? Was she not happy to be drinking? Didn't she always say that life is a path and that there are only two things that will ever let you step off of it—alcohol and dreams? You have to believe it was humanity and not the good Lord who came up with repentance: to live and spend your life blaming yourself, inventing drugs only to lock up the addicts, vinting wine and then deploring the alcoholics. I thought she drank to raise a middle finger to the bigots and religious fanatics. That she was saying *to hell with the world*. She the prude believer and the imam Lèye-Miro's daughter, who, after B, acquired a taste for sass and revolt. That little bastard, whose whereabouts no one knew, had she brought him into the world in the simple spirit of provocation? Did she carry that child just for its capacity to shock? Or did she drink to lighten the crushing weight of her shame? I'll never know. We were the only ones who knew of her penchant for Guiluxe and the unsolvable puzzle of the letter B. Outside, no one could guess anything. She was still the ideal woman in everyone's eyes, her soul as smooth as her dresses, permanently pressed.

She fascinated me. Her finesse, her tastes, education, but also her innate sense of freedom in a society run by despots and marabouts. In her house as at the Oxygène, you took life as it came. You didn't inflict prayers on or sermonize to the living. How could you expect me to understand anything about humanity after that?

Yâyé Bamby brought to mind a fallen angel and the Oxygène a metaphor for destiny. A vague, impersonal place where people would meet unexpectedly, eat, dance, smoke, drink, occasionally take their lives, very often fight, before vanishing with no goodbye.

You talk to everyone as soon as you meet them, but it takes two or three weeks to distinguish Kefala from Pivi, Mariama from Kesso, Famanin from Tierno. And then one fine day the bosses summon you for a business proposal. You find yourself under a patio umbrella, first in Bonôrou's office, then in Kâkilambé's larger one. At the Oxygène, you don't trifle with the hierarchy: Kâkilambé comes first, then his associate, Bonôrou, then the others—an insignificant mass of others. But before you get to the holy of holies, you brush by touched-up mannequins and jacked meatheads, you hear yourself giving orders. You're talked to like you're in the movies, showed things you only see on film. Everything is so well organized that you don't worry, you don't tense, don't panic. Oh, it's just a game. We're just at the movies, right? By the end, you're fooled. You have to change your name. And nothing surprises you more than when the boss Kâkilambé, so disfigured from all the whisky and blow that it looks like he's wearing a mask, announces:

"Listen, Clara: you're at the Novotel. Your team is Marilyn, Greta, and Rita. The job being what it is, it won't be as stressful with your pals. Tomorrow at 3 o'clock, Makhalé will give you final instructions. Greta's your team lead, you'll obey her orders at all times."

We doubled over laughing when we realized Raye was named Greta, Saran was Marilyn, Penda became Rita, and I was now Clara.

That's how it happened, Madame Corre. It was a game, just like in the movies. Euros, dollars, yen—just like in the movies. Not allowed to accept any other currency. Bread, dough, the grease, just like in the movies. Gringos, bosses, big medicine, just like in the movies. What were the gringos looking for, stepping off the plane? Booze, coke, and pretty women. And for that, they didn't have to lift a finger. They just followed us and the whole Oxygène was theirs. He was crafty, Kâkilambé, and his associate Bonôrou a skilled gunman who was quick with a blade. Of course, you couldn't call it a job. It would have been pointless to talk about it with Yâyé Bamby.

The Novotel bar worked perfectly as our headquarters. A fantastic pool was there at the ready in the middle of the patio, and it gave us an unobstructed view of the Loos Islands. We would set up at 4 o'clock, around the time the planes land. Very quickly, the guests would start hovering around us. We had everything for it: the clothes, the bodies, the talk, the makeup. And Saran, born in Sierra Leone, spoke perfect English and could get by OK in German and Spanish. I'm telling you, Madame Corre, it was just like in the movies. Our job was to privilege the whites: they weren't the best looking, but they were the richest and quickest to pop a bottle of champagne or rum. Everyone else carried a flaw that made them unapproachable: the Guinean franc. Apart from the diaspos, of course—diaspouris, those Guineans who, to jealous minds, left us to rot so they could twiddle their thumbs in Paris, New York, Honolulu and wherever else, who spoke the right languages and banked with the right currencies. A few glasses at the Novotel and we were soaking these charming tourists in the Oxygène's steam. There, we pushed them to drink until their wallets were empty. Then we'd take them by the shoulders to drop them in a taxi. Kâkilambé would do his accounting, his otherwise threatening face lit with satisfaction, and then he'd give us our share.

Yâyé Bamby was fully aware we'd grown up, that we were going out every weekend and that she couldn't do a thing about it. "Live however you want, it's in vogue. Just don't mess with drugs, that's all that I ask." It paid well and only took up two days a week. We'd come home on Mondays knowing that Yâyé Bamby had succumbed. Evenings, we'd wait for her in front of the TV, imagining that after she left the office she'd make a stop at Provençal for a round or two of Pernod. But the tightrope walker held firm over Niagara: the gulf down below, its water spiked by an evil spirit, had no effect on her; that height no longer made her afraid or even nervous. She'd come home serene and unbothered, take down her manga and her yoga books, eat dinner after a few Pacheco tunes, and head to bed early so as not to rouse the devil. "I admit it. I didn't know her well enough," Ray gloated, her eyes bright with admiration. "An aunt? No, a goddess!"

A month passed, then our biggest fear came true. That night, we saw her cross the courtyard, her face vacant, her footing unsure. We were already prepared to call Stumpy Togba, our handyman, for a case of Guiluxe. She gave us a quick hello, threw her bag on the table, and slumped over with a long sigh.

"This whole Zen thing isn't for me. No matter what I do to feed my soul, it won't fly any higher than the ceiling. I need something else."

Next to the Anglican church was a Bambara man who knew about bark and herbs. His charms and talismans could allegedly save you as much from alcohol as the throes of depression or a spell.

"Right, why Zen when we have our ancestors' recipes?"

He weaved amulets into her hair and had her drink down a few concoctions.

That was when our little business flourished. Yâyé Bamby didn't object when we got the idea to paint the little villa and renovate the kitchen and living room.

"Bravo, girls! I imagine you wouldn't have gone this far if it was from drugs."

It wasn't from drugs, Madame Corre, it was just from the movies. It was Bonôrou who managed drug sales. We had no problem turning down customers. There was a corner of the basement with some sinks, syringes, and arm ties—someone, obviously an Andalusian Arab, called it Alhambra. It was swarming with rats and roaches, spider webs and questionable stains on the walls. But to our eyes Alhambra was a palace, just like in stories from the East and tourist pamphlets. We didn't go down often, though. I was happy enough with some yamba, and my friends would only touch tchondi on birthdays and over the holidays. I'm telling you, Madame Corre: movies. A flirt and some champagne, no more than the length of a film. Although sometimes connections were made. Some would send us cards from Brittany or California. Others gave us gifts: smartphones, purses, watches. The more realistic of them sent cash.

Alfâdio could disappear for months and reappear as if we'd said goodbye the night before. I didn't ask him anything, and he did the same. He would set me on fire and douse me with gifts, then we'd make love.

Alfâdio would turn up and could equally well be coming back from Dakar, Freetown, Lomé, or prison. He was my love, my yârabi, my kélé, my mârafandji. Whatever he did there was his business. In those days I thought the whole world lived that way. Like Yâyé Bamby, like Raye, like Saran and Makhalé, Bonôrou and Kâkilambé. We lived freely, no ties. No contract, no family, like we were living in the first hours of the world, when nothing was forbidden. I learned to avoid him when it was necessary. I knew what would happen to me if he saw me with a gringo, even if we were just getting a drink.

"Do you really love him?" Raye asked. "The guy freaks me out." Yes, he was weird, yes, he was scary, and maybe that's why I loved him. I guess if he hadn't been weird, I wouldn't have loved him so much. What did I know about love? No one ever mentioned it before I left home jumping off the balcony. Yes,

I'd committed a crime, yes, I couldn't wait to forget about it. I couldn't wait to find something other than what I'd seen struggling between Dick and Nantou, between my dad's absence and my mom's calculated indifference.

I missed the world. It's a mega geography, the world, with its streams and rivers, volcanoes, jungles, and, in the most secret heart of all this chaos, love—a poisonous fruit, a wonderful, forbidden fruit. And it had a name, this love, along with a gun and a face, or several: a demon's and an angel's. A python and a cherub. All lovers are like that, they come in twos. In Greece, Rome, Persia, Guinea. Eros and Psyche, Romeo and Juliet, Zal and Zadabh, Atou and Alfâdio.

Yes, Madame Corre, I'm not ashamed to say it: I was madly in love because I felt madly loved. We had the same tastes: in beer, wine, rap, reggae, salsa, weed. He'd yell at me sometimes—or slap me—a few seconds after whispering sweet nothings.

One day he found me under the coconut trees talking with Saran.

"Come here," he said. "Right now, I have something to tell you. Come here right now before the good Lord changes his mind."

He hoisted me onto his shoulders, jumped with his feet together on the beach pebbles, then ran like he was trying to escape from a pack of wild dogs. When he was out of the Oxygène thugs' line of sight, he set me down on top a rock and took a few seconds to catch his breath.

"Well, Atou. The dream's finally come true."

"The dream?"

"You don't remember? The ticket, the passport? The visa, all that? Well, it's done!"

He lifted me up again like he might have done with a cotton ball and laid me down roughly on the sand.

"Hold tight, babe, and listen close. I'm talking a visa with a stamp, a seal, signature, the whole bit! I walk out the German embassy and, hand to God, I lose it. How could I not after that? I went nuts and there's nothing better than going nuts. I've been crazy two times: crazy for you, and crazy about leaving this fucking country. Hamburg. Any idea where that is? Me neither. All that matters is getting there. *And* getting there safely. Check the visa, look. Real as the sky above, true as our love."

The questions rattled around in my head. Words formed, urgent and messy, in the middle of my throat but lagged and faded by the time they reached my lips. He was delirious, impossible to cut off.

"I'm going to marry you, Atou, understand? No, not like this, not this wild animal here in front of you. Another me. One you've never seen, who's waited too long to clean himself up and get out of this cangue and show his true face. Me, yeah, the guy you can't hear or predict who's still right there at your fingertips and who no one else can see because of all the smog in this fucking country. Only when the plane lands, when that shithead customs agent pops open the lock... Give me two years, just two years babe. Two years is more than enough to become a man. Yeah, Atou, I want to be someone, be someone for you. One heart for you and two strong arms to pull you out of here, cherish you, push you, protect you. I'll move heaven and earth. Out there, when you move around you find things. And look, the visa is here! Here, here, here—it's a done deal! I'm tired of talking. Now, it's our wedding night. Right now, this minute, when we're through eating and drinking, we'll smoke yamba. And then, after that, we'll smoke another one. Nothing's truly ever happened before, if you think about it. Not for me, not for anyone else... But tonight's our wedding night. Two years and I'll have it all together: the residence card, the job, the apartment. Then you'll come up and you'll see plain as day, the true face of the man who loves you, and you'll love him because you won't be scared anymore. Right there, look, that's fear freezing you. Fear of abandoning yourself to the dream, fear of searching, fear of never finding it. You find whatever you dig for up there. Here it's all rocks. Let's go, drought is on the horizon. Two more years here and bam, we're nothing but dust. Sure, we'd be standing on two feet, yeah, but with two fossilized souls, two decalcified bodies, two beings fallen into ruin. I don't want to dry out standing here, or watch as my hair chars in the heat, my toes and fingers turning into sand... Oh no, not up there! It's right here where we're digging our graves. Five, six years—ten max—enough time to get some money together, and we'll come back to remake everything those fucks demolished, not just the roads and bridges, but especially here [*he indicated his head*] and here [*palm over the left side of his chest*]. That's what they're aiming for, and it's not just bullets coming out of their satanic artillery, but lies too, tons of lies, and hate, tons of hate. Every heart is dead, here, that's where they take aim first... Let's go, come on babe, it's our wedding night."

Room 13 was available that night. The ideal number, according to him, for a couple like us, for a night like this one. There was blood. He thought it was his outsized manliness. It wasn't. But it was simple: in my mind I was still a virgin, my body untouched, untouched in my soul. Untouched by perverts and demons.

He talked to me the whole rest of the night about my thighs and breasts and schemed up the most plausible plans for our future life together.

When the day came, I went with him to the airport. He kissed me.

"If there weren't all these idiots around us, you know how I'd say goodbye. But hey, in Hamburg we'll have a bed that's just for the two of us... Hey babe? You know what you're risking if... [*He made his fist into a gun.*] Oh what the hell, you're free to do what you want. Faithful chicks are a thing of the past. Don't tell me you can go two years without a guy! You're no different from the others, Atou… The heart, the heart! Yeah yeah, the heart. It's all lies! The heart says this, sex does that—that's how it was in the first hours of the world… Tell yourself that this shithead Alfâdio loves you."

He held me a long time before he went through customs. Words came out one by one from my mouth, choked by my sobbing.

"Do what you want in Hamburg. But, please, don't tell me anything. I'll die of jealousy."

"OK, Atou. OK!"

He called me the very next day. I was expecting it. Still, it made me keel over. No one had ever called from so far away. He told me it wasn't a dream: Hamburg snow had actually crunched under his feet. It was cold, and that's just what he'd set out to find. "Nothing better than -12°C to put some balls on you!" Before his eyes was everything little Black boys dreamed of in Africa: skyscrapers, trains, factories, cathedrals. Soumah had been waiting for him at the airport with a coat, boots, gloves, everything he needed to keep from catching pneumonia. He'd warned: "It's going to be hard." That didn't discourage him. In fact, it gave him a titanic energy that radiated from his spine. It was Hamburg that had to watch out: he'd come to win, and nothing could keep him from winning, especially since his love for me quintupled since his plane touched down. In two years, he would have the time to change. He'd throw the flaws of his past down at his feet and in suit and tie he'd greet me at the airport. Soumah had promised him a contract with the security company he worked for. After the contract would come the residence card, and, after that, paradise. Soumah was more than a friend—he was a true brother.

"Armstrong's foot on lunar soil, and mine on the promised land. Seriously, anything's possible here. I'm straight up a poet already."

He'd known him from high school in N'Zérékoré. Together, they played volleyball, screwed girls, and dropped out
of school. That forms a bond. He was going to take care of him
until the good Lord sent something his way: a soft mattress in
a corner of the living room, a Greek sandwich so he wouldn't
die of hunger. And, of course, all the rest: tips on picking up
women, yamba, booze, how to ride the Metro for free, how to
get away from the cops. We agreed he'd call me every Sunday at
7 PM and that I should braid my hair and wear perfume like it
was a real date.

Ears buzzing with Hamburg this, Hamburg that, this
area of Hamburg, that Hamburg neighborhood, I could—if I
sprouted a pair of wings—have found him instantly, without
losing my way. I would take care of his laundry and, later, the
studio apartment he'd move into after leaving Soumah's. The
city of Hamburg had jumped off the map and wedged its port,
all its avenues and monuments, in a corner of my brain. In the
living room, they were waiting for me, eyes brimming with curiosity.

"So, this contract? How long until the residence card?"

"Does he speak German already?"

"Not that fast, even if he's in Germany! Let it happen!"

Raye turned toward her aunt, giving me a side-eye.

"Did you notice, Auntie, how her eyes didn't even get
red? I would have cried if my Romeo were so far away. I bet she
doesn't even love him. It's all just so she can see Hamburg."

"To see Hamburg, I'd do anything," Auntie replied. "Hamburg, Rotterdam, Barcelona! It's a shame, a city with no port.
And what about you? If Ousmane left?"

"I'm all about America, with or without a port. If Ousmane has to leave, it's going to be New York or Montreal."

"No way, it has to be Hamburg. That way we can double
date."

"Hamburg or Montreal, what matters is getting the hell out of here."

"I'd leave too if I were your age. But—"

Yâyé Bamby never finished that sentence. It looked like she was trying to hold back tears. She swallowed some corn mush and made her way to bed, not paying attention to our conversion. Strange, she'd always been that way with her little caprices, her depression, pain, frustration. Deep down, Guiluxe or not, I'd always seen her like this: her face serene, looking nonchalant; but her spirit was prey to some secret agitation.

Her cure only added to her manias—she wasn't the one generating them. She'd flit between the courtyard and her room, turning the lights on or off, letting the faucet run or shutting it off, complaining about everything and nothing. The Harmattan breeze would dry out her skin and, thanks to the Bambara drinks, she suffered vertigo and migraines. She claimed she was seeing an herbalist to treat it, that that was why she was late coming home from work so often.

■ ■ ■

Two months later, Alfâdio still didn't have a job or residence card, but he'd learned how to get by. He started sending me gifts: jewelry, underwear, shoes. Then came the phone call where he announced he was going to leave Hamburg for a city with some unpronounceable name.

"Nothing to worry about, starting this April you'll get fifty euros a month, and that's a half a stack back home. See how much this dope Alfâdio loves you!"

There were two Western Unions after that and two or three emails telling me to be patient, that this could take years. "I won't be able to call you every day. What matters is that I love you." The very last email was terse but touching: "I may have to disappear for a bit, but you better believe I always reappear."

Yâyé Bamby's ailments calmed down and soon I was the one with bouts of vertigo and vomit. Raye brought me pills and tablets from the pharmacy. The treatment did nothing.

One morning, tears rolled down from Yâyé Bamby's eyes. She collapsed on the couch after inspecting me from head to toe.

"This is bringing back so many memories. Oh no, good Lord! Oh no..."

A heavy silence fell over the house, punctuated with the clinking of mugs and muffled steps, hiccups, sneezes. A few minutes later, Yâyé Bamby's gloomy voice broke through, and it gave me the feeling of being licked across the face by a flame.

"Sit down on this chair, Atou, and look in my eyes and tell me: how long has it been since you had your last cycle?"

"I wasn't keeping track—I didn't know you were supposed to?"

"Oh my God! So that's it?" shouted Raye, visibly on the brink of tears.

"Oh no. Anything but this. You should have warned me, Atou! Oh my God, oh my God!"

It was my turn. I started to weep. It was tormenting to have made Yâyé Bamby grieve.

"How would I have warned you, Auntie? I don't even know what that means, *having your cycle.*"

"OK, OK, it's not your fault. It's thanks to this goddamn existence that's only satisfied if it's playing tricks on you."

Anger gave way to an uneasiness we weren't used to. There was certainly sulking from time to time, sudden out-bursts, but the three of us still got along well. We had matured and this wasn't our first shock. The surprise, though, had quite literally struck me. Instantly, I was hurt, horribly hurt, and I couldn't think about anything: not Alfâdio, not the baby, or the future. Raye, who wasn't saying anything, looked at me like I'd just grown a third eye. Yâyé Bamby was crying, and I could tell it wasn't for me but for herself. Yes, it brought her back memories, things she'd struggled to bury that were now emerging with an air of vomit and the violence of a bludgeon. The same scene was playing out twenty years later. She must have been my age, with my inexperience, to feel the fullness of my desperation. The snake of love had bitten her in the stomach, too, and she was alone, naïve, and no one said anything to her. You didn't talk about those things here. Girls grew up fast, without their parents knowing. There was so much they were unaware of, including the perfidy of men and their own body's mysteries. It was even more cruel in her day. Passersby were given an index of transgressors, and the imams had the fatal voice of an inquisitor. At least I wasn't the daughter of the imam in Lèye-Miro—no one even knew me in this region. I had no father, no mother, no spiritual guide or guardian angel. Plus, yesterday and today have never once been the same thing.

Yâyé Bamby and I were the same species, with the same fieriness, the same distress, but not the same time.

T HE NEXT TIME (we were on the square, I think), barely seated, you shot your foul mood right into my face.

"Discretion's not necessarily a good thing, Countess. It could simply be a mark of indifference."

"I don't understand."

"You didn't ask me why I don't like balafons. That's the first thing people love about Africa: the music and the food. If I don't like balafons, there's a reason."

It took great pains not to plant you there and take a nice stroll along the Seine. Five minutes with you and, right away, I had the urge to find some fresh air.

"It's your right to spit at a balafon, Madame Corre, but if you have reasons for doing it, for goodness sake, keep them to yourself."

"If I hate balafons, it's really because of the niâmou."

"The niâmou?"

"You know what it is: that mask that's ten meters tall and

covered with little mirrors, made out of glass and straw, and that dances with its legs over the roofs and treetops! Well, it was then, on that day. And those sacred balafons rang out entirely for him. The musicians were under the bridge, and you couldn't even see them the crowd was so thick. But we heard them, that's for sure, we heard them, the sharp *doh* of the balafons over everything. And the people who'd brought me there were pushing me in the back with a force as strong as the crowd was big. And the people danced, sang—they yelled out much more than they sang. It was only afterward that I understood why the cars coming off the highway were circling the roundabout and why their hordes of kids poured out under the bridge before leaving along the ledge, thick black smoke sputtering behind. One look, with their hats and uniforms, and you could tell: they were pioneers of the Party. They jumped out of the bus and ran to join the crowd, imitating the acrobatics of the niâmou.

"It was already 2 PM, Countess. I'd been there eight hours, hungry, tired, half roasted by the sun, and I was having a very hard time keeping my son close. Waves of people threatened to take him from me at any minute. At 5 AM, they'd knocked at my door and ordered me to get dressed and follow them without a word. After the pioneers came the parade of schoolchildren. They also had their own flags and uniforms. The balafons quieted every so often to give way to the loudspeaker-armed militiamen bellowing out slogans that the crowd would repeat at a decibel that could raise the sea.

"At that moment, the sergeant who'd brought me there turned my son over to his assistant. 'The boy is no longer your son, Madame Diallo. He is a son of the Revolution.' 'Are you saying I won't see him again?' 'It would be better for you and me both if we discussed other matters.' The sergeant had no reaction when I grabbed his uniform to keep from falling. My eyes, hallucinating, strayed from the breaking waves to the movie playing before my eyes. Then he suddenly locked eyes on the throngs of restless schoolchildren shouting out. I saw a child wobble in the mix, clinging to anything he could so he wouldn't be trampled under the crowd. That was him. He was more slender and lighter-skinned than the others. He took a blow to the head and staggered. It's always the fairest ones, the skinniest, the most mussy-haired who get beat up.

"That's when an uproar exploded from one side of the Palais du Peuple. The door of a Jeep swung open. Four men stood on the platform, hands tied behind their backs, with long beards and gray tunics. The Jeep came right up to the bridge, cutting through the booing crowd. What did it all mean: that crowd, that Jeep surrounded by soldiers and militiamen? Was it a new concept for Party pageants? And why these four men with their shaggy beards and hands behind their backs? What role were we playing for them? I had already attended this kind of parade where, to recall our colonial past's horrors, scenes were staged of whites in colonial helmets whipping Blacks. What horrors did they want to recall that day? Those of slavery, it seemed.

"The niâmou left the roofs and treetops to display his acrobatics around the Jeep, terrifying the poor passengers with the grimacing face of a boogeyman. The Jeep continued to roll at a snail's pace toward the bridge. I was having difficulty staying upright, staving off the vertigo. 'Commander, Sir... I'm going to die of thirst.' Eventually the man who had taken me there showed his stripes and ordered a militiaman to find some water.

"The niâmou, the balafons, the variegated crowd undulating as if moved by swells. A violent apprehension took me by the stomach. The Jeep was no more than a few meters from me. Then I recognized him. And, for the first time, I knew what was going on. My mouth opened; no sound came out. Gathering my strength, I stepped forward, swimming against the current, making way with my hands and feet across the tight mass of the crowd. I put a hand out in the vague hope of reaching the Jeep. A militiaman knocked it back with a swipe of his baton.

Taken by the tide, I was tossed a few meters away. I clung to the sergeant's uniform to keep from falling. The scene was repeated two or three times. I never managed to reach that goddamn vehicle and touch his cheek. I never managed to catch his eye. He didn't hear me saying his name. However hard I tried, my mouth was like the soundless bottom of an empty cave. Then the Jeep disappeared, swallowed by the crowd.

"I looked the other way, toward the rows of schoolchildren shouting whatever slogans the militia had ordered they repeat. Always the lightest and skinniest of them. And their resemblance had never been so striking as in that moment. I still tried to move my hands and feet and did manage to inch a few steps forward before realizing it was pointless. He was too far away, I didn't have enough time.

"They weren't in the Jeep anymore. They'd reached the top of the stairs by the time I looked away from the rows of schoolchildren. They moved forward with gliding steps, almost airborne, eyes fixated on nothingness. They knew where they were going and it was as if they were already there. Once they'd reached the bridge, one wearing a white bubu robe—who looked like a master of ceremonies—silenced the crowd, whose hellish swells softened at the same time. They were presented in alphabetical order, beginning with him, Diallo. Each of their names was punctuated with boos. On the other side, the kids were having a harder time bringing their screams to a close. And sure enough, he was the lightest and skinniest of them all, only he was shouting like the others, laughing like them. Did he know what was happening? Had he recognized him? That beard altered his face and he was too short to see high up from where he stood.

"Everything after that happened very fast. The rope was cinched around their necks in alphabetical order. In alphabetical order, they were thrown into the void. And everything doubled in intensity: the clamor of the slogans, the undulation of the crowd, the crushing beat of the balafons. I still wonder if he was already dead when I fainted.

"At the hospital, I was still on an IV when they came in. There were four of them and only one was wearing civilian clothes. He was the one who talked to me, in a slow, delicate voice, the voice of diplomats. One tasked with coating the poison, making the pill easier to swallow. 'I trust you believe in God, Madame Diallo? We all need him, especially in times like these. Don't worry, everything will be done to bring you back to good health. Here's my card, if you ever need anything, please don't hesitate to call.' 'I just need to see my son.' 'Don't complicate things, Madame Diallo. Follow through with your treatment, forget the rest. Take care, Madame Diallo, and safe travels.' He felt he had to go on since I looked stunned: 'Go home, Madame Diallo. It's better for you, better for us. Your flight leaves tomorrow. Please, do not belabor this for your son. It's better for you, better for us.'

"Do you see now, Countess, why I don't like balafons?"

I listened the whole way through without coughing or sneezing, as they say back home. Without a teardrop either. Back there, that story is as well known as a song's chorus. In those days, when conspirators were being hanged, their white wives were expelled and their children, declared a national heritage, were returned to the State. I understand, Madame Corre, I understand, but your son had the time to get to know his true parents—believe me, that's something special.

All the same, I let a week or two go by before coming back to it.

"What are you waiting for to go find him?"

"I'll never set foot there again."

"He's your son!"

"I know he's dead. In that country you aren't long for this world if you're mixed or albino. You know that."

"Human sacrifices! Here we are talking about it again. It seemed like it was happening everywhere: in the stadiums, on public squares, right up to the presidential gardens."

"You see? A mixed child, the son of a conspirator at that! He had a thousand and one reasons to wind up cooked or in a cell at Camp B."

"Why do you think he's dead?"

"It's a real thing, maternal instinct. And I won't say I have proof of it, but just about. A veterinarian cousin did an exchange program there, go figure, just after Sékou Touré's death. He searched everywhere—*everywhere*—for five years. No trace of Dian Charles-André."

I gave you a napkin and paced around long enough to let you dry your tears. It's long, "Dian Charles-André," for a single baby. Long and so incongruous! It was your deceased husband who came up with it, you said. Charles-André. It was your father's first name, and Dian, *his* father's first name. The little one's mixed heritage must have been in his horoscope, he said. He insisted that he read the Bible and the Qur'an, that he be half black, half white, half Christian, half Muslim. Alas, dreams don't last long—especially in those countries. Anyway, I have in front of me a widow who's seen her husband hanged and who's heard no news of her son.

If it's even possible, we're on the right track in Conakry. The gentleman in question has a white mother. Even better, he has some vague memories of Dijon—of a certain Gammie in particular. What in the world could Gammie be? A person? A filly? A poodle? You may not know a thing about it, Dijonnaise as you are. The fact remains: it wasn't enough for you to visit my country, to wed yourself to one of ours. You'd also married his fate and plunged up to your neck into his shit. Oh yes, that forms a bond, Madame Corre, that forms a bond. I need to make an effort to see you differently. I have to get used to treating you better. You're not a simple neighbor anymore, one I have to tolerate just to kill time. You've become a friend.

We shouldn't be afraid of words: kindred.

ON THE FIRST DAY OF SCHOOL, in Yâyé Bamby's day, vaginas were inspected and unwanted pregnancies made the front page news. The ones deemed guilty were exiled from their families and school benches, stigmatized by the griots, cursed by the praying masses. In my time, you weren't hanged for so little. But still, harpies would cry out from behind the courtyard and the young folks shunned you and your spoiled meat, but you weren't any more alone than you were before. I didn't live through the same misery Yâyé Bamby did. It had been twenty years since she'd seen her son and she didn't even know where he was, or if he was still alive. Things had changed. The city was teeming with perfectly happy bastards and teen girls with round bellies. I was going to be one of them. I was going to be the mother of my son and wife to Alfâdio.

I thought I should let him know as soon as Yâyé Bamby brought what happened to my attention, but how? I didn't have his phone number, he always called me.

I stood up to go to the cybercafé, but Raye pointed out the clock on the TV.

"It's closed right now—you'll have to go tomorrow."

I was restless all night. How would he respond? The pregnancy didn't bother me; I just didn't want to do it alone. It's only in moments like these that a man's shoulders have any use at all. It wasn't supposed to happen this way. It was just our wedding night. The kid, if there would even be one, should be born up there, sheltered from malaria, from discrimination and hunger. Up there, where I was constantly told that, with the magic of a residence card, the hinges on heaven's gate would turn as easily as a subway turnstile. "Well. I hope they hurry up and come to an end, these stupid two short years. Get on with it, giddy up, knuckle down and spare no expense. Find a place to stay in this town with an unpronounceable name where, you say, the cold has sharp teeth and the fog a lead blanket. I'm coming, Alfâdio. I'll be a mother already if you take any longer to legalize your papers. You'll come to the airport dressed like a kingpin, surrounded by your friends. If it works out this way, I'll have found a job before we celebrate her first birthday. It's going to be a girl—my little finger tells me so. It's going to be a girl and I already know her name. She'll have your round and cheerful face, so her femininity will be all the sweeter. You'll be a nightshift security guard or taxi driver and I'll be a cashier (absolutely not a house maid or a personal care assistant). On weekends, we'll meet up with expats and listen to music from back home over fonio and mafé. We'll make love every night and you'll touch me from head to toe not with the barrel of a revolver but the soft skin of your hand."

It amazed Raye to touch my round belly and feel the donkey kicks the baby used to remind her mother of her existence. "Some real wrestling moves! That's not a girl, Atou." Yâyé Bamby, coming back from work, would bring me milk and cheese, and, kissing me hello, never failed to check on us. "So? Little Bamby doing good? Mama too, I hope." She'd shed torrents of tears the day I announced the child would take her name if it were a girl. It was almost two years ago that she stood poised on her wire over that Niagara of alcohol bubbling fifty meters below. Women who seem frail always outdo the others when it comes to prowess and stamina.

My conversations with Raye were getting more and more heated. As always, we couldn't agree on anything, but on this subject it turned into twin rivalry.

"OK first, it's not milk and cheese you need—I wonder who planted that idea in Yâyé Bamby's head. What you need is sorrel. Sorrel, soumbara, and ginger. Nothing better for toning up that fetus. But you won't listen to me. *Listen* is a foreign concept to your little mule head."

"It needs calcium. And milk has calcium, unlike all that stuff."

"And you really shouldn't just sit there doing nothing. You need to run, jump—the gym's not far away."

"What if I hemorrhage?"

"Hemorrhage! Oh, mother. Come on, get up! Hurry up, I'm taking you jogging. We'll go to the concert after a shower."

Alpha Blondy was playing at the Palais du Peuple.

When we got back that night, the house was empty. Yâyé Bamby wasn't in her room, or in the shower, or at the sink. She came in a few minutes later, stumbling.

"Hi, my babies! Let's call Stumpy Togba for a case of Gui-luxe, how about!"

At the Oxygène, an Irishman died of an overdose and a girl was found in the landfill by the ocean with a knife in her back. I wasn't hanging around the Oxygène anymore given my condition, but Raye would bring back fried yams and fresh news.

Yâyé Bamby took us out more often to take my mind off things.

One Saturday night, she was driving me to the Palm

Camayenne, where the port festival committee was having a reception. Suddenly, she turned from the musicians and acrobats switching out on stage to elbow me.

"Look behind you."

He was standing with his back against the door, arms crossed, his red panther stare like a nail in the middle of my face. You could see his ringed fingers and count the scars streaking his cheeks.

The panic didn't only hit me, it also took hold of sweet, carefree Yâyé Bamby. You could see the sweat forming on her forehead and trembling lip.

"Let's get out of here right now, before the end of the show. We'll see what he does."

Once outside, we jumped into the car without giving him time to react, and took a long detour beside the Nigerien highway. But, beside the stadium, Yâyé Bamby made a huge swerve after looking in the rearview mirror.

"Look, right behind us! Look!"

It was him, at the wheel of his car, unfazed and enigmatic, with his indigo bomber and eerie sunglasses.

"Let's go to Nongo! We can lose him easily in Nongo's alleys."

After Nongo, we followed the mountain ledge and pushed all the way to Lambanya Beach, where she cut the motor and let out a breath with her chin on the steering wheel.

"That son of a bitch. What does he want from us? Truly— what does he want? He's waiting for us at the house, that's for sure! What are we going to do? What's going to happen to us?"

Two hours later, Yâyé Bamby's face had changed. It seemed to tense up as night fell. With a nervous hand, she started the car again.

"We're going back. Let him stop us if he wants. Why doesn't he just gut us, impale us. It'd be better than all this unbearable waiting."

At the house, no one was waiting for us.

Yâyé Bamby opened the door and sprawled out on the couch.

"Just show up already! Just show up, you dirty indigo bomber cop!"

No one came knocking at our door that night or any of the following. Indigo Bomber had vanished, dissuaded no doubt by Yâyé Bamby's temperament.

As for Alfâdio, he seemed to have sunk into that town with an unpronounceable name where luck had cast him. I was glued to the phone for nothing. I'd go ten times a day to the cybercafe, desperately hoping for a reply to my emails.

"What if he's dead?" shouted Raye.

She had the look of a bad day, an illegible and irritated one, so you couldn't tell if the idea terrified her or gave her some secret pleasure. I remember I was making us some plantains when she opened that beak like a bird of ill will. It took everything I had not to throw boiling oil at her.

But it wasn't true. Alfâdio wasn't dead.

A few years after Yâyé Bamby was born, Stumpy Togba told me he'd come back and that he knew where he was staying.

"In prison, I hope."

"No, Foulamadina. With his parents."

"So he has parents, then?"

I should tell you, Madame Corre, at that time I was living alone with my daughter in a two-room apartment I rented in the Hamadallaye neighborhood. Yâyé Bamby's place had gotten too small for the four of us. And Stumpy Togba, who had a soft spot for us, would come by from time to time to see if I needed anything.

"You seem suspicious."

"If you're telling the truth, we're going there right now. I have his kid and he has no idea."

I washed the little one, dressed her in new clothes and sprinkled her with talcum powder. You'd have thought we were celebrating her first day of school.

The taxi made it to the luxury villas along the seashore after sputtering a while by the tin shacks, the piles of bagged coal, and the papaya and mango vendors. We left him at the edge of the asphalt. The smell of cullet and burnt tires was getting sharper, less bearable to the lungs. A rocky path led toward the mangrove. We walked down it on foot, narrowly avoiding the motorcycle taxis and the soccer balls from the players in the street. Five hundred meters below, the path got smaller, eventually the size of a headband running through little houses with narrow doors and yards where women were busy around pots and washboards.

I recognized him as soon as we got there. He was wearing a tie. An old man in a thickly-embroidered Phrygian cap—surely his father—was sitting beside him in the middle of the yard. Behind them, under the narrow veranda, sat four women—one of whom was white—on low chairs. His mother and co-wives? A kid was shouting and running in all directions trying to get a ball. Not everyone was black.

My visit surprised him, but he didn't look embarrassed. He didn't bother to stand up and kiss me hello.

"Hey, it's Atou! I'm so glad you came... Father, this is Atou. She's an old friend of mine."

His gaze wandered back to his wives.

"Come here, Martha—yes, come here! This is her, the one named Atou. I'm sure I've already talked to you about her."

We were offered peanuts and some ginger juice.

I was not in a position to hit Martha. I had to be court-eous. I didn't stutter, didn't sweat or tremble. Stumpy Togba would tell me later that I'd kept perfectly calm, indifferent even, my face serene and with a smile as natural as someone who'd come to greet her cousin. Martha spoke at length about her two kids and her town with an unpronounceable name. It was the first time she'd been to Africa.

"This continent is marvelous!"

"What? All this noise and filth—"

"Oh! Like when we did New Delhi..."

I took another drink of ginger juice, spurred by the lovely atmosphere, the right words and laughter.

"Martha's a big traveler, Atou. It's not just India she's been to—Colombia, too."

"I'm glad for you, Alfâdio. You got it, at least? Your resid-ence card?"

"Martha helped me out a lot. I got a job as a warehouse-man in her father's company. Oh! Who's this little sunflower?"

"Umm... My niece."

"You have a niece? I never knew you had a sister. She's such a cute little girl."

As soon as I got home, I dropped off Yâyé Bamby at a neighbor's and hurried to the Oxygène, where friends were wait-ing for me with an a gleeful excitement that didn't surprise me.

"So? When do you leave? Was he wearing a tie?"

"You really think I'm going to waste my time with an ob-scure warehouseman from Leinfelden-Echterdingen? No way. Who do you think I am, my same-mothers? Good riddance—to hell with him and his German wife."

"He came back with a German?"

"Yes. A slut with greasy hair and two little ones about this big."

"That bastard! What an oaf!"

"No, no, my lovely same-mothers. One lost, ten found! We're going out—tonight it's all on me."

We drank all night chanting at the top of our lungs: "One lost, ten found!"

Saran, who couldn't stand upright, was looking at me with eyes full of admiration.

"How do you do it? I'd have broken down. It's honestly hard to believe a girl of your caliber even exists."

The next day, she was at my side, and Raye and Penda and Barenga and all the others with her. They surrounded me with their looks and catastrophic whispering. I had a hard time moving because of the bandages and infusions. My throat wouldn't swallow my saliva and my ashamed eyes wouldn't fix on them. They were wiping my forehead, taking my pulse, whispering the most comforting words.

"I would have done the exact same thing."

"There's no shame in it, seriously."

"In moments like this, yes, it's beyond thought: it's this or a bullet or sulfuric acid—however strong your character is."

"What a shit! How is anything like this even possible?"

"I wouldn't have killed myself—I'd have gutted her!"

Of everyone in the group, Raye had the hardest time holding back tears.

"When I heard the sirens, I thought of you first thing. And yet there was no reason. You seemed so strong last night! Luckily it was more fear than real trouble. Three or four days in the hospital, according to the nurses. They got you there just in time."

My suicide attempt was quickly forgotten. Down there, Madame Corre, no one would think to write a book. You have to understand: that would mean you had time to kill. Life being what it is, it's better to leave the seeds of the past in the ground and ready yourself for the next ones. You don't give books to the deathly ill, you give them opium. Forgetting is what's needed in that critical moment of distress. This doesn't mean we've turned amnesiac. Our amnesia is artificial, our amnesia is momentary. Memory returns with the thaw, when the thunder quiets, when the wind softens.

At the Oxygène, we didn't have time to dwell on the past's little dramas. There would always be funnier, more palpitating ones, not to mention trippy.

A week after leaving the hospital, I got a phone call from Sergeant Karim Bah, our "man at the airport": a well-dressed and very dark-skinned man who was flying in from Mexico by way of Casablanca on Royal Air Maroc, taking a cab to the No-votel with 100,000 dollars in a briefcase. I alerted Bonôrou and the mousetrap was quickly set. The idiot got shot at the top of the Kâkimbo bridge because he didn't want to let the briefcase go. The newspaper told us the next day he was one Manuel San-chez-Quispe, a new consul of Peru. Kâkilambé called me in so I could receive my customary 10% and bottle of Jack Daniel's.

I was able to make ends meet with no issue. All the money Kâkilambé gave me each weekend, the tips from gringos, the consul of Peru's cash, it meant I could pay rent, feed my daught-er, pay for her school. I was watching her grow up and telling myself deep down: "It's better, much better this way, to live without a father, a father like that. Mama's here, don't worry. Mama is here. You'll have everything you need: loving arms, lullabies, trinkets, and caramels. She'll keep you safe from hun-ger and danger, from the witch's red eye and the cackling of the hyena."

I had no cause for complaint. I was eating three times a day, living in a house that didn't let in rain or wind. The good Lord had saved me from mange and leprosy and typhoid fev-er, my broken heart had been definitively healed from love. My daughter was feeding me with happiness, friends, joy, and care-lessness.

Saran came to find me one day with a calabash of papayas and avocados.

"All the money you've earned here, what are you going to do with it? You don't know? I got an idea: we go to Bamako!"

I said yes without thinking. Bamako, not Leinfelden-Ech-terdingen! That trip needed to happen. The world as vast as it is, I only knew one city. Not even the dust of the islands jutting out from it, not even Coyah's arms of ocean, not Smoking Dog, the mist-shrouded mountain that natives of Jakarta and Honolulu claimed to have summitted.

We rented a bush cab and Stumpy Togba offered to come with us. What a great idea Saran had—those dollars the whole Peruvian consul ordeal brought me might have been lost on a few weeks of food, on clothes and perfume, partying. But by in-vesting in Bamako's famous bazin, in the bogolan of the Bam-bara people, in Tuareg jewelry, in Dogon masks, we could ex-tract five, ten, fifteen times their worth. I was going to be rich, buy myself a house, a little café or cosmetics store. Alfâdio just had to disappear—along with Santa Claus. I didn't need anyone anymore.

Everything went according to plan in Bamako. We came home confident, cheerful, our heads full of dreams about cash and flourishing business. After some reflection, I wasn't satis-fied with a little café. One day I'd have my own Oxygène—or I'd buy the original if Kâkilambé were ever willing to sell it. I'd test the waters as soon as I got there. Saran had a good idea. We were rolling up in a covered pick-up, weighed down not with gold but with almost five tons of bazin, kilos of jewelry, dozens of masks. That can change your fate, five tons of bazin.

We bypassed Bissikrima Junction to avoid any run-ins with highwaymen. Stumpy Togba, who had made the drive five times already, led us toward the mountains for a direct route to Dogomet. One of his friends ran a hostel there full of young women on the run and truckers from all ends of the earth. We ate a badly cooked chicken there (there were still feathers in it) along with oily black fries. It was a long day's travel. We slept happily, not paying any attention to the awful state of the mattress and sheets.

The next day, Stumpy Togba let us know we had time for a hearty breakfast: he was leaving for the marshes with the driver to wash the truck.

By 10 o'clock, there was still no truck.

Dogomet was swarming like a hive. And Dogomet made me think of the Oxygène: another metaphor for destiny where people crossed paths without knowing each other, without any plan. Where were they coming from, these multicolored semis, covered with naïve logos and verses from the Qur'an, overloaded with onions and red oil, smoked fish and fabric? Where were they going? From the termite mounds in Senegal to the raging rivers of Côte d'Ivoire? From the ocher walls of Timbuktu to the colonial banisters of Freetown?

One day, two days, still nothing. No truck, no Togba.

"How do you explain that?" Saran said, her head in her hands.

Yes, how do you explain that? Two days to wash a truck.

Dogomet had the color and salt of the Oxygène: the booze, the sex, the clamor, the fights. No one was from here. No before, no after, nothing but the now, the thick, intense now, ready at any moment to blow up from a grenade or joie de vivre. No ancestors, no spiritual guardians. You could do what you wanted, no one was going to hold you accountable. I felt relieved to see that the Oxygène wasn't the only of its kind, that you could have a good time in broad daylight in some other place without being vilified.

After some investigation, we wound up running into a

stranger at a gambling house on the North Side.

"A truck, huh? Three days ago the shepherds saw it careening up the trails toward Sierra Leone... Ask the shepherds!"

That's what ultimately solved the puzzle. All the semis from Dogomet were hauling to Sierra Leone. You just had to ask the shepherds.

We didn't have a sou to save us: I'd trusted all of our money to that lout Togba and got all of Saran's resentment for it. Togba the magnificent, the one who made sure Yâyé Bamby got her Guiluxe and my daughter her medicine. Where, gentlemen of the clergy, did this assholery come from? Was it essence or existence? No, never mind. All that was just the start of a thought. 10,000 dollars gone! A real ruin in a country like this. I decided, however, to hold back my tears for other uses.

I've told you before, Madame Corre, here, you don't need tears or books, you just have to hold on, keep holding on, forever. One peril overcome, two more to weather: how would we pay for a hotel? How would we get to Conakry? Yes, how, in a country where men won't offer you a thing unless there's a little nooky at the end of it?

We thought it would be easy to sneak off in the light of dawn to leave the hostel undetected. But the early mornings had become uncertain and the night watchmen more and more clever. One surprised us as we got to the side of the highway, a wild glimmer in his eyes and a little revolver shining in his hand.

"You paying here or at the hotel?"

"We don't have any money."

"We'll make it in kind, then."

I was the first to undress, once we were back at the hotel. The guard let out an animal grunt touching the charcoal shock of hair that shone at the fork of my thighs.

"I'll show you," he snarled, "you nasty little bitch."

Saran put a karate hold around his neck just as his mind was reeling from the effects of his erection.

Not one logging truck would take us. Apparently, no one believed in the existence of a billionaire aunt, and, if ever she did exist, no one was sure she'd open her purse to pay for our transportation to Conakry. Still, we had to get the hell out before our friend from the hostel came to.

Hitchhiking wasn't something done in this corner of the world, but, around 9 o'clock, a sedan pulled up to us, pulled in no doubt by our half-bare chests and our kaftans pushed up to mid-thigh.

"Where you going?" a fat man grumbled in his embroidered, starchy bubu.

"Conakry."

"I'm headed there too."

"We've got a long road ahead of us, then, Monsieur....?"

His name was Laye Oularé and he served as the director of finance for the prefecture of Labé. We were perhaps relatives when the Oularés all lived in the same village, spent their days spinning lies over gourds of dolo, hollering at women and hunting elephants. Seated in the back, I pretended to watch the countryfolk march out into the fields as well as the shade trees to keep a lookout for that little merry-go-round, Saran, who was now sticking a piece of gum in her mouth after getting dangerously close to him.

"I'm sure you like to dance, Monsieur Oularé, seeing how charming you are."

Of course Monsieur Oularé liked to dance. But in places like the Palm Camayenne, for example, or the Club des Îles. He would take us there for champagne.

"Mmmm...Champagne!"

The audible kiss Saran planted on him almost sent us into the ditch. The ice had been broken. She didn't hesitate to dig around under his bubu as a little treat. Eyes half closed, Monsieur Director whistled between his teeth, drunk on pleasure. There was no risk, the car was going as fast as the pedestrians.

I was struck on the head and sat thinking a few seconds before I understood: Saran had just thrown something at me. I ran my hand discreetly along the floor to gather the pile of bills held together with rubber bands. The spoils from the director of finance came to the tidy sum of 30,000,000 Guinean francs. Enough to make us forget Stumpy Togba for a good while.

We laughed making our little calculations as we closed in on Conakry. But I couldn't fully shake my constant apprehension. I knew the good Lord hadn't spoiled me as far as horoscopes went: as soon as life smiles at me, the jinx of calamity scoffs in my ear and a big black cloud covers the horizon. What was about to happen to me this time?

Nothing. Nothing happened to me. Everything went so well in those following months that when my daughter got sick I never thought to blame the genie for his jinx of calamity. Bad weather punctuates the seasons the same way illness does our normal course of existence, especially at that age. There was nothing to be alarmed about. Still, the spoils we got from M. Oularé had been exhausted and the gringos almost never came back because of the epidemics.

She was throwing up, spending the clearest part of the days in a lethargy that worried me sick. The doctors couldn't tell me anything. They needed to run x-rays, blood tests, urine tests, before possibly moving forward to surgery. I almost fainted when the clinic's accountant slid me the bill. Years of income for the average public employee! So, for the first time, someone told me about Lebanese Jamal. He actually wasn't Lebanese. He was born here, had grown up here, spoke our languages, stole and lied with the same ease as the sons of bitches from here. He just had a Lebanese last name, which he got through a misunderstanding. Around 1880, his great-great grandfather, a Maronite Christian dogged by the American dream, had decided to leave in order to pull himself out of poverty, but he boarded the wrong boat and wound up, despite his best efforts, on the shores of Conakry. That was why you run into all these Jamals today in Coyah, Forécariah, Mamou, Pita, Kankan, N'Zérékoré, and everywhere else. I wish that kind of story would happen to me: I take the boat to Port Harcourt and wind up in Hamburg. Bordeaux, Rotterdam, Nagoya, Anvers, Port Harcourt, Valparaíso—anywhere on Earth—just not on nasty Jamal's couch.

That's exactly what happened, Madame Corre, and I very nearly lost my skin. Jamal was a criminal, one of the most dangerous of his time. He killed by Russian roulette. His weapon was not cut from metal but from his own flesh: his weapon was his dick. He could send you out to pasture on the other side with a single stroke. I had never seen that, someone who can kill with the potent toxicity of his own organ. But someone told me about Jamal and said it could be worth a try. Put yourself in my place, Madame Corre…The girl was vanishing before my eyes, and no medication I bought was helping. The operation seemed indispensable, and every mother is ready to sacrifice her life to save her child's. So I decided to go to the Millenium Hotel, where the recluse had a suite.

Imagine, Madame Corre, this oaf had a secretary who'd wait for you in a little office he used as a waiting room. She'd offer you chocolate and juice and then introduce you after he stepped out of the shower in just an open bathrobe, cigar forever hanging from his mouth. He'd be holding a magazine, leafing through it, without paying attention to his stiff upright cock, on which bulged some fully dilated blood vessels.

"Everything was explained to you?"

"I wouldn't be here otherwise."

"And what do you know?"

"That you have AIDS and you pay twenty million."

"Twenty million for a go with no condom, take it or leave it. So?"

"I don't have a choice. My daughter is sick and the cure's expensive."

"What are you waiting for? The shower is this way."

I don't remember the exact moment I came out. I spent the whole night puking and crying. The next day, my daughter had the operation.

After two or three months, the vomiting came back. My whole body ached. Three or four illnesses took over me at the same time: the flu, lumbago, colic, and malaria. One night, exhausted, I decided to reveal everything to my friends at the Oxygène.

"Stay away, I have AIDS."

Convinced I was saying that to make fun of them, Saran planted a loud kiss on my lips.

"We're not the kind of idiots you want to be showing off to, Atou! You'll have to try something else. We're sensitive souls."

They averted their gazes from my bulging eyes to my scabby forearms.

Not one chair squeaked across the ground, not one girl disappeared. I heard a cathartic laugh burst out in my left ear.

"AIDS or schistomiasis, you're going to die one day. Why do you think the good Lord put us on earth?"

Raye, already overstimulated from the detonating mix of red wine and vodka, called out for Makhalé.

"Hey sweetie! Someone at our table came down with AIDS. Bring us a round, we need to commemorate this."

Then she stood up to go dance.

The next day, it wasn't AIDS I was preoccupied with, it was my hangover. I was putting it off with a few cold beers when

Raye knocked at the door.

"Are you going to report it to the hospital? They have lots of things for that now. They can extend your life ten or twelve years."

"Oh yeah?"

She turned toward little Bamby, who was playing with her straw dolls in a corner of the room.

"How old is she now?"

"Almost four years. If I have it right, she'll be fourteen when I die. You can get by when you're fourteen. I got out of the house at fifteen, remember?"

"Where'd you have your test done? At the hospital or the Polyclinic?"

"What test?"

"Well, who told you? That you have AIDS, Atou?"

"No one. You know you have AIDS when you get sick after you sleep with Jamal."

"You slept with Jamal? Have you lost your shit?!"

I dodged the empty bottle she threw at me and heard it break into pieces against the wall behind me.

"How else would I have paid for the girl's operation, huh? All ears."

She carried my daughter on her back and dragged me to the Polyclinic like I was a suitcase.

A week later, she called out for Makhalé again, but with a tone ten times as vehement.

"Bring us a drink, Makhalé! Néné Fatou Oularé doesn't have AIDS, we need to celebrate this."

The test was negative. It was only typhoid fever.

"You are good for nothing, Atou! Sleep with Jamal and all you get is typhoid!"

I didn't have AIDS, my daughter had her operation. The epidemics receded and our little scam at the Novotel was starting to go south, but it was still going. I could run and jump, reflect and breathe without worrying about the jinx of calamity.

Yâyé Bamby looked like me, but the piercing brightness of her soul would bubble up under the skin. When she wanted something, she had to have it, and fast.

Leaving Jamal's, an incredible idea started through my head: "Neither love nor hate will save you, Néné Fatou Oularé. Your life preserver? Curiosity. That's it, more than anything, that's what ties you to the rest of the world. Arm yourself with curiosity! Open your mind to people, things, principles, causes. To love, to life." It's curiosity that connects us. It's a matter of circuitry, Madame Corre. The light goes out the moment curiosity quiets down. And I'm not talking about intelligence. I'm talking about heart, about flesh, life. Look at Alfâdio and me, Madame Corre. What feelings did I have for him today? I don't really know. Maybe not love, but certainly not hate, either. Did I still love him after the painful discovery of Martha and his kids? For me, love, that precious resource, is never fully exhausted. Passion is always there, fed by the ardent fire of pursuit. I need to go to the root of him, need to understand him. Understand his being, understand his awful fate. He was the first man of my life. But I'd never completely known him. For that, I would have had to climb back to the summit, explore his crevices and ridges, his traits and vulnerabilities. Make a tour of his being, the way a globe-trotter journeys the world. I won't hold him in my arms again, won't open my heart to him after what happened. But I wouldn't turn my back on him if we ever crossed paths, even if it were in that unpronounceable German town that swallowed his future. There's one feeling, Madame Corre, that's never suited me: resentment. No question it's why I'm so wary of the past. Who's strongest in the end? The ones who try to forget or who allow themselves to remember? I certainly want to love, and I especially want to understand. Why did he get me pregnant exactly when he was going to leave me, leave me for good, never to come back unless as a ghost flanked with loudmouth kids and a blonde German and who knows nothing about me, nothing about either of us, and less about our daughter?

Why did he ask me who the girl was? I thought life was an act of collusion, that we'd all been born to vibrate in concert. It was impossible for me to imagine nothing occurring between a father and his daughter. Genes speak to genes, hearts to hearts—especially cases like this. Why do believers still think of God when they've never seen him? Because if their conscience forgets, their pores still recognize the breath that made them.

We're told everywhere we go, Madame Corre: blood doesn't lie; it's the spit, that slime, that handles the dirty work. Not too long ago, in our provinces, you were considered a witch—or at least an unfit mother—if you didn't quiver with fear when, a hundred kilometers away, a viper bit its offspring. No, I didn't love Alfâdio anymore, but I had a mad desire to travel through his soul and touch a finger to the mysterious springs that made him so fiery and unpredictable. I know the sensation of doubt had never brushed against him—or the feeling of regret. Which kept you from ever knowing what he was going to do after making love to you: smoke a joint while railing against Sékou Touré? Lodge a bullet in your genitals? Maybe his own? He could alter fate from one minute to the next without losing the boyish smile that hid his carnivorous soul. He was sincere when he told me he loved me. He had no trouble telling me that. I had no trouble believing it. I didn't give a shit which chick he'd just dumped. He was mine; I wasn't thinking about anything else. And poof, innocent and cool, he's on the other side of the world, clueless that I hold in my arms a life that came from his.

MARJANEL DOESN'T CALL YOU "Mathilde." He calls you "Suzanne." You and your goddamn heavy makeup! It can transform your face, your hair and your dresses if you're a real artist, Madame Corre—but not your marital status. So what is it, Madame Corre, Mathilde or Suzanne? And what in the world is *Corre*? A swear word? A tagline? Pseudonym?

We were at the Vésuve that night, and I could tell by your face you'd reached the end, that you were through lying to yourself like that; that, suddenly, you needed to see yourself as you actually were. Hear your real name resonate, offer your true face to the mirror. A vital necessity, that precious whiff of air into the lungs that a smothered person begs for. When you went back to Dijon, you were nothing. Tatters. A woman empty of self. No bones, skin, nothing left of a brain. You only wanted one thing: to escape yourself, get out from that wreckage. To become another person.

Only how can you escape yourself? What shell do you have to crack? Jumping which wall? Breaking down what door? You were ready for all of it. It wasn't tenable anymore, *Suzanne* disgusted you. The name stank like shit. So you'd tossed it the way things are tossed into the dump. You'd tried several of them, all of them just as uneasy and oppressive. Then in a superhuman effort—a desperate passenger jumping a sinking ship to latch onto a makeshift raft—you arrived at *Mathilde*. That name, or rather that material, had a consistency, a faultless solidity you found reassuring. It would hold firm against everything: storms, swells, undertows, raids.

Mathilde, Saint Mathilde, your Sunday school idol. The German empress, so pious, so generous, she who gave so much to the poor that her own children rose up against her. This was, as a kid, how you imagined your heroes. Not generals bedecked with stripes, just big hearts like that one. Ready to love, to share, save, protect. You only saw your future in fire departments or the Salvation Army—that or, with a little luck, at the opera. *Give to the poor.* That was what they said at church. *Defend the workers.* That was what you heard at the dinner table from your communist father. You were a teenager. Fifteen, sixteen, maybe seventeen years old.

And one fine night your life turned upside down. Coming home from a Party meeting, your father brought home a handsome Black man. Total chance, that encounter. You were supposed to be in Roanne that day for a friend's birthday, but you'd cancelled at the very last minute. It was this change that put a certain Bôry Diallo on your path. It was this friend—what can I say?—this comrade of your father's who plunged you into my country and all its bullshit. In those days, love and love of revolution went hand in hand. The life of an individual was inseparable from that of the collective. Nothing like today. I have the impression that the world turned its back on us, left me in solitude without a voice on the icy dock where no bench was open to me.

Your engagement was brief. It had to happen quickly: Bôry Diallo was finishing his engineering studies and was about to return home. Independence was awakening across

Africa, the third world of revolutionary romanticism. There wasn't just one alliance formed that day. Ideas and dreams united alongside you under the aegis of the moment's icons: Sékou Touré, Kwame Nkrumah, Lumumba, Ben Bella, Nasser, Castro, Che Guevara. Images impossible to forget. Intimidating names to your frail eighteen years on earth.

Beautiful, naïve, idealistic, and in love, you had everything you needed to make the leap, to get yourself hooked. The descent into hell was waiting for you the way a wild dog awaits his prey. Oh yes, after that you had to change your name, your face, your memories, fingerprints and vocal chords.

"*Mathilde* I get, but *Corre*?"

"I found it in the phone book. It's such a stupid name that I decided I'd adopt it, monstrous dragon that it is. You know that mask people wear in the streets of certain cities in the South for Mardi Gras? That's what I'd become in my mind: an abominable stone tortoise that spits water and frightens kids."

"And what name is the dragon *Corre* masking?"

"Farjanel."

"Hey! Don't tell me you've been married to him since birth!"

"You've got your threads crossed, Countess. I'm not a medium or telegrapher or food cart operator. I lied to you. I'm not Stéphane's wife—I was born a Farjanel. I'm his niece. His stepniece, anyway."

You talked for an hour or two without pausing to breathe, without letting me say a word.

Your grandfather had a plantation in Vietnam, on the coast of Da Nang. After your grandmother died, he married his Vietnamese cook, who turned out to have been his lover. It was from that bed that Stéphane Farjanel was born, and his mother had served as nanny to your own father. Vietnamese—the language they had in common—hit your ears as often as that of Voltaire and Hugo. And it's in Vietnamese that you always place your orders at Ái Vân's.

"My genealogy's not simple either, is it, Countess?"

"I'll grant you that, Madame Corre, now that every single thing has been accounted for."

"Ah! See, we almost have twin lives! I had good reason to bother you that winter afternoon on Rue Mouffetard. Otherwise, you wouldn't have known we had so much in common."

"Both of us thrown into this *brutal adventure* Simone de Beauvoir talked about."

"That's not all. Our identity is fluid: we're both going non-stop from one character to another."

"Yes, but my roles have been imposed on me. You chose yours."

"And our relationship to country? I perfectly understand that, for Philippe, for you, it's France. But what is Guinea to me? Now that they killed him, there's no more Guinea. I'll never set foot there again. Besides, they took my Guinean passport when I got on the plane."

"Even if Dian Charles-André is found?"

"That's the only condition."

Then you buried your face in your hands for a moment. I almost left you there, but you didn't cry, you didn't bring up the balafons or niâmou. You just sighed.

"Those people kill everything they touch. They strangled my husband, his neck at the end of a rope. And it was enough for them to inoculate me with self-disgust—it's ten times more fatal than hemlock or strychnine. I'd never told anyone about it. You're the only person who could understand. Everyone else is so far removed from it... The poor souls think their barbarity is behind them. It's true they don't understand a thing about seasons. I learned a lot there, in Africa. The world is round, Countess, it moves in cycles: the roundness of the seasons, of flowers, dishes, words.... Do you know, Countess, *La Ronde des jours*, the famous poetry of Bernard Dadié? My husband would read it to me often. 'I'll take you to Abidjan one day just for Bernard Dadié,' he'd say. Go figure, he was informed the night before his arrest of an upcoming mission to Abidjan. It's there, that thing we call happiness, right within reach, free of charge. Why is no one ever able to capture it?"

You never told me about your husband, just the balafons and niâmou and the little métis taken away by the crowd, a single straw in a raging sea. You fished through your bag and took out a photo.

"That's him in his office, he'd just been named minister. Look how handsome he is!"

A handsome young man indeed. Oval face, thin, copper complexion. He certainly had the head of a Diallo, those mountain people who are said to be gorgeous, clever, and cocky.

"He didn't drink or smoke or flirt. Meanwhile I had a weakness for bourakhé and palm wine. Anything for his country! Anything for his work! Anything for Dian! Anything for his little Bunny Rabbit—yes, that was me, his Bunny Rabbit. We never went out. Every once in a while, an excursion here or there: the Loos Islands, Bel Air Beach, the fragrant hillsides of Yembereng."

He'd studied in Dijon, at an institute for engineers in the food industry. He and your father had met at the Paul-Vaillant-Couturier chapter of the Communist Party, hitting it off right away despite their age difference. They resembled each other somewhat: both reserved, both regulars at meetings, both loyal to the Party. Their rare doubts or reservations about the USSR were never heard outside their dormitory walls. They handed out issues of *L'Humanité* on Sundays and played belote with their comrades. And sometimes they'd take a pot of coffee to the bottom of the garden to chant Nâzim Hikmet and Walt Whitman."

It felt good to hear you talking like that. No tremolo in

your voice, no veil of sadness over your eyes. I had the impression that you'd just left him and that you'd find him right after we said goodnight.

"My one and only love, Countess! I'll never know another man. I don't give a shit about faithfulness, it's just that I'd throw up if another man touched me."

By turns, he'd managed the Mamou cannery, the fruit juice factory in Forécariah, followed by the Guinea Brewers' Society. Then Sékou Touré, who had a lot of respect for him, appointed him Minister of the Economy and Finance. In fact, he dined at the presidential palace the night before his arrest. Sékou Touré didn't lack for heart: he invited his ministers to dinner before locking them up in Camp B. And these poor souls were the first to be stunned when the soldiers would break their villa doors down with combat boots: "What? Me, a conspirator? Does Sékou Touré know about this? Give him a call, hurry, you'll see there's a mistake." And, of course, Bôry didn't escape that morbid game of dunces.

"Your generation may not know it, but that's exactly what happened in Moscow in the '30s."

"That's what happens everywhere all the time, Madame Corre. Even today in 2012!"

Your parents understood everything when they saw you coming. They didn't ask questions. But they were less prepared than you were. Your father had a heart attack and your mother sank slowly into the darkness of Alzheimer's—a night with no morning. Bôry Diallo was almost family: he had visited them often before he asked for your hand.

"One question, Madame Corre. *Gammie*. Does that mean anything to you?"

"That's what the little one would call his grandmother. His grandfather he'd call *Nononque*. Why do you ask, Countess? Who told you about Gammie?"

"I can't remember who. I don't remember where it was.

Here, on the square, or maybe back there in a Conakry bistro. Doesn't matter."

We said our goodbyes very tired that night. Much more tired of talking than drinking.

"Am I allowed to call you Suzanne Farjanel now?" I said, shaking your hand.

"It's too early, Countess! Too early. Just let me get used to it again."

O N MY DAUGHTER's fourth birthday, there was an incident.

We'd spent the night downtown where we bought her gifts, rode the merry-go-round, and had some Lebanese ice cream. On our way back, Goulo, the yam vendor, was waiting for us in front of the church.

"Someone was here."

"Who?" Raye asked, worried.

"He had scars across his left cheek. He was wearing big sunglasses. He stood for a long time in front of your door, then cased the building. He left without a word."

"How was this someone dressed?"

"He was wearing a blue bomber jacket."

This time Yâyé Bamby was the first to panic. She decided to take matters into her own hands.

After talking a while on the phone with someone I didn't know, she announced, "Atou, you're getting out of here. There's no other solution. A smuggler will come find you tomorrow at

8 PM. 8 PM is the best time: any earlier and it'd be daylight; any later and the light and traffic would ease but patrols would ramp up. He'll take you by road to Maferinyah. Once you're there, he'll turn you over to some canoers who'll help you cross into Sierra Leone. I have a cousin there, Malal, the Philadelphia one's brother—they're the only ones in my family who haven't turned hostile."

She put together a little go bag and gave me some money. We all agreed that no one would leave the house until the smuggler arrived.

The next day, we were snacking on cashews, watching soap after soap, trying to calm our nerves. Around 4 PM, as I was washing my daughter's hair, Raye's voice came to me in the bathroom. Trembling and abnormally sharp.

"You'd better go, Atou. There's a visitor here for you."

"Who is it?"

"Indigo Bomber!"

My instinct was to run away or at least save my daughter. But there was no window, just a skylight that would barely let a hand through. I squeezed her against my chest and leaned against the wall, fully resolved, come what may, not to budge. My shaking, however, would not stop.

Five minutes later, the door started to creak. I saw Raye's shadow in the doorway. She wasn't holding herself together any better than I was.

"Atou, this is fucked!" she said, her face ravaged with fear. "You better come here."

He sat in the middle of the couch, sipping a Coca-Cola. He finished his glass, in no hurry to open his mouth.

"I'd have come earlier, but I couldn't make up my mind."

"I don't want my daughter to go to prison."

"Come see me Thursday at 4 PM."

"At the police station?"

"No, no, my place."

"What's the address?"

"24—two doors down from your father's villa. And please, come alone."

Between the three of us, no one could remember what happened over the next few days: fear had plunged us into a half-unconscious state that kept us from noting the time and day, events and actions, what meals we ate, or any sign before us.

On Thursday, I found him alone. He had no guard or gun, no handcuffs or nightstick. He started by showing me a photo: a charming young couple dressed like Europeans, clearly just married.

"Your name isn't Néné Fatou Oularé. You weren't born to Dabola de Oumou Sow and Oussou Oularé."

As I was completely inert, unable to make a sound, he thought it was fine to continue.

"You are the daughter of these two here."

Zero emotion in his voice and movements. He finished smoking a corn-paper Gitane and was already lighting another. He stood in front of me, imperturbable and stiff, his sunglasses sitting on a pile of paperwork, with the air of a scornful schoolmaster about to give a lesson.

I stared shamelessly at his scarred cheek and his eyes made red by the ill effects of yamba. He disgusted me. I wasn't afraid of him anymore. He'd already disgusted me when he started in on his awful lecture.

"I was your father's—or, well, Colonel Oularé's—deputy. Commander Fodé Soumah."

"You worked in Central Brigade, too?"

"Colonel Oularé never worked at Central. Me neither, for what it's worth. That was just a cover."

The two strangers in the photo, my "true parents" according to him, had names that meant nothing to me. The woman's name was Rama Baldé and the young man was Jean-Pierre Bangoura. She was a midwife; he was a diplomat. They met each other in high school and had imagined that ever since then they'd be together for life.

I looked at this strange photograph for a while, surprised not to find one tear streaming down my face.

"For the love of God, how did you know these two, and how can I be sure they're really my parents? There's no resemblance."

His tone turned professional, as if he were explaining an intake form.

"You resemble them both. Your figure, your nose, forehead, eyebrows, fingers, and toes are your mom's. Your skin color, smile, lips, cheeks, earlobes—that's all your father."

He brought out another snapshot, this one of a woman in prison clothes with her baby.

"You, strapped to your mother's breasts, on your first birthday. She insisted we take a picture. She kept insisting that we owed her this exceptional favor. It's the only photo from the camp as far as I know."

A baby girl with hollow cheeks, her shaved head eaten away with ringworm. I had no desire to recognize myself. I turned the photo over mechanically and read what was written: *August 20, 1979*. According to my papers, I was indeed born on August 20, 1978. Everything had been taken from me except my date of birth.

"Your father had already been executed," he went on, not noticing my reaction. "You were eighteen months old when your mother was executed."

"Who killed them?"

"In your father's case, Colonel Oularé. Your mother, me."

"And why?"

"They were condemned to death. That's how it went back then: you were judged, condemned to death, and executed."

"And why were they condemned to death?"

"They were accused of plotting against national security."

"Are you sure you're talking about me, Commander Fodé Soumah?"

"I was there the day you were born. There's no mistaking it."

"Where was that, where you witnessed my birth?"

"At Camp B. That's where we were working, Colonel Oularé and I. But no one was allowed to know."

"Oh yeah? People were born, too? I thought they were only put to death there."

"You wouldn't be here to ask that question."

"You mean I was conceived in that hell?"

"Of course not—your mother was already showing when she was arrested."

My name isn't Néné Fatou Oularé, Madame Corre. My name is Véronique Bangoura. The day I learned that, I understood exactly what a name is: it is a prey's shadow, the sound of a coin, the inestimable value of packaging. Who are we trying to fool: the customs agent or the goods themselves? Names are chosen to deceive, and I almost fell for it.

Leaving Indigo Bomber's place, the first thing I did was lock myself in the bathroom and take a long look in the mirror. The magic didn't work. I still had the same dismayed face upon which, once and for all, fate had engraved the signs of bad luck and stubbornness. I can't remember who said it, that we change faces when we change names. Old Ténin Condé, with her esprit d'escalier, thought the opposite: "Changing the name of a tree doesn't make its branches fall. But be careful, Atou—a genie is in love with you. He wants no man at your side. None!"

But I needed names to stick with me. You can't lead a normal life without one. It might be easier to remove your bile or spleen than it would be to change your name. And I do have names: enough to fill a kid's notebook! So many names, so many roles. Just like the movies, Madame Corre. Names can't hurt, but they can disfigure—actresses can tell you a thing or two about that. Here's what I'd say if someone asked me what I was put on earth to do: stray from one place to another under different names, different faces. *Countess* makes you laugh out loud. Well, that's the name that suits me best. Nothing incongruous about that, a countess with black skin. Everything is passed on to Black folks once it's fallen out of use: leftovers from the day before, old slippers, old outfits, titles of nobility fallen into disuse. I wear it with arrogance. I know it's unsettling to more than one person behind closed doors. I also use it for my own amusement: not so long ago, it would have meant my head on the chopping block. How many crooks escaped the gallows or gibbet just by changing their name? I won't escape the fate in store for me, but I do enjoy changing names as often as I change dresses. I enjoy it now—now that I'm used to it.

"No one survived more than two years after getting out… We were put to work in three categories: red, brown, and green. Each had their quotas. Your mother was category green."

"If I heard right, the first two categories meant death."

"Yes. Red by hanging, brown by black diet. Green meant you'd eventually be eligible to return to life."

"Black diet. I've heard of that: BD was etched on the cell door and every morning they'd look through the skylight to verify the detainee was still moving. Is that true?"

"It is. No food or drink. The strongest managed fifteen days."

"My mother was eligible for release, right?"

"She was. Colonel Oularé was the one who transferred her to red status."

"Why?"

"Because of you. He wanted to take you home to his wife, who wasn't able to have kids."

"So you hanged her, then?"

"No, I cut her throat—we didn't have any rope that day."

He lit another corn Gitane, his cold eyes still planted on mine.

"You want me to tell you something else? I didn't like Colonel Oularé. I'd have killed him if you hadn't. That's why I didn't arrest you."

"Oh yeah? You hated him?"

"We'd agreed to split your father's belongings: the Dixinn villa for him, the one in Kipé for me. And the Kouria plantation, fifty-fifty. But the son of a bitch kept everything for himself."

Before, I went by Néné Fatou Oularé. I wasn't embarrassed by it. I thought I'd been born like everyone else, that I'd even have that name on my grave. Then Indigo Bomber showed me that picture and I started to doubt the real value of words. So I learned how to lie and slid like an eel from one name to another, from one life to another, one truth to another. It's not enough just to be yourself—you have to become yourself.

I did my best to become Véronique Bangoura. I had the story and the photos from Indigo Bomber. That was all I had to imagine the rest. This young woman, this Rama Baldé with the face of a pharaoh, was born in a village in the mountains. Which one? Commander Fodé Soumah knew nothing about it. The man, Jean-Pierre Bangoura, was from Boffa. They met in high school. Rama studied midwifery and he became a diplomat after studying law in Belgium.

"I have to tell you, mademoiselle, your father was well

known. He was a star in Addis-Ababa, then in Havana, then Dakar. At the time of his arrest, he was our embassy's chargé-d'affaires in Bonn. He was expected to oversee the one in New Delhi. See?"

He would often finish his sentences like that: "See?" Without the slightest sign of repentance, which gave me an urge to slay him. It was comically indecent, Madame Corre, our little tête-à-tête. Two criminals behind closed doors. I came so I could be arrested and found almost the same thing: he'd killed my mom and I my dad. I didn't take notes, my memory had no trouble soaking it in, the way a fax machine's stupid paper receives messages from who knows where. I was looking at his salt and pepper goatee, his red eyes, squinting through the yamba smoke, and thought, "Get yourself a cyanide pill, you dummy, before you finish off this snake in shades. It'll be better. For the moral, for the beauty of the story." But our death would only do service to the moral, not to my curiosity. Curiosity, again, Madame Corre! The desire to know prevailed over my inclination to kill.

"Oh no, mademoiselle, it was nothing out of the ordinary back then. One or two conspiracies a year. That was the culture at the time.... What? Did we buy all that crap? That's not why we were there. Our role was to arrest the culprits we were designated, get them to talk, hang them, shoot them, or subject them to the black diet. It was the Revolutionary Committee that decided. Our job was purely technical—and believe me, that's not a cynical stance."

Chargé d'affaires in Bonn! So fate had tied me to Germany from the cradle! In Foreign Affairs, everyone remembered Jean-Pierre Bangoura, but no one knew whether or not he still had family. He was executed at the same time as Tierno Oumar Barry, his childhood friend, with whom he'd gone to high school, followed by law school in Liège.

And Rama Baldé did indeed have a cellmate who was liberated after the death of Sékou Touré, but she died a year later.

No chimera to hold on to. No archive and no witnesses. Those people left nothing to chance. *And in order to kill, you have to be calm and lucid.*

"Did they have other kids?"

"I don't think so, mademoiselle. A mother can't live for months in jail without talking to her kids."

When I finished giving her my new biography, Yâyé Bamby just flicked her hand like she was shooing away an annoying bug and Raye had the same phlegmatic reaction as the night I killed my father.

"Who cares! We're still calling you Atou. *Véronique Bangoura*, we'll never get used to that."

NOW HERE'S MY QUESTION, Madame Corre: why haven't *you* considered writing a book? Why do I have to be the one to do it? Lives are like fingerprints, they're never exactly the same. Your son is still living—should it turn out to be true— and your husband died before your eyes. That's a kind of favor, an almost lavish gift. Whereas I was twenty-two when I even heard tell of Rama Baldé and Jean-Pierre Bangoura. In some ways, it wasn't until age twenty-two that I was born. My father was thrown off a cliff, my mother expired under the blade of a filet knife. My family history was summarized in one photo. A photo I received from the murderer of the woman who carried me nine months in her belly. These things have been discussed. Besides Primo Levi, can you count off how many witnesses were present at the Holocaust? And how much did it cost them in blood and sweat? And beyond that, in Siberia, Tomsk, Irkutsk? One Solzhenitsyn and two Zinovievs out of the 18 million mowed down, scrofulous and crawling with worms. No one's looking for the limelight in these cases. They're tucked away in the thick woods of anonymity. Here, the only thing expressed is shame. Shame on us all, shame forever. And shame, Madame Corre, isn't cried out from the rooftops. I assure you, if all those people dared to speak up, there'd be no earthly corner to spit out its disgust, not one library shelf to wedge a book. We talk about our triumphs, our diplomas, our achievements, not our hernias and boils. A cripple doesn't show off.

You still think it's time well spent to drone on about your past? Camp B, the Bridge of the Hanged, your husband, your son, my two fathers, my two mothers—why don't you quit for a second? Nothing's around us anymore. Not the Panthéon or Les Arènes. Not Prospero, not the street vendor, not even the ghost of Sartre, or the memory of Cohn-Bendit and his cocky bunch of brick throwers. Nothing but the two of us, shut in this foggy, gray-walled cubbyhole, emptying glasses of Sancerre, sobbing about the past. But how do our little hiccups square with the infinite madness of men? Are you familiar with the histories of Blacks and Indians, Jews and Hereros, Soweto and Sharpeville, Sabra and Shatila, of Sobibor and Treblinka?

Do you know how much it costs a writer to scratch his balls? To dig through the latrines of the past? Could *you* write a book? Admit it, you'd never perform on the public plaza, detailing what happened on that bridge the day you were jostled awake at 5 AM to go give the balafons a listen and watch the niâmou dance. You left your pharynx there and your bile, your myocardium and your spleen. You're one hell of an egotist, Madame Corre—you'd throw me down and spare yourself to gauge the depth of a well.

Believe me, there will never be enough books and movies to contain men's bullshit. It's not memory that will heal us, it's the hard drug of amnesia, the end of the end, that snug bed of nothingness. As long as there are men, so too will there be bullshit. And bullshit's not the only thing we know how to do, it's just what we do best. I wasn't in school very long, Madame Corre. Nothing besides Raye's school notebooks and Philippe's library. But I do on occasion indulge in the snootiness of a citation. Here's one that's not the most celebrated, but to me it's the truest, the most honest, most touching of them all: "We often compare the cruelty of man to that of beasts, which insults the latter." That was Dostoyevsky, I think, unless it was Socrates, before the hemlock. And hemlock isn't just used in Athens. Everyone's forced to drink it—anyone who thinks, loves, or dreams.

Which makes me want to repeat what I often said to Philippe: "Hitler, Stalin, Sékou Touré, Franco, Pinochet, and Pol Pot aren't dogs or pigs or hyenas or lice or polar bears or spiders. They're men, they're our brothers by blood. They're you and me." And don't tell me about context. Climate, skin color, and mores have nothing to do with it. It's been like that since the beginning. Here, there, wherever.

We're disarmingly stupid and hateful. And when evil is done, when blood and tears spill over everywhere, we pour out prayers and speeches. There we are, in front of churches and mosques, protest signs brandished: NEVER AGAIN! The slogan is firm in our mouths. But our minds aren't fooled: two, three, four, five years, ten years max, and Camp B will have spawned little ones in Tibet, in the Yucatán, in Bechuanaland. Sobibor, its grandbabies in Peru, Siberia, Botswana. And, again, prayers and speeches. Again, stirred-up sensitive souls and protest signs over the heads of the outraged. And no one will think to lift up a mirror: "Look, open your eyes. What devils? What monsters? It's only you and me. Leave the devils alone!"

Philippe had a funny idea one day. He wanted to introduce me to Ambar, Nera, Gnoap, and Adhylia. He'd brought Gnoap back from Cambodia, Ambar from Chile, Adhylia from Congo, and Nerea from Argentina. He wanted to know how it would go. If we had anything in common: a tic, a brief memory or—who knows?—some fragment of a gene. It was one of his anthropologist friends' ideas. Four girls born in tyrants' prisons had to have some small thing in common. My reaction made him cut ties with his anthropologist friend. And he spent the whole week after offering apologies and foot rubs to ease my anger. "Sweetheart—honey! I'm the dumbest idiot, I know that now. I shouldn't have listened to that prick. And I know, that's how the doctors at Treblinka thought, too. Open more laboratories to prove what monsters the Jews were.... No, no, no, you aren't going to see Adhylia, Nerea, Gnoap, or Ambar. Forgive Philippe's carelessness. Please, forgive him!"

Would you have granted, Madame Corre, that anyone had a right to ask whether you and I had something in common besides X chromosomes and our condition as earthlings? That something meaningful should come out of that shared experience? It's one's environment that determines everything, if we believe the scholars. The victims, even indirect ones, of Sékou Touré should necessarily have something in common, some visible characteristic, like the wings of airborne animals or marine life's fins. We would have recognized each other, we would have addressed each other with our own signals. No! To each species its own language! Dogs communicate, crabs communicate, but humans don't understand them. God, more mysterious than magnanimous, raised towers everywhere among beings long before Babel.

And yet it doesn't show on the nose, those beatings. They never leave a trace: the mark of a true criminal. Once they're done breaking you, it's on to the sulfuric acid bath or the mass grave, where they pile the dead dogs and goats, the ones who don't ask to be remembered. If they do let you go back home, it's because your scars are internal: broken ribs, mangled spleen, memory in tatters. That's their little trick: no trace, no witness, no proof, no document. That's what allows them after a few years of respite to find successors. The old cycle of life that feeds itself and that neither you or I have the means to break.

Let's be real, Madame Corre: I'd have fled if you brought up Camp B first thing. If I'm still there to hear your nonsense about balafons and niâmou, it's because you trapped me somehow. Yes, you were wily enough not to telegraph the color to me.

I'd have turned my back on you. What bothers me with those recited stories is that memory is almost always one of disgust. This day is remembered, and not that one, because this day was most dismal. Like Kundera said: "Memory doesn't film. It photographs." I prefer film. A photograph fixes the moment. And the moment has nothing to do with other moments. A photograph is yesterday. A script is tomorrow. And a film, real footage, is today. The day containing all the others.

On the topic of film, there's one Philippe loved more than any other, a little Soviet film, *Fate of a Man*, that was projected when he was still with Young Communists. The memory he had of it was, all in all, somewhat vague, but the emotion he'd felt watching it for the first time never left him. His soul would take merrily off when he thought back to it. He'd give a sigh I couldn't interpret and rave about everything that stood out from his childhood: *Tintin, Les Pieds Nickelés*, books by Péguy, Vallès, Saint-Exupéry, tennis courts, Abby Guichard's homilies, vacations in Saint-Raphaël. "Yes, I've been conditioned like everyone before Vian, Lautréamont, the Surrealists, the scoundrels in *Le Grand Jeu*, Sartre, and others taught me how to take care of myself," he'd say again and again in those nostalgic episodes. Apart from the anthropologist incident, *Fate of a Man* was one of our rare bones of contention. I don't know why this movie I've never seen—and will never—opened the floodgates in him to a theory that riles me up so badly: humanism. OK, Madame Corre, poison my life with your stories about balafons and niâmou, but, I beg you, please don't ever bring up humanism. I'm just not ready for it. In all honesty, I'm not a human being. I'm a little blade of grass. I got none of what's supposed to feed Man's offspring: caresses, lullabies, morality, religion. I'm clueless about Islam, Christianity, Marxism, and Buddhism. My parents never said anything about it. I don't get one thing about humanity. My own humanity consists of Dick the dog, Nantou, Raye, Yâyé Bamby and the hyped-up populace at the Oxygène. Plus I'm for life, not *Man*. And life encompasses everything, Madame Corre. Man is never more than a laughable segment. Turning on the TV last weekend, I saw the Dalai Lama watch the conversion of some unhinged man. You know what he said, that unhinged man? That on a geologic scale, our lifespan on earth doesn't even touch five seconds. We're not the foundation of the world, we're a teensy fraction of it. If you say God created Man in his image, you have a pretty feeble idea of God. Sure, we invented the bow and arrow, shaped stone into a wheel, created vaccines and the submarine, the atomic bomb and football. We walked on the moon and summited Everest. But I ask you, Madame Corre, are we worth any more than a bee or a lion? Bacteria? Plants? They're heroes in their way—heroes that don't need a statue. Be modest, humanoids. We're not the beginning or the end. Life existed before us. It'll go on with or without us.

He didn't like to hear me talk like that, not at all. To get me to shut up, he'd send me off for a glass at the Antidote, and afterward we'd make unhinged love.

THE EPIDEMICS KEPT DIMINISHING. The airport was once again full of tourists and businessmen. Kâkilambé organized a little meeting in his Alhambra-styled office: everything was ready at the Novotel. But first he needed to find a new Rita to replace Penda, who'd left to get married in Malaga.

The new one was Niépou. She'd just come from Yomou. She was younger and more touched up than the rest of us. Still, we came back empty-handed several days in a row: nothing but couples; or else old single men drinking water and going to bed right after dinner. We killed the time watching football matches or splashing around in the pool. By 9:00 we knew it was another day pissed away and would sweat our way down the Folto-Falta trail until our legs couldn't support us. Sometimes Ousmane would haunt the area, sometimes not. His absence had begun to mark two lines on Raye's cheeks that made you think of a scar. When he was around, though, she'd manage to get close enough to confide in me. I knew she was going to disappear for an hour or two. I especially knew that I wasn't supposed to ask any questions. I knew Ousmane didn't lead a simple life. I knew Raye worried about him a lot. His frequent, prolonged absences sowed a panic in her that she struggled to hide. At the Oxygène, she'd abruptly cut off a conversation and drop her head in her hands. At the house, she'd race to the bathroom in such an unnatural way that we knew she wasn't just answering nature's call. Ousmane wasn't some little boyfriend like you find in a corner of the Oxygène. He was the love of her life. On that topic she'd soliloquize without any prodding: "He's the only one and it's forever." Of course, life had other plans in mind. But at that age, it's what every girl tells herself. It's our way of exorcising ourselves from risk, of bridling our apprehensions. After Ousmane there would be another, then another, then another. Meanwhile, that kind of nonsense would have left her head. You can still imagine that, even in someone else's arms, it was Ousmane she'd be thinking of.

Go figure, Madame Corre: I've never seen Ousmane. We'd have crossed paths, though, on that wild night I found shelter in that unfinished house where—I would later realize—men like him would hide. Who was Ousmane? A guy of Alfadio's ilk, only more enigmatic, more frightening, more dangerous. Raye wouldn't tell me that but she didn't think any less. I remember one of our conversations: "What! A photo? You'd think he's never had one taken. But he's obsessed with recognition." Maybe we bumped into each other in the hallways at the Oxygène or riding in a magbana. Maybe I heard his voice. Maybe I caught a glimpse of his silhouette.

My scattered memory wound up establishing a vague connection between him and my uncle. They both slipped out of view, which left me predisposed to love them. Two ghosts who will never stop haunting me.

My uncle would have added life to this photo, which had discolored and shriveled so badly over time. He'd have given me the chance to dream up a father for myself. The one I knew had assassinated the other before I assassinated him in turn. And the one who should have been my stand-in, I don't even have a picture of him. Jesus Christ took it from me. Not a word.

Not a handshake. Buried alive behind the clay walls of a convent, of an old leper colony, and by the madness of an era, by the Lord's grace. He occupies the same mystery and importance in my mind as Ousmane. One could have been my uncle and the other my brother-in-law. I'm spending my time on earth rebuilding a humanity for myself. No sooner traced than gone. Maybe she was right, old Ténin: a genie loves me. I must be made for him and for him alone, for his pagan desires and ravenous jealousy. I'll say it again, Madame Corre: Raye is the sister I never had, the sister I made for myself. Ousmane is my brother-in-law, the brother-in-law I never had.

Ousmane and my Uncle François! I miss those two souls I never met. I entertain myself imagining them in my head. To me, they both have the same head as the man in the picture. We missed each other from the start, Ousmane and I, since that wild night when I devoured the shawarma intended for him. Some kind of irony—it was their love nest that old Ténin had sent me to. "Be patient," Raye used to tell me. "You'll run into him one day. I'll make sure you're ready for it."

A meeting was organized at a maquis in Madina Foula.

Raye's phone rang the exact second we sat down on some rickety chairs in someone's backyard where we were served kebabs and beer.

"Hey! Allah! Late again, you're always late… An hour, you think? Two? Don't sweat it, you won't be bored. Got good music going on here and some damn good kebabs, mm-hmm."

An hour later, she tried calling him back. No one picked up. She tried again and a pale glint of worry started showing on her face.

"You never know where he'll turn up, never know what he's doing. But he always answers his phone."

Two beers later, she jumped as if a snake had bitten her, and grabbed my arm in desperation.

"He's with someone else. Come on. I said come on!"

We started at the Oxygène. Then we tried the 36–15, the Dallas, the Kosovo, and ten other maquis scattered along the marshes of Kakimbo and Sonfonia Marina's worst-smelling watering holes. In desperation, we ventured out to the famous unfinished house, the one where we first met the day I killed my father. No eye had seen Ousmane, no ear had heard from him. On the way back, it made me think of a panther brushed by fire: provoked and snarling, full of sound and fury.

I knew the house's idiosyncrasies by heart now, and that niece and aunt alike could make the world uninhabitable in the event of a setback or disappointment. They had the same sensibility but opposite reactions: one would lose her mind and start clawing at, or biting, friends and enemies just the same; the other would sink into the recesses of her being, tensed shut, and eat her heart out. Anyway, I didn't pay attention to the yelling or kicking of empty packages or the broken corned-beef boxes littering the sidewalk. Upon entering, I ran to take refuge in the kitchen, pretending to munch on something while, slumped on the couch, she went on threatening Ousmane with a Muslim hell and Jove's lightning.

I imagine she didn't close her eyes for a second that night. Still, she didn't leave the couch: that's where I found her when I woke up, in the same state I was in when, at the convent, my uncle had refused to see me. Haggard, mouth hanging open. But no tears ran down my face. Her phone was lying next to her, on the ground at arm's reach. Certain she wouldn't be able to respond, I didn't say anything to her.

She spoke without my prompting and her words rang out in my ear, precise as a verdict.

"They beat up Ousmane."

No more than two words were exchanged that week. Yâyé Bamby and I worked around each other in hushed steps between the kitchen and living room, not daring to give our wounded feline the wrong look. Then there was a sudden change of wind. The atmosphere set its electricity loose again. Raye found her boundless energy, that awkward humor and her bursts of laughter.

One night, after shutting herself in the bathroom for an hour, she yanked me out of a daydream, a diamond of a smile on her lips.

"What if we went to the Oxygène?"

All the girls were there and, within a drop of beer of each other, the same scene played out as with Alfâdio and his German wife: "One lost, ten gained!"

In a way, we had just concluded our initiation cycle: to each her own master's exam!

That day, we'd completely done away with the principles of our schooling. Life seemed easier to endure for us, more comprehensible, at least easier if you put aside a few small things. Our new psychology went well with the nicknames Kâkilambé had minted for us. They were stars' names, shiny and easy to remember, like at the movies. A star's coat of arms. Distinguished. We'd just jumped the velvet rope, up and changed our status. We weren't girls anymore. For starters, we had to take ourselves seriously and master our fantasies—along with our excesses. From then on the Oxygène was only on Saturdays, and no more than three beers a night. Our suckers from the Novotel had no reason not to trust us: we'd learned what shoes to wear, how to style our hair and hold a conversation like any other in the grand salons. We weren't pretending to be students anymore. Now we were professors and lawyers, all out for a round because we lived alone in mansions to keep safe from the brutality of the men around here. It was the kind of story that delighted them. That kind of story made connections. We accepted invitations to upscale restaurants and fine hotels on the islands. We'd go upstairs to flirt in their rooms—enough time to empty their pockets—and then we'd lead them to the Oxygène where we'd leave them in the hands of Bonôrou and his gang.

We weren't the only ones, of course. Kâkilambé was careful enough to plant a club beside every hotel. At the Camayan Palm, Liz was queen. She told me a funny story one day after asking over the phone if I'd meet her at Toes in the Water.

She'd gotten word that a Frenchman fresh off the boat had been talking about me. What was strange was that he called me Véronique Bangoura and not Atou Oularé. He seemed to know as much about me as Commander Fodé Soumah.

"He said my name?"

"Yeah. He heard you come here often."

"And where is he currently?"

"Here, in Alhambra—Kâkilambé›s office. He's waiting for you."

That, Madame Corre, is how I met Philippe Claude Célestin, Count of Monbazin.

My heart didn't exactly thrum the first time I saw him. I more felt the way I would meeting a census-taker. The atmosphere was ripe for it: he was sitting in Kâkilambé's office, his messenger bag perched at his right and a pile of papers about me just in front of him. The documents absorbed his full attention. He didn't give me any more than three glances. A purely administrative meeting—dry questions, cold answers. I signed a paper or two and left without saying goodbye.

Now, I should explain why he came to Conakry just to meet me.

I told you, he's a soixante-huitard, a boy put on Earth to betray his own class and take up causes that have nothing to do with him, like Che Guevara, Régis Debray, or Conrad Detrez. He'd studied law. For those people, even the renegades of the family end up attorneys. His feet itched right away—he couldn't stand being confined to a firm. He had to be there in person, meddle in every corner of the earth, lob a grenade with the guerilla fighters in Mozambique, break bread with the Tupamaros, pose with the bearded men of Shining Path. It wasn't that he hated Sartre. He adored his books, admired the acuity of his thought, the precision of his theses, the courage he defended them with. But he had to be at the front, take the enemy's bullets without flinching, or else he'd be Sartre. Instead, Old Piker, as he called himself, was content to be an unrealized Sartre of the cafeterias and bleachers. "Ah", he'd often say. "The world would've been saved if Che or Hemingway had a mind as sharp as yours!"

You know what dreams like that turn into: nightmares you can't get rid of. He was waiting on the fall of the Berlin wall, hoping for it. But he wouldn't tolerate seeing the Castros, the Sékou Tourés, or the Mugabes turn into monsters. Great causes weren't showing up on that side anymore. You had to resolve to look elsewhere—to human rights. With some colleagues in law, he founded an association: Living Memories. Their objective was to locate and denounce concentration camps, find the victims, and help them find satisfaction in life again. He of course knew about Camp B and learned I'd been born there. He'd already come once before (Mariam wasn't lying), but he didn't get the right person and so had to take another plane in a hurry: pressing matters awaited for him in Argentina, Chile, Congo, and elsewhere. His research had confirmed several births at Camp B, all of them adopted by their parents' torturers. I was the only one he'd been able to trace. Given the wrecked state of the country, it wasn't easy to find people again: some had left the living, others exiled never to return, and still others were hiding in convents and caves. A nation at the end of its rope— unburied dead, the living immured in silence to try and hide their shame, to sidestep insanity.

He knew the country when it was in ruins, when it had no landmarks or sense. He had four ways out: get drunk, put a bullet in his brain, force himself to forget, or else hover ghost-like along the unlikely walls of the real. He'd already been here and come back—both times stumbling at the thick barrier of silence. There were those lying in the tomb and those who'd preferred vegetating in towns around Paris and New York. Those who knew but didn't want to say anything. Those who knew you didn't have to say anything. Camp B is our collective prohibition. Impossible to talk about, impossible to forget.

Two or three other meetings followed. He expected me to deliver on everything: the sadism of the guards, the humility of the prisoners, the conditions of the cells, the art of their torture, the variety of executions. He even expected me to talk about the journal my mother may have left—*my* mother's journal, I being barely over a year old when her throat was slit.

So there you have it. There weren't just two photos, there was also a journal. The shock sent me running to Indigo Bomber, who had no trouble confirming it.

"And what happened to this journal?"

"Colonel Oularé took everything: you, the journal, the Vuitton purse, the Astrakhan coat, and the golden molar. She'd just come home from Bonn when she was arrested. She got on a plane the second she heard about her husband's incarceration.

"Philippe was still convinced that my father hadn't thrown out the journal, that he must have kept it in a dusty drawer somewhere. Go figure, Madame Corre. He tried to find it by ringing the colonel's doorbell, the fool. No one answered, not even Dick's barking. Which made me realize no one would ever want to live in the house where a daughter had killed her father. Mom had to run away somewhere to hide her shame and sadness. Not in a convent—she wasn't Christian—but in one of the villages where witches and outcasts live in isolation. And Dick and Nantou? Where could they be now if not here, on the left side of my chest? That's where their home is. They represent my tiny humanity's very first creatures. My own little planet is no larger than that, and still I manage to cram all my humanity there: Raye, Yâyé Bamby, Néné Biro, Philippe, and the others, all the others, provided they have some heart and energy to spare."

Now that I've mentioned this, I'm delighted to imagine what gusts of questions are swirling in your mind. "So, how does a man show up from the antipodes to investigate a sordid concentration camp end up becoming your husband?"

One fine day, he knocked at my door, this white guy I didn't think I'd see again.

"OK, I've learned some things: your mother is from Sâré-Kali. Which is near Télimélé, after the Konkouré rapids. Also, according to what I've heard, your grandparents are both alive. If I were in your place, I'd go have a look."

I got started pinpointing this godforsaken Sâré-Kali on the map. If you took a rapid bus at six in the morning, you could get there by midnight. It was only three hundred kilometers, but three hundred kilometers of trails where, daily, the wounded and dead were counted by the dozen.

That was the second trip of my life, and it would be the most epic of all of them.

"My guide drove me to a hastily-built house, in front of which was a half-circle of huts whose straw-thatched roofs sloped down to the ground. An old man, the spitting image of Haile Selassie, was going through his prayer beads in a yard decorated with multicolored gravel and lemon trees while the large radio a young man was holding belched out the day's news, which you couldn't make out, thanks to the dogs and insects.

He cleared his throat three times and greeted us for about ten minutes, according to custom. The young man barked out an order and three girls came out of the huts to lay down mats and goat skins. We were invited to sit down.

"*Kori dian*? Has peace brought you to us?"

"*Dian toun*. Peace, nothing but peace."

We followed the same ritual among the old folks in town, but those didn't last as long. Here, you had to spend a long time listening to the dogs and watching the chickens peck around between the mats and through the vegetables in the nearby lougan before asking what you needed.

"As you can see, I'm not alone. This young woman here with me is researching her blood line. That's the only thing that brought us here. Conakry isn't exactly next door—she would have come last night, but the Konkouré Bridge was acting up again."

You take your time in those villages. And when you're well educated, you should never show your impatience. Which meant my imagination was hard at work.

The solid house, with its unfinished floor and stairway still covered in gravel, had to be where the patriarch lived—the far-off author of my existence—and the huts around it, the homes of his wives. While my guide talked to him, I stared at the old man, trying to make a kind of communion with him, to see if our thoughts might cross, if our genes had something to say to one another. But nothing clicked. No point on his being seemed willing to open to me. He continued, unphased, through his prayer beads. No concern for me, for my guide, for the wall of ferns separating us from a bleak and solitary hut under the big kapok tree. His half-closed eyes only seemed to look inward, no doubt more vast and luminous than the sky, which was starting to show its first stars. "Dear God, please don't let this be my grandfather!" Why had I told myself that? His soul hadn't recognized mine, or his blood mine. Maybe it was all wrong: the photo was simply edited, and Indigo Bomber even more cynical than I thought.

The guide was still talking about the rain and how great the weather was, the state of the pastures, and the livestock's good health. Good manners dictated that we beat around the bush before trying to barge through it. "Better to bypass the river from dawn till dusk than drown in happiness," as the song goes. He recited a lovely couplet about the intrepid Baldé family line that didn't seem to warm or chill the noble old man and that referred to a sad era the country had known when a person lived by the rhythm of its deprivations, speeches, and hangings. Suddenly the feeble old man got up and without a word disappeared into the gravel-covered spiral staircase.

The young man at the radio also stood up and with a nervous hand pointed to the standalone hut under the big kapok tree.

"You might have better luck over there."

"I knew I shouldn't have," the guide moaned, passing by the fence's vine-woven gate.

"What?"

"Uttering the name Jean-Pierre Bangoura. That story made a lot of noise around here. And in this village, resentment is handed down from father to son like a precious heirloom. You should have known that before you came. I don't know what you're going to find in that hut, but if anything seems unusual, I suggest you get a hotel room—there's one on the other side of the village off the road to Télimélé—and get back on the rapid bus first thing tomorrow morning."

He cleared his throat three times before lifting his hand to knock at the door. An old woman with a smoke-blackened face appeared.

"Excuse me, elder-mother, there is a young traveler in need of hospitality."

"And where is she coming from?"

"Far away!"

"And what is her name?"

"I haven't asked her. Give her something to eat and drink

and tomorrow she'll tell us who she is. It's nightfall—I need to get going."

She offered me a bowl of fonio and a calabash of curdled milk. A storm lantern only barely revealed the glowing hearth and two small earthen beds, but I didn't need to see her. I could sense from her first words that this was my grandmother. This time, genes had spoken to genes. There was no question: we had joint molecules.

The next day, the guide found me wrapped around a bowl of corn porridge while not far off the old woman was busy watering the chickens.

"You didn't sleep well. How should I interpret that? Overjoyed or overly anxious? What did you talk about?"

"We looked at each other."

"I was careless yesterday. Today, I won't talk about Jean-Pierre Bangoura. I won't even mention his name."

He dusted off a mat on the ground and, as soon as he sat down, raised his voice in the old woman's direction.

"She's not bothering you too much, our young outsider?"

"She's educated enough for a young city girl. But that's not what brought you here, is it? A hut like mine here isn't the best choice to treat a young girl like that with hospitality. You have bad news, Pétel. I felt it in my bones right away…"

She peered at me from the corner of her eye and went on in a voice choked with emotion.

"Is it about my daughter?"

"Um… not exactly…"

"You can tell me everything. There's no news anymore I can't handle. You can survive anything when you've lived through what I've lived through… My daughter, then? Is she really dead or—?"

She interrupted herself to stare insistently at me again.

"Unfortunately, my elder mother, unfortunately..." the so-called Pétel said. "But God is just—he doesn't put everything in the sack of misfortune."

"You mean...?"

"Yes, I mean..."

"In *that* hell?"

"In that hell!"

"And why was I told nothing?"

"No one knew anything about it."

She let out a sound she meant to be a laugh, but it made me jump.

"Come, so I can see you up close! Don't be afraid, I won't cover you in tears—I don't have any left."

I spent the following days relaying what Indigo Bomber told me, but it felt useless. She didn't need to know any more. She avoided my eyes and would endlessly repeat, as if to dissuade me from going on, "I know...I know."

On the fourth day, she asked me to go with her to the creek to wash clothes.

"Sit here," she said, pointing out a flat rock. "Sit and look at the kapok tree over there... Good. You can stand up. Your reflection in the water touches those water lilies. Same age your mother was when she told me about your father."

She tried to get used to my name: *Woronyiki*. In their language, *v* doesn't exist, and the silent *e* is a conundrum. I almost told her I'd been given a Muslim name in a past life, but that would needlessly complicate things. I sensed on her wrinkled face the effort she was exerting to hold back the torrent of memories and muddy waters of the past.

"She could have given you another name."

"She didn't have the time."

"That's true. She didn't have the time. You know what

we're going to do tomorrow after the midday prayer? We're going to say hello to your grandfather."

"You think so?"

"He'll come around—he'll accept you. He's not mean, he's
just full of pride. That's what ruined Sâré-Kali: that violent prison of pride. All you have to do is dress like the girls around here
and everything will be fine."

She explained that she hadn't always lived like that. She
used to live with the others, on the other side of the fence,
where she occupied the biggest hut. Tierno tore it down after
my mother's marriage to keep her confined in one meant for
servants in the bygone chieftaincy days. In the end he wound
up building this unfinished house.

"Oh, what a story. If only your father were willing to con-
vert!"

But Coastal folks are hardheaded: impossible to get that
Jean-Pierre Bangoura mule to swallow a single Qur'anic verse.
So Tierno took out his gun. The village still remembers it—her
words becoming confused, hesitant, as she voiced her question,
as if this one proposal would upset everyone's thoughts and actions. It was a close call. Our two lovebirds had to zigzag on their
motorcycle to dodge Tierno's bullets and curses. "Do not touch
my daughter, evil Coaster! You Christian dog! Pork eater!" The
great wheel of despair had carried Néné Biro behind them to
the bridge over the river. She stopped there, to watch them go
down the slope and risk their lives on the cliffside before the
hills could swallow them up.

"For me, that's where she died. An awful griot filled in the
rest—I won't go into it."

She took me by the hand and crouched down at a respectable distance from the goatskin where Tierno sat, with the thin-
ness of a biblical character, his Phrygian cap and prayer beads
phosphorescent. Priestly, detached.

"Lower your heart, Tierno. This is your daughter's daughter, the fruit of your beard and my bosom. Take her hand, say something to her."

That lasted until dusk. Tierno focused on his prayer beads without giving me a single look. The whole village was there. The scene recalled that distant day when he'd taken out his gun, when my future parents—the two cursed fiancés—had to flee on motorcycle.

Néné Biro didn't cry. I knew she didn't have any more tears. I still had some but chose to save them for another time.

She sent a message to Pétel so he could find me a seat on a bush cab the next morning.

"Come," she told me. "We're going to cut a chicken's throat. Nothing better than guilé-pepper chicken to escape whatever disaster's stalking you."

That night was my party, the only one I'll never forget. An inward fireworks display, my soul in motion, heart in every state it knew, ready to love every creature on earth: lizards, beetles, Hitler, Sékou Touré, and even that unthinkable character that Raye, with her phenomenal need to laugh at everything—herself especially—had named Indigo Bomber.

Her hut was in poor shape, but it was neat and fragrant. The smell of caro-caroundé, the wonderful smell of caro-caroundé! Between us, nothing but that, the smell of caro-caroundé and a nourishing sea of quiet. Flesh doesn't speak, Madame Corre. It was on that day I understood the magic effect of genes.

It took me a long time to fall asleep, repeating incessantly to myself these words that had come to my mouth without passing through my head: *The intimate seeps in through your pores, dishonesty and hate by the fetid breath of the mouth.*

Her speech turned abundant and nervous as my departure drew near.

"He loves you, Tierno, he does. He can't bring himself to say it because of the prideful clot obstructing his heart. You'll come back and he'll fall into your arms once he realizes his mistake. Do your best to understand and not judge him. People are made of skin and bones, anyway. Not Sâré-Kali. He's bone, nothing but bone. Bone from head to toe. Nowhere to put a heart…"

It was the season of plenty, that brief interlude of aromas and ripe ears of corn that separates the winter lightning and the blistering Harmattan winds. You could see far beyond the rattan and bamboo fences, over the fern hedges, up to the banks of the stream, and even farther, after the oval huts and the rows of termite mounds, the smooth wind on the swaths of fonio, on to the dusty trail and bright valleys behind which loomed my destiny. I couldn't wait to get out of there. I was missing the Oxygène and, with it, the nauseating smell, the mosquitoes, and the bewitching Conakry nights. I knew I wouldn't come back to Sâré-Kali. I wouldn't see Néné Biro again. I didn't feel the need. Those few moments spent together filled my emptiest void. I gained a grandmother. It was a good start for cobbling together a genealogy. A grandmother who talks to you, a grandmother who loves you, who loves you in silence, who passes it all on to you: the wreckage of the past along with the lights to come. As for me, I became everything in her eyes; I was redeeming both her vanished daughter and her life, which Tierno had wasted in sixty years of marriage.

"We are one and the same person," she said before helping me into the van.

"She offered me her left hand: that's the one you give when leaving someone close, to stop the witches and demons from separating you forever with distorted omens. When Pétel took my suitcase to hoist it onto the roof, I insisted on keeping it with me. I didn't need to talk or drink or eat or look behind me until twenty kilometers separated us, still because of the demons and sorcerers.

I thought about her the whole trip. But, leaving Sâré-Kali, I swore I'd crush every louse swarming the rags of my memories, that I'd see more clearly and look straight forward. Not just forge ahead, but surge, make if not an exciting life then at least a tolerable future. I wasn't just living for myself anymore. I was living for her, for her daughter with no grave, and for everyone who would be born of us.

I started yawning as soon as the tabletop mountain ranges unfolded like a dream: the brush in flower, the river shimmering, the ocher valleys coiffed with hibiscus, bubbling waterfalls, kids armed with slingshots to scare off the snitches.

I assumed that, like me, she slept very little that night. In the same movement of the soul, we were left thinking, ahemming, ruminating on what couldn't be said, our ears open lazily to the nighttime crackle of the bush and, far off, the heartrending music of the koras and flutes. "We won't see each other again. Why would we? Make sure our family line doesn't end, that's all I ask. Go, my child, go. Wherever you are I will feel you." She said all this in a voice soaked with tenderness. Still, we'd spent the afternoon arguing—in total opposition by the end—in the amused tone of a girl and her grandmother. She was eager to sell her cow so she could send me gifts and pay for my travel. I lied to her and said I had some money and didn't need hers. "OK," she finally allowed. "All the same I bought you some sandals and robes from the region. You can't turn them down. My granddaughter isn't leaving my home empty-handed. Now, go tell your grandfather goodbye! It's never good to leave in the middle of a quarrel." Grandpa refused to come out. She took the blame and, to alleviate the pain, sang me the lullabies she'd sing to my mother on the way to the bus station. Then she tried in vain to stuff some bills in my bag, then my bra, before I got in the van.

The bush cab reached Conakry and, of course, there was no electricity. The city had rekindled with its old demons: the hold-ups, the curfews, riots, water shutoffs, power outages. But that wasn't what worried me: I didn't have any money and two burly men, one on the steps, the other perched in the arch of a bridge, were watching me with suspicious interest.

We were stopped at a first police checkpoint, then a second, then a third. Too risky: that kind of place is relatively well lit, thanks to the generators and police lights. But fortune smiled on me in Rogbané: a strong burning smell came out of the engine and the clutch disk gave way. The two burly men jumped down to the ground to open the hood, swearing at the top of their lungs. I got out of the car without drawing any attention, like someone wanting to stretch their legs or satisfy some little need. One of the burly men saw me jump over the roadside school's chain-link fence and immediately understood why I insisted on keeping my bags so close. He jumped it too, and the chase lasted about a half-hour before I managed to disappear into the maze of a slumland.

When I told them about my last few days, my girlfriends at the Oxygène almost strangled me.

"That cow needed to get sold so we could have the cash! Cash actually has value here. Out there, they just drink kinkéliba tea and cow's milk—which is free, mind you. By the way, I ran into Miriam yesterday."

"Was she in Mamou?"

"Yeah, and her grandma pampered her so much she managed to get by without cocaine."

"Miriam with no syringe to save her! If that's not a miracle—"

"What time is the Royal Air Maroc plane getting in?" asked Saran, cutting me off.

"1:30!"

"Alright, girlies, let's make our move. I've got a stunt for you."

Three hours later, we found ourselves at the Mariador pool around a bottle of champagne. Saran, who had a pulse on everything, found out that a team of geologists were coming from New Zealand for the mining town of Sangarédi. And at the agreed signal, she drew the fearsome weapon of a polyglot.

"*Would you like to find a night club?*"

Of course these young people from Down Under wanted just that, to get a taste of Africa at its finest: booze, dance, girls, all the trappings.

We had enough time in the interval to smother them with kisses and empty out their pockets. No, we couldn't possibly go back with them at such a late hour, we had work waiting at home. But we could call them and party together, and why not pay them a quick visit to Sangarédi once they settled in? Taxis were on the way to take them to the Oxygène.

The rest went back to Bonôrou and his little tigresses. There were four of them, so they needed four taxis, each visitor in the backseat surrounded by two escorts. And boom! Once they'd reached an obscure place, the Kakikombo Bridge for example, the taxis would all stop at the same time and, armed with PK3s, the tigresses took it from there. It was our twelfth time executing that plan—there was no reason it wouldn't work.

From the bar, we were on the lookout for our partners, certain nothing could have happened to them. When the four taxis passed through the arch hanging over the maquis entrance, Kâkilambé, who was watching just behind us, knew he had cause to celebrate. We were operating as a group of four, at the Novotel, the Mariador, the Relais, the Palm Camayenne— all the palace hotels where gringos and diaspouris with fat wallets stayed. You can bet, Madame Corre, the police were in cahoots with us. She always managed to bring back passports and empty bags while shedding crocodile tears: "But, sirs, you should have asked us for an escort! You don't just go walking around in a country you don't know like that. Here. We were able to get your papers back, but as for your money... Those thugs are already in Sierra Leone by now." That's how it went, Madame Corre, nothing special, nothing strong, nothing profoundly human without a butcher knife and crocodile tears.

...

The Oxygène was a respectable house. I never saw a police raid there. And apart from two or three settled scores, no one ever died of anything but malaria or overdose. Same as a palace or skyscraper, really. Yes, from time to time couples would clash and break out a knife in the bedrooms, or the same would happen to others kissing on the beach or under the jagged covers of the water, but what could be more innocent?

We weren't angels but we weren't devils, either. We were just young and used to an insatiable urge to feel alive. The Oxygène had everything we needed for that, with no lender's fee or doctor's note or priest's morals, no astrologer's dismal omen. I watched love kindle there, and hatred explode. I watched vocations take shape as other fates crumbled. If I had Gorki's pen, I would have called this place *My Universities*. I swear, Madame Corre, there's no better school than that one.

We weren't exactly daddy's girls and boys. Single moms, lawbreakers, overqualified students bent on driving motorcycle taxis or polishing shoes. Most were happy just to have a bowl of corn porridge and bank on some luck. We'd get restless, get by, fight life tit for tat and try to stay sincere. But it wasn't just hopeless and feral rebels who ventured there. During the day, you could see families from beautiful homes sitting on the patio—spouses, offspring, and all—to try braised fish or garlic squab. That type never ventured to the Motel or Toes in the Water. They'd disappear with dusk's ocher colors and emerge after 2 PM the next day. Apart from Dr. Diallo. The most respected doctor in the city, from the Barki and Tchellal clinic.

Little was known about Dr. Diallo, except that he studied in Cuba and his reputation as an OB-GYN reached well beyond the country's borders. He'd saved lives, Dr. Diallo, which meant no one—not even the badly brought up kids from Coronthie—had the right to judge him. He was prompt in a country where lateness is considered the mark of a good education. He only came on Fridays and would always show up at 6:52 PM. He was handsome. He was elegant as a baron and courteous as the people of Tokyo. The kind of person who inspires respect but still has an art for cultivating their own manias. Makhalé was the only person allowed to wait on him. When she was gone or busy elsewhere, he'd take his newspaper, plant himself under the Kapok tree by the street, and pretend to read, his back seemingly turned to us. So Kâkilambé would have to go apologize and beg him to take his seat. Then the boss would start nagging the staff so Dr. Diallo would see how important he was to the establishment. "Move heaven and earth if you have to—I want her here in five minutes. We are not making Dr. Diallo wait any longer!" We'd sprint to sweep the patio, clean the tables and chairs, and change out the placemats the moment his Toyota appeared at the Ambiance intersection before making its way to the Oxygène parking lot. By the time he'd go to the restroom, he made sure we knew everything had to be cleared away: the poire africaine, the sanitation bucket, mops, old boxes, whatever was lying around. Makhalé would eventually materialize. She knew he'd start off with a glass of pineapple juice before the Guiluxe beers and half-bottle of whisky. Then she'd slip away undetected. The ritual never varied. After the last glass of whisky, he'd collapse on the table, face in hands. To sleep? Cry? Meditate? No one would have dreamt of asking him. Sometimes, without meaning to, these inscrutable phrases would cut into his quiet reverence: "The one meaningful question, how to reconcile sex, alcohol, and faith?" Around 11, a young woman would come looking for him (his daughter perhaps, or his wife or lover). She'd whisper in his ear and take him delicately by the hand to guide him to the parking lot. "Kill the mind and the heart! Are we sure we've done what we needed to do?"

That exalted voice, hovering high above the clanging rumor that was the Oxygène, gave the night a kind of density, something deep and mystical. I would go home feverish afterward with a head full, not of Bob Marley lyrics but of the concise and impenetrable words of that troubling doctor, who knew just how to penetrate my soul with questions that had no answer. "A tree without sap, life without love—are we barbarians?"; "In what sense, prehistory? Yesterday, today or tomorrow?"

Does Dr. Diallo still come on Fridays to charm the Oxygène standbys with his unsettling voice and his handsome mixed complexion? Do they still keep it for him, the big secret that makes him so moving, so human, every Friday between 10 and 11 o'clock? You'll know soon, Madame Corre. Raye and the two Bambys are on the trail and it could be the right one. "Prepare the Arc, the Flood is coming!"

For a change of scenery, Yâyé Bamby invited us to spend a Saturday on the Loos Islands. When we got back, Goulo left his pots of boiling yam to intercept us.

"A white guy just came by. He left a phone number."

Naturally, it was Philippe. He picked up as soon as I called.

"I've got a trail leading to Boffa. Is your dad from there?"

"I'll go to Boffa tomorrow."

"I'm coming with you," he said with authority.

I knew by his tone of voice that any discussion would have been useless.

Boffa after Sâré-Kali! After my maternal side, after the mountains of Fouta-Djalon, now I had to explore the mangroves of the Low Coast to trace my paternal line. To complete my genealogical tour and cobble together a semblance of civil status. I saw it as a privilege: being born at my present age. Yes, it is a privilege to attend your own birth, a favor afforded to gods and found children. And I wasn't the only one this time to go rifling through the shitheap and choose the parent I wanted. Philippe was with me. I wondered why he quivered so badly to restore my whole genealogy. "You understand," he said to me with a clenched fist, "it's the only way to take revenge on these bastards. Their whole goal is to reduce you to nothing. To do that, they start by erasing you from everyone's memory. Then bam—you don't exist for anyone anymore. You don't even exist in your own head anymore. That's the worst way to kill someone." I felt so stirred when he said that, as if it were his own father who'd been hanged, as if it were his own memory that was falsified. "Don't worry, Véronique, I'll be at your side until everything is clear, until your past leaps from the shadows where it was thrown. We're nothing without names. The real name you were given and that goes so well with your soul. Yes, yes, yes, Véronique! Not 'Atou,' Véronique! Véronique, the scathing rod that lashes their face, the posthumous calm that finally allows Jean-Pierre and Rama to rest in peace."

There, among the mountain's prideful shepherds, Néné Biro was able to fulfill what she'd lacked and ease her grief. What was I going to find in the coastal rice farmers where I owed my boiling paternal blood? We had a few clues before getting in the bush cab. I knew according to Indigo Bomber's claims and the meager information I gleaned from Foreign Affairs that the man in the photo was from Boffa. Philippe was able to learn that he'd been born to a certain Albert Bangoura.

At Boffa City Hall, we were received by a kind, old but goitrous official who could barely stand with crutches.

"Here it is, madame, monsieur, right here: 'Jean-Pierre Bangoura, born in Boffa on March 31st, 1939, to schoolteacher Albert Bangoura and homemaker Véronique Conté.' Your namesake is from here, but your grandfather seems to have come from Colia, two hours away by car. If I were in your position, I'd go there first thing tomorrow and present a kola to the village elder. The elder will understand, everyone will understand: nothing more normal than tracing one's roots. The trouble is you're not the only one in this case."

He screwed up his face and wiped his eyes with the sleeve of his bubu.

"Things have happened here, child. Things have happened."

He took us to his place to sleep and, without knowing it, sparked a bright hope in my little head.

"I didn't think he was the only one. It's rare here, you know, only children! Maybe you have uncles and—who knows?—an aunt or two. But they wouldn't have been born here, otherwise they'd be in my registry. Schoolteachers moved around a lot back then, they'd go north or south as assignments changed. They'll tell you everything in Colia. I have a cousin in Colia, I let him know you're coming."

The elder in Colia knew my grandfather well and even, when he was a kid, his father before him.

"They were from here, Susus like us: enthusiastic, generous, short-tempered, with a love for dance and quarrelling. But there's not much I can do for you, child. Your grandfather never came back to the village after his father's death. And he was still unmarried at that time. You see... Well, maybe my wife knows more about it than I do."

The woman stood quietly frozen, twisting the end of her camisole, then fixed her round eyes on me and I almost hugged her when she opened her mouth.

"Jean-Pierre wasn't the only one. Véronique had three children with Albert: after Jean-Pierre there was François and Pascaline."

I didn't dare ask the question that was burning on my lips. Philippe did it for me.

"And where are they now?"

"I don't know."

"Think back, please," insisted Philippe. "Did you ever seen them, I mean with your own eyes?"

"A long time ago. In Conakry. Their father had become a school inspector. He was living in the same neighborhood as my cousin Mâfoudiya. François was destined for the seminary, but Pascaline was still too little to choose."

This time I couldn't contain myself. I jumped to my feet and threw myself into the old woman's arms, patting her back.

"Thank you, Mother, thank you! Thanks to the whole village! Pardon my disruption, but this was worth the trouble. Everything is better now: I know where I'm from."

The day after, back in Boffa, Philippe turned down the hospitality of the old goitrous man. He ordered a cab to drive us to the best hotel in the city, where he booked two rooms.

"Two rooms, please—adjoining."

After a shower, the receptionist guided us to the bungalow where dinner was served. Avocado salad, red konkoé stew, and a pineapple carved into a boat. Two or three words, that's all we could muster after spending the whole afternoon on the bumpy roads of the bush. Then came a mug of kinkéliba tea and everyone went back to their rooms.

I had a dream about Pascaline. She was running an old merry-go-round, dressed like a fairy. Everything around her was red: the platform, the wooden horses, the clowns' oversized clothes. She asked me to come closer. She pulled candy out of my nose with the sound of a whistle. She didn't ask if I wanted the candy, she just stuffed them in my pockets and then in my mouth. "Is it you, Aunt Pascaline, is it really you?" She didn't answer. She just smiled and shook her long magic wand overhead.

When I woke up, I found Philippe sprawled out beside

me. He was stroking my hair.

Hearing the news, Yâyé Bamby had streaks of joyful tears and Raye cackled and slapped my back.

"You're going to be born, Atou! You're going to be born for real."

Then Philippe stormed in and jostled us to our feet. He demanded we take the Honda he'd rented to see the bishop.

"What sweet revenge if you could find them! For you, obviously, but for us too. That's their strength: they don't leave a trace. Only now, with a living, breathing person, we're left necessarily with traces," he was turning red opening the glass door to the lobby.

We were taken to the archives, where an old priest was waiting for us in a white cassock and round glasses.

"François Bangoura, is it?"

He said the name about a dozen times flipping through his old files.

"How am I going to do this? We've got several François Bangoura priests in just the last twenty years. This country has a cruelly small imagination: four or five last names for twelve million residents... When was yours born, where? To whom? Come back tomorrow—I can look more carefully in peace. I'd better look since you came just for this. But tell me, is it for a pension or is it something else?"

"It's for a genetic test," Raye said without laughing.

"A genetic test?" the old priest choked, not sensing any humor.

I spent the evening shouting at Raye.

"We were this close and you had to trot out your dumbass jokes!"

"Sweetie, you know I can't see a monkey's red behind and

not try to put my hand on it."

The next day, the old priest gave us a lukewarm reception, still not recovered from Raye's thoughtlessness. But Philippe, who knew better, showed his diplomacy and soon the prelate brought out his registries a second time.

"We're making itty-bitty progress, but progress nonetheless: I found two that matched your description."

"Both of them born to an Albert Bangoura and Véronique Conté?"

"Unfortunately. And both of them born in Boffa."

"And where might they be now?"

"One is dead, the other is living in Kindia. In the bishopric or the convent."

I don't know why, but my mind was made up. I said so to Philippe.

"That's him, I know it. The one in Kindia, that's my uncle."

"Why do you say that?"

"The one who died was 'born near...'. Back then, only the kids of government officials had exact dates and places."

Philippe vanished again and I knew he was hot on some trail. Once he got back, he asked me to pack my bag and follow him without saying anything.

The convent was at the top of a mountain. We had to borrow a 4x4 first, and then a dirt bike. After that, on foot, we followed a path along the ridge leading to an old leper colony that smelled like goat piss and soumbara.

The elder who greeted us spoke for a long time under a tall mango tree, as if he wanted to prepare us for a challenging task.

"Dear Lord, who put such a thought in your mind? It's

been thirty years since he was here, you see... And out of the blue a visitor! Who gave you such a thought? And this is the first time he's had a visitor, you know. We eventually thought there was no one left who knew him outside these walls."

"I didn't know I had anyone inside these walls either..."

"And who's to tell us you're really his brother's daughter? No one came out of there alive, let alone a baby."

"You're telling me he doesn't want to see me?"

"I'm not saying that."

"But you'd assured me in your letter that... Philippe, you try."

"Yes, that's what I thought, and what he thought too... It's not an easy decision to make, please understand."

"I just wanted to—"

"Please don't abuse our patience, mademoiselle... Go, I beg you. And please, speak softly. This is a house of God."

Philippe and I made the trip home without a word.

I told you, Madame Corre, I'm not looking for ink to doodle with. I'm after a magical forgetting potion. When it's all over, when there's nothing left to do but look back through the book of my life before I take my last breath, that will be the hardest image to look at. You understand, don't you? The man stuck here to his wheelchair, with nothing more than an eye that twinkles for the rest of his life? I had the time to fathom his body, gauge his soul. My father, though, I only ever touched his photo. But there would be an image engraved, not on the cold material of film, but in the living flesh of my memory if I just had the chance to see my uncle—who, it seemed, resembled him like a twin. But here I am: the only person ever born to parents who never existed. Sharing can relieve anything. Real tragedy happens when there's nothing: in my case, not even a glance at one another. What memory was my uncle holding onto? Some wet, straw-covered huts daubed with kaolinite? A yard thick with horseflies and foraging goats? Tell me, Madame Corre, how can you make ends meet when you can barely put the pieces of your family together? Yes, I know, your son disappeared. But there's a chance he'll come back. Your horoscope is stuffed fuller than mine. You knew your mama and papa, your nephews, cousins, and—I'm willing to bet—your ancestors and aunts. As for me, the only papa I was given I killed like a dog. And I'll never know what became of my mama. I'd die of shame if fate ever dropped me in front of her: shame for killing my father, shame for running away from home. And still, never forget this, Madame Corre: I won't have any other father besides the fuckhead that raped me and no mother apart from the cold, distant woman who left me in the hands of a maid so she could go meet her lovers. A photo isn't enough to fill a child's emotional void. A photo is meant to call to mind the existence of someone close. A stranger's photo brings nothing to life, not words, not flesh. You learn how to console yourself quickly when you're born in a country like mine. It's such a disaster that, however deep the pit, you're never alone. The whole world lost someone in the cesspools of Camp B, even those born like you in Navarre or Burgundy. There are some who not only lost their mother and father, but their uncles, aunts, grandmothers, their hired help and dog. I'll only ever be the one-eyed woman in a kingdom of the blind.

And yet, just the same, a miracle unfolded in Sâré-Kali. God gave me a mirror in whom I recognized myself from hair to toe. Through Néné Biro's voice I could hear the young woman in the photo. She breathed life into the static material Indigo Bomber had given me. On that side at least, my ancestry is certain. Néné Biro is brimming over with joy, truth, generosity, life. Néné Biro is enough to me. As for Tierno, I've gotten nothing from him, no thoughts, no gestures, no chills, no flesh. No fruit to pick from that tree. Pride and fanaticism swiped away its buds and sap.

YOU KNOW WHAT Prospero told me the other day? "The vise only gets tighter, Countess. Around who, you ask? Well Lady Smaragdine, of course! The one who's always in emerald green! Last night, on my way back from the movies, I noticed some cops in civilian clothes pacing in front of the gate to her building. The whole neighborhood's atwitter—the florist, the baker, even Monge plaza's homeless. Everybody. This is the day! The Rue de la Clef murder is going to be fully revealed! Have a waffle, Countess, here. You know what, here, take two. They're not annoying you too much, I hope? 'Who? Who?' These Gauls, for heaven's sake! Especially Crotchety Anne with her foul mug. Because if they colonized you, Countess, we've colonized them back. But hey, to each one's owners. If they're annoying you, let me know and we'll cross that Rubicon again. Not just Caesar and his generals this time, but also the Camorra, Juventus, AC Milan, the Commedia dell'arte, Berlusconi, Cicciolina, the whole gang. They'll have no way out. You really buy this story about the son she apparently left in Guinea? Not me. She's a phony, I'm telling you, just spinning yarn for the attention. And yeah, Countess, I'm Italian. Guilty. I'll never speak French like the French do... A minister husband! *She* has a husband and he's a *minister*? And my old lady's the Queen of England. She's an odd one, that woman—odd and shady."

And yet, you did leave a son behind in Guinea. Is he still alive? Does he remember you? I had to have run into him, just like I have millions of others since coming here. Millions of people who mean nothing to me. At the Oxygène it was different. Everything meant something: bodies, voices, looks, gestures, even silence. Anonymity didn't exist at the Oxygène because the chain wasn't broken—the chain of life, I mean, the thing that allows us to love and vibrate in harmony. Maybe I saw him right there at the Oxygène, but nothing is certain. I don't want to give you any false hope. That would be unforgivable, given I've carried the same cross as you. But he pops in my head like an intuition, so maybe I'll ask Raye, Yâyé Bamby, and my daughter to see if my doubts had any basis. Let them do it. I'll fill you in the moment the news is credible and reassuring, but not before. Given the life he lived, you never know: you don't get out of their hands unscathed down there. Kids aren't hanged. They're not even snapped into a pillory. But they take their young brains, their developing memories and fragile identity.

You were right, Madame Corre, you had your own problems with genealogy, only with a shimmer of hope for a consolation prize. I'd known for a long time that, as far as I was concerned, the good Lord omitted the word *family* in the pages of my fate. I'd get the same therapeutic effect I was expecting from my trip to the Kindia convent if you ever saw your son again. Our lives have some resemblance after all. No, there's no resemblance—our lives have an intersection. Two parallel lives that suddenly came together. Both drunken boats trying desperately to echo the other.

I owe you an apology, Madame Corre. Ultimately, you did well annoying me that winter afternoon in front of the pastry shop on Rue Mouffetard. I wouldn't have known anything about all this. I've already told you—you're no stranger anymore—a simple passerby with no voice, no face, no name. We come from the same torn-off piece of fabric. You're the other side of my mountain, the other version of my story. There are family ties more solid than genes. Sometimes your presence irritates me, I look at you and think, "Who created the two of us, this one and me? Was it the good Lord or was it Sékou Touré?"

Despots aren't on the same level as the good Lord, but they all try to topple him. Good God, the energy! The will! The sense of intrigue, of imagination! They blur our memories, break destiny apart, rewrite genealogies. Anything that can be taken from those monsters, even an engagement ring, is a colossal victory for the people of Camp B, their ancestors, their descendants, and the descendants after them. Philippe would never stop repeating it to me: it's on the soil of memory that we have our last chance to win. If we lose on that soil, we'll have legitimized all the concentration camps—yesterday's and especially tomorrow's. Bastards! Memory, Madame Corre, is the one weapon they're afraid of. He fought all his life so the smallest injury, the lightest scratch, the smallest microaggression could be collected, recorded, and indexed. And now here he is, stuck in this contraption, damaged as if he'd fallen into the hands of Pol Pot, Pinochet, or Sékou Touré. Earthquakes and epidemics will never be enough. Nature alone is too little— man has to tack on his own bullshit.

Did you know, Madame Corre, that in some countries political prisons outkill epidemics? Therein lies the whole human comedy: epidemics we'll overcome, but political prisons— never. You're helpless when you're up against the bullshit of human affairs. I've long vowed that no one will see me bellow slogans or chant hymns with people who think if you lose your hair and walk on two legs, you suddenly have the right to take a shot at anything that moves. This earth was not created for people, it was made for life. What do we understand about life? What does that mean? Taming nature? Only by asking ourselves these kinds of questions will we stave off all the perils we set in motion.

These were the sorts of ideas running through my head that morning on my way back from Cluny. Prospero waved me over as I was coming down Rue du Cardinal-Lemoine.

"Over here, Countess, over here! Have you seen the paper?"

"No, why?"

"She asks me why. Feast your eyes on this: the crime on Rue de la Clef has been solved."

"So?"

"That's the whole drama, Countess. It wasn't her. It was a burglary gone wrong. Some kid beat the old retired lady to pay for more dope. They suspected her because she'd just left the victim's place an hour before the crime. She was going every week to take voice lessons. Did you know how into opera the woman was? And no, the thug wasn't from the suburbs. Kid lives on Rue Saint-Jacques—his old man's a professor of medicine! Rotten times we're in. Just vulgar on every level. Doesn't sit right with me, doesn't sit right at all, Countess. I don't like being wrong... All I can do now is put my tail between my legs and go back to brushing against the walls of Barisciano, my old Abruzzo hometown. But Crotchety Anne, well, I'll never look her in the eyes. I had her pinned as Suspect Number One for nothing. Oh, mamma mia! Countess, tell her from now on she can have all the waffles she wants. She eats free starting today. That's the price point on my regret. Nothing makes me crack like regret. I'm Italian, in case you didn't know. You thought it was her too, yeah? Just like the baker, the street vendor, the garbage men, like every respectable person in the neighborhood. Look how wrong we all are! What are we going to do now? I'm asking you... Lie down at her feet and apologize? Saying sorry's just not a thing I do. *I-ta-li-an.*"

Yes, even Prospero knew it: we were all wrong. You're no criminal, Madame Corre. But the whole neighborhood took you for one. The trial's been going on forever—well since Kafka—and it works by that same logic. You create the culprit before inventing the crime. One minute, you come around to accepting your own indictment. The next, like Joseph K., you start defending yourself. And the next, you're already at the end of a rope like your husband. Or, your hands and feet bound, thrown from the top of a cliff like my father. You're the ideal culprit. It would never have occurred to anyone to think otherwise.

Our poor people didn't get the chance to defend themselves. Under Sékou Touré, the "culprits" were presented before a mic (not a courtroom), their confessions drawn out by electric shock, broadcast on the radio, and thus the trial was closed. I have no doubt, however, that while being led to death, like Jean-Pierre Bangoura, Bôry Diallo ever thought he was guilty. Tyrants aren't on the same level as gods, but they have a resemblance: their will is always done.

The next week I got an email from my daughter:

Dear Maman,

Pretty sure we're on the right track. The guy's mother is, can confirm, from Dijon. Like I said, he talks about *Gammie* all the time. And at the mention of *Nononque*, he has a clear response: his face goes straight into his hands (can't tell if he's crying, praying, meditating) and words gush out of his mouth—each one weirder than the last. He's got a vague memory of his father but seems to think he was a minister? He's not fun to deal with, this gentleman, but we're all trying to stay positive, Raye, big Yâyé Bamby, and I.

I'm starting to hesitate about med school. "Surgeon" sounds tempting now—pediatric surgeon, it's more modern. Straight pediatrics is kind of old-fashioned. But right now I need to pass the bac, and with honors. I'm not your daughter for nothing. Kisses to Philippe and hang in there!

Yâyé Bamby la Petite

P.S. You'll never be able to thank big Yâyé Bamby enough for everything she's done for me.

IN THE FOLLOWING WEEKS, our life was nothing more than comics and video games. We had to be careful. The awful memory of that sour visit to the convent portended others to come. Philippe was drinking whisky after whisky, taking drags off his cigarette and grumbling about his archest enemies: the puppet masters of the world, the despots, prison overlords, every sordid man who ever called in a busted kneecap, a broken skull, a gag, a Judas Chair, the torture fanatics and crusaders in the name of debasement.

"You understand, kiddo, it's not enough they throw you down a pit, they have to take the lives of everyone who survives you. So the world is nothing more than their private farm and all living things an army of zombies. You're right—let's quit accusing the dogs and pigs and rats. Pinochet, Hitler, and Sékou Touré didn't come from them, they came from us. They're hum-an beings like you and me. And that's the tragedy, the tragedy all the others live off of: Auschwitz, Phnom Penh's S-21 'hotel,' the ESMA in Buenos Aires, Santiago's stadium, Camp B, here in Conakry. Out of this earth, they made one immense concentration camp.

Raye, who never had the courage to face reality when it went gray, didn't hold back her swelling critiques. "You shouldn't have visited that animal Indigo Bomber. You shouldn't have! Some things are better left unknown." I knew Yâyé Bamby had a sickly aversion to bugs: fleas, spiders, and cockroaches, to her, represented the most abject form of existence. But pessimism meant something even more atrocious, beyond the roaches and chameleons. And she had her own way of exterminating it: just like someone taking out a fly with a magazine. Until I left her for France, she hadn't again said a word about the patricide, or Aunt Pascaline, or my visit to the terrible Kindia convent, or any other sad episode in our shared existence. She'd swept it all out of her mind, or at least wedged it into her gut, where it ate at the deepest part of her being, in secret.

I'll die without knowing what the letter B means.

Then Philippe pushed his bottle of Jack Daniel's away and disappeared for a few days. I wasn't worried: my mind offered no bad intuitions and I knew he didn't go back to France—he'd have told me. It was serious between us from then on. It had happened the way water runs: with no sound, with no hurry. I didn't say anything the morning I found him in my bed, stuck to me, as if we'd known each other forever. No shock, no disgust—no rage or euphoria. He still felt comfortable calling me *Petioute* taking me by the hand, caressing my cheek, planting loud kisses on my lips. He didn't say so, but I knew that to him *Petioute* was the equivalent of every word meant to sweep women off their feet: *my sweet, my love, honey, baby, ma chérie, mon amour, déwi an, marafandji, yârabi, mi habiba,* etc. Two weeks of little gestures, of short but tender words, before getting serious. His sense for the symbolic was strong, my beautiful leftist. There's a picturesque hotel in Dalaba where, back in colonial times, the elites of the white world would stay: the famous Fouta-Djalon Hotel. It was nowhere else but there that our first true night of love unfolded. As the sun rose, before the arms of Morpheus replaced his own, he whispered something in my ear. I just smiled and didn't say a word.

One week later, back in Conakry, he took up the cause over an ice cream cone on the Novotel patio, where we were living from then on.

"*Petioute*, you never answered the question."

"Which one?"

"Do you love me?"

"What do you want me to say?"

"*Yes*."

"I have a way better answer than that."

And I led him up to our room.

After our love, he opened a bottle of Dom Pérignon.

"You know where I'm taking you for our honeymoon?"

"Tokyo! Miami? Honolulu?"

"No. The Canary Islands. I have a lovely house there in Agüimes—thirty kilometers from Las Palmas. It's in the mountains. It feels almost like Fouta-Djallon, but it's not Fouta-Djallon. Some would compare it to the Pyrenees, but it's everything but. You might think Kabylia, but it's not. There's just nothing stranger than the Canary Islands. It's not Africa, it's not Europe, not America—it's all of them at once. It's there, in Agüimes, where we'll really, *really* love each other."

My daughter had started to call him "Uncle Philippe," Yâyé Bamby "my nephew Philippe," and Raye wouldn't stop heckling him. "That's my sister, don't forget! *My* sister. And my aunt is now her aunt. We should be added to her crazy genealogy. You're not marrying my sister without paying the custom: a hundred kola nuts or she's not walking through that door! What? That's how it goes here. No roses, irises, gardenias. Kola, good old Nzérékoré kola! You get it, my beau, you understand?"

He came back one night with his arms stuffed full of gifts.

"Have them all, ladies. Don't hold back—I don't get to spoil you often."

And while we were busy opening packages and gorging on chocolate, his booming voice rang out without us knowing where he'd just been.

"Have you heard? They just built a new village, somewhere near Tanéné."

"And what's in this village?"

"I don't know, *Petioute*. We'll have to go see."

"Go see what?"

"There could be a surprise."

"You know I don't have good luck, Philippe, on expeditions to the bush."

Yâyé Bamby was watching us with the half-shut eyes she'd get when a whiff of panic went to her head.

Sucked into a soap opera, we didn't see her get up and go to her room. She came back out an hour later. Siesta always made her voice scratchy.

"Don't go, Atou. Don't go to Tanéné. There's nothing good in Tanéné."

Her voice shook like she'd had visions and that an assembly of demons was waiting for me in Tanéné.

Raye came to her aunt's rescue with her usual wildcat energy.

"She's not going anywhere!"

"It does involve a certain Pascaline," Philippe insisted.

"'A certain Pascaline'! Oh, OK. You still want to make your little collage of hypothetical relatives? Forget it, my beau. We're his real relatives. Her family's right here and nowhere else."

"Please, Raye! That's my aunt, if this turns out. My Aunt Pascaline."

As we got closer to the village, he had me sit under a kapok tree. In a voice that seemed to tremble, he said, "I have to warn her, OK?"

"Here we go," I whined. "Same blow to the chest as the convent. I should have listened to Raye and Yâyé Bamby."

"It's a basic precaution! She isn't exactly young anymore, and if there's any strain beyond what she's gone through already—"

"Let's not tempt the devil, Philippe. Please."

He disappeared for a while, paying no mind to my apprehension. I saw from there what awful scene was in store for me: an old senile woman who'd lost her vision, her hearing, her teeth, her mind, and who—

A sudden need took over me: to bring my knees to my neck and jump with all my heart into the arms of the two benefactors the good Lord had planted in my path. Raye was right: I didn't need any more than what I had for family. Why go waking up the dead?

Philippe appeared and gave me a signal. I followed him toward the thorn and bamboo fence enclosing the village, boiling with anger at the man responsible for this place. Why did I have to be born like this on a dungeon floor? A father thrown off a cliff, mother with a throat cut through. An uncle behind the walls of a convent. An aunt here, in this village a Norwegian NGO built to house the destitute: witches, rejects, the half-mad. And that Haile Selassie look-alike back in Sâré-Kali, who had nothing left but inconsolable wrath and the prayer beads of a fanatic.

A muddy path snaked between the lougans and round huts, their walls painted identically with kaolinite. It smelled like castor oil and basil, chicken poop and sumbala. In the backyard of one of them, an old woman girded with a tunic stretching from her knees to her breasts, surrounded with clay statues of pregnant women, was working some clay with the meticulousness of ritual.

"We are over here, Pascaline. And we do hope we aren't bothering you."

She didn't turn around. She just muttered something without stopping her progress.

"Here she is, Pascaline. I promised I'd bring her to you. This is Véronique. She has her mother's name. Come here, Véronique. Come say hello to your Aunt Pascaline."

It was no use. All his stage-setting had no effect. The old woman kept on with her chores as if she didn't hear anything. And I was stock-still, literally hypnotized.

Then she inched toward the well and drew water from it.

"Go wait for me on the other side. I saved you something to eat. Just need to wash my face!"

No matter how hard I focused on her voice, none of her words stirred any emotion in me. But it wasn't her I was upset with, it was Philippe. The look I gave him was so furious that, his legs shaking, he sat down on a pile of wood and invited me to do the same.

"Father Foromo, you know, the one from the bishopric... You with me? It's thanks to Father Foromo... "

At his insistence, Father Foromo had investigated further. They were right, the folks in Colia: Albert Bangoura didn't only have two sons. He had a daughter, too—a girl by the name of Pascaline. She had married several times without bearing children. That's all he knew about her. But, again at Philippe's insistence, he kept digging around. And he remembered this village that a Norwegian NGO had made to house old women like her, with no husband and no offspring, to protect them from the crowds that assumed they were evil spirits. The task was Herculean: he'd managed to reunite an aunt's ghost with her aborted niece.

Pascaline came back from her wash and served us something to eat. Afterward, she squinted at me two or three times and addressed Philippe.

"Our skin color on her mother's body! Who would have imagined that, a child in that hell hole."

She went back into her hut for a long while. When she returned, she handed me something.

"Your grandmother's necklace. She inherited it from her mother, and now it's your turn... Ah! I forgot. There's a bit of palm wine. You don't mind a little palm wine, do you? Everyone drinks it nowadays, Christians and Muslims alike. Times change without asking our opinion."

I hadn't calculated any of this, I swear, Madame Corre. The palm wine had nothing to do with it. I walked over to her without realizing it, and then we embraced without a word. After that I went to the bottom of the lougan to a cabin with toilets. I stayed there a good long while. I thought I was crying but I wasn't. My mouth was open, but no tears ran down.

When I came back, she closed her eyes and touched a trembling hand to my face.

"You see, I don't dare look at you. Don't worry, I'll end up getting used to it. Don't listen to their lies, my child: they didn't kill your father, he rose up to heaven by himself to answer Jesus' call. It was the best thing that could have happened to him... Things have happened here... Forget, forgive everything... God is love and forgiveness."

"Pascaline, my tante, do you still have photos?"

"I burned everything the day Papa died. When they arrested Jean-Pierre, he was talking like you and me. It was after that that he was locked up in a barn and not allowed to see me; I fed him through a crack in the wall. Mama died before him and François was already at the convent. Since then, I have no need for photos."

"Do you ever see Uncle François?"

"He's gone the way of Papa—doesn't want to see anybody. Those were dismal times… Did you know you had an aunt? Don't blame Uncle François, don't blame anyone. Those were dismal times. A kilo of human flesh was worth less than a kilo of goat."

"I have a daughter, Auntie."

Her face was beaming.

"How old?"

"Almost eleven."

"So she'll live for all the others. Don't tell her that. Let her live her life. We'll all be resurrected if she makes it."

Later that evening, as she was walking us out, she turned to me for the first time.

"What's her name?"

"…?"

"Your daughter!"

I had to explain that it was Yâyé Bamby. I told her about Raye, too. Still, no word about Indigo Bomber, about Dad, Mom, about that crazy night when I had to leap from the balcony and throw myself into the world. I who knew nothing about the world.

We went back every Sunday. By the end, Philippe would sit under the kapok tree at the village entrance.

"Go on alone, you have your own things to say. I don't want to intrude on your family affairs."

"Oh wow! Do you have family, yes or no?"

"Of course I do, yes, but she won't say anything serious when I'm around. If she does, it's a lie—she still has the photos.

If that's true, then she has to know some piece of this story about the journal. Trust me, for these people manhandled by history, there's nothing more terrifying than the truth. I met an old woman in Chile who refused to admit she'd been raped in the camp where she was imprisoned."

"But Philippe—"

"If she asks for me, just make something up. That I'm traveling or something."

Once, she showed me the mortar where her mother would mash yams, the crucifix she'd collapse over so God would watch over her son, the rake she'd grate kola with, the gourd she kept her palm wine in...

"I'd give them to you, but they'd be a burden for a city dweller."

I would come back, she'd show me her clay statuettes that she talked to as if they were dear, living beings, she'd take out the wine and we'd drink in silence. When the sun would disappear behind the mountains, she'd touch me on the shoulder and smile. "It's time for you to go, my child. You know you have a long road ahead."

One night, she insisted on coming with me to the kapok tree. Nothing awkward, though: Philippe, who'd seen us leave the muddy trail, had enough time to skitter away. For a full hour, she talked to me about her statuettes.

"People don't understand. These aren't statuettes, they're revenants. It's very cold out there among the dead, which means the ones who can return do it so I can find them in the clay, so I can give shape to them, warm them up a bit. People think I'm crazy, that I'm talking to myself. I'm not. I'm talking to them. They're shy, revenants. They only talk to me—they're afraid of everyone else. And there's more from Camp B than anywhere else. None of our own have come back. Not Mama or Papa, not Jean-Pierre. Which proves they're plenty warm under the cover of Christ! You believe me, don't you? Of course you believe me.

You have the same blood as me. Your blood has faith in mine."

She turned around, and shot a burning look at the Dubré-ka Mountains. She was muttering as if addressing a prayer to a deity perched on the peaks.

"Now leave me, my child! It's nighttime, and you have a long road ahead. Tell me, my child, why in all this time did you never consider giving me a photo?"

The following Sunday, she put the picture of my daughter in her pocket without looking at it. She let out a chuckle at my confused face.

"He-he! She's pretty, your daughter. I've turned into my ancestors: I look out the back of my head, with the eye that sees everything—especially what's forbidden to be seen. That's how they spoke to those initiated in the secret of blessed caves. But why bore you with stories about sacred caves when you've never set foot there? He-he! I'll hold on to that one, it's worth keeping. The others carry no meaning anymore... Tell me, child, why did your friend stop coming to see me?"

"Oh, did I not tell you? He's my fiancé."

"Are you getting married soon?"

"Yes, after Tabaski Feast. I wanted it to be in Paris, but he wants to do it here. 'Here, marriage is a celebration; over there it's an administrative formality,' he says."

"So you're a Catholic? Like us!"

"I'm not sure. I love church choirs just as much as I do the muezzin's call to prayer."

"What faith do you pray in?"

"I've never prayed. Religion isn't a choice, I don't think. It's inherited. And God Almighty didn't think to give me an inheritance."

"And where is he, your fiancé? His name's 'Philippe,' is that right?"

"He had to travel... To Labé or Kankan? I can't remember."

That was the last time I saw her.

The night before leaving for Paris, we came back to tell her goodbye. It had been one or two months since I'd seen her: Philippe wanted me to make a grand tour of home before we left.

Strange, so strange! No tools in the yard. The hut was closed shut. Behind it, no statuette in sight. The clay earth was completely dry.

Pulled into such an odd scene, I didn't notice that at my side stood a kid with a shaved head and a hula hoop in hand.

"Please follow me!" the child said politely.

He led me to the bottom of the lougan where the bathroom cabin stood.

"There it is," he said, showing me a heap of dirt topped with a bamboo cross.

Philippe took me in his arms and raised a corner of his shirt to dry my tears. Then he handed the kid the bags weighing us down—toiletries, clothes, and food for several months.

"It's been like this since Eve. The living inherit the dead."

We left the premises, but not without covering the mound of dirt with leaves and flowers plucked from the surrounding shrubs.

WE MADE OUR WAY slowly to France. He wanted me to experience Dakar and Cape Verde before getting to his house in the picturesque village of Agüimes, tucked deep in the mountains. He wanted to show me off, but in small doses. The world's marvels in a single take would have disoriented me. I still had never left Guinea and only four times been outside Conakry. I'd never ridden a plane or train or boat.

"I should have brought my ethnology notebook so I could record your amazement at all these new things," he said.

He wanted to introduce me to his country with slow and gradual changes of scenery. Dakar, he thought, would make a good first scene. I felt somewhat at home in Dakar: the same odors, same images, sounds; the same jewelry, same dresses, the same swaying movements, same old buses rippling through the dust. We didn't have the time to visit Rufisque or Gorée. I did insist, because of the famous story by Birago Diop, on climbing the Deux Mamelles—the two hills that make the city so distinct and that a stupid monument covers now.

In Praia, I heard Portuguese spoken for the first time over a bowl of cachupa. It was in a charming restaurant run by a man from St. Malo who married a Cape Verdean. For hours on end, he brought 1930s Conakry to life.

Every one of those picturesque steps presented Philippe the opportunity to return to his favorite subject: Man. The prodigious human adventure, the human condition, Man's dream, Man's genius, Man's triumph. It exasperated me to no end.

"Look at Cape Verde, for example, this little piece of Brazil floating off the coast of Africa. It alone explains the torments and wonders of our species. Slavery brought it about, Petioute: this new race, this new architecture, new food. It's from the depths of barbarism, you see, that hope springs back up. You know what they represent to us, these teensy islands you see here? The world of tomorrow! One of merging and reconciliation after we've healed from the demons of the past. Every race, every tribe, every gender, every social class on the same line, hand in hand and gene to gene. I love Léopold Sédar Senghor. And I love Carlos Fuentes. They talk about mixing. But I suppose you haven't read Senghor. You have some catching up to do, Petioute. I'll take care of that once we get to Paris."

In Praia, he spoke at length about Brazil—the city reminded him of Salvador, Bahia. In Las Palmas, he could see the columns of Havana and the old churches of Mexico.

"Latin American civilizations owe everything to Cape Verde, the Azores, and Canary Islands. These islands served as breeding grounds," he said in a fevered voice.

Digging through whatever's left of my memories, I still recall this Guinean man I met on the Ramblas in Barcelona. He'd noticed me the same way you did that first time: I was talking on the phone with Raye and he was surprised by that flurry of Fulani words colliding one lovely morning with the venerated column of Christopher Columbus. He abandoned his magic act and the little crowd surrounding him to run toward us, spouting out a stream of words—passionate, curious, and uninterrupted—from which I gleaned only a snippet, thanks to the distance between us and the street's rumbling. Once he was at eye-level, he led the way to a bench.

"Let's have a seat here under the plane tree. It'll be better for a chat... Oh my God!... Oh my God! And so it is! And so it is."

He imprisoned my hand in his for five long minutes, planting audible kisses from time to time.

"And where is the sister from? Conakry? Mamou? Kankan? Nzérékoré?"

"I was born in Conakry."

"I'm from Labé myself—Popodara to be precise. But this is still a miracle, more than that! To meet a fellow citizen on the Ramblas on a beautiful morning like this! Men, sure, but women—that's so unusual. But come now, come on, I haven't finished my act."

He pulled a whistle out of his pocket and right at my nose blew a sharp, awful sound. Two streams of candy poured down from my nose, which he distributed to the onlookers pointing at me and writhing with laughter. Then he turned toward Philippe.

"And what have you done with your belt, Sir? No, wait a minute. You haven't lost it, you say? So why is it over here?"

He opened his hand and there was the belt. He murmured a few *abracadabras* and the innocent leather band became a cobra that scattered the little gathering that had formed around us.

"Ladies and gentlemen, do not leave! He only bites if I give him the command. Go on, be gentle, Amitash: give this pretty young woman there a kiss."

He put the reptile to my cheek and it very affectionately ran its tongue over my face. He went around doing the same thing to two or three other young women. He pointed to a woman and the color of her dress changed. He pointed again and everything went back to normal.

"Go ahead," he told us. "It's time to leave."

He scraped his money together and thanked the audience as if he were on a trestle table at the circus.

"This just rounds out my funds at the end of the month. I'm a sailor by trade. I've learned all sorts of little tricks like that bopping around from one continent to the next. You learn a lot when you know how to open your eyes and perk up an ear. The world's not lacking for genius: I've seen it on the Kuril Islands, in Kerala, Papua New Guinea, the Amazon. You all think it's magic, but it's not, it's science. Science when it still amazed people, when it had music and poetry to it. Today we use it to manufacture this and that. In India, I saw a priest make a woman come just by meditating. Didn't undress or lay a finger on her."

We learned about his life and the city's at the same time. He'd been roaming its alleys for more than fifty years, haunting its brothels and bistros.

"Well not exactly fifty years, not really. Half that, maybe. It's pretty, Barcelona, but it's not the only one! I've been met with open arms at every port in the world. But I admit this is where I feel at home. Barcelona's my old girlfriend."

His name was Aly Touré. Like so many Guineans, he'd walked hundreds of kilometers to escape Sékou Touré's henchmen. In Dakar, a Guinean told him about Nouadhibou, Dakhla, Smara, Agadir, Casa, Tanger, Algeciras, Valencia, and Barcelona. Names that sang to his ear, dream destinations for a young man from the bush. In Barcelona, he was told, he could earn money in spades and have any girl he wanted on his arm. But it's always Man who's in a hurry, not the good Lord. He'd hung around Dakar for two years selling coal, teaching night classes, stitching hats. He needed a lot of money to pay the smugglers. Then again, the Sahara wasn't what it is today. Fatigue and thirst, that's all you had to worry about back then.

And once you'd traversed it, Black folks could make a living outside selling drugs or kicking around a ball. You don't exactly choose a career at sea. A port is the first destination to an arriving foreigner. That's where the pubs and no-nonsense girls line up. That's where you get a chance to hum through a whisky and some cigarettes, work as a docker or errand boy until a kind-hearted captain invites you to set off for Kobe or Valparaíso.

Around 2 PM, he slapped his belly. "You guys hungry at all?"

We both admitted we were.

"I know a little joint around the corner with the best escalivada in the city. Mind if I tag along? I am your guide, after all."

A man of the land, he ordered both the wine and food for us. I discovered what the thing he called escalivada was, along with pan con tomate, serrano peppers, calçots with romesco sauce, and, my favorite, a magical fish stew called suquet.

When dessert came, Philippe turned toward him.

"You told us this morning you'd come back last week after a ten-year absence. Where were you?"

"On an isle in the mainland. Tortosa."

"That's right next to us!"

"To me it's more remote than the Tuamotu Islands. You see, for me an island is a removal, it's solitude. And there are three expressions of removal and solitude, three things I knew perfectly: exile, boats, and prison."

"So you just got out of prison?"

"Come on, I'll explain."

We wound up in front of a cemetery after an hour-long taxi ride. But there was still journeying from there. Only after walking for half an hour between hydrangea beds and graves covered with flowers and etched in gold lettering did we reach two parallel little tombstones. African tombstones: no name, no bouquet of flowers.

"This one here is my wife. That one, my cousin, Amadou Diallo. I'm the reason he came here, poor bastard. The plane ticket, the certificate of accommodation, everything. I fed him, gave him a place to stay. I even paid for his computer science degree! I had suspicions my child wasn't mine but I had no proof. Only then, on that night, a suspicion came over me as I got off the banana boat that brought me back from Guayaquil. I tiptoed up the stairs and gingerly turned the key in the lock. There they were in our marital bed, wrapped up in each other. Wailing and huffing like two seals in agony. So I took out my revolver."

Philippe stepped forward and took him by the arm to keep him from spinning out. All three of us sat down, on a grave, a rock, and a tree trunk, to come back to our senses—to let the demon pass, as they say back home.

Later, in the taxi ride back, he whistled a Bob Marley tune.

We ate chicken fricassee and washed it down with a bottle of Tarragona, then Philippe asked him to come up to our room for a nightcap.

"At least the boy wasn't there," he added on his way out, "to see it. He died of pneumonia. He was about to turn seven. You didn't ask about her name, my wife's: Mireia Viapuig. A real cigar woman from Barcelona. Everyone in that family's a cigar woman, mother to daughter. I'm the one, me and my bullet, who put an end to that legacy."

And again he started whistling. Philippe was shaking. Aware I'd noticed his intense emotions, he told me:

"That's an old tune my mom used to sing. I must have been eight years old, ten at most. My whole childhood in the mouth of a Guinean sailor from Barcelona! Do you believe in chance, Petioute?"

And he followed me to the bed, tears shaking his voice:

Les cigarières de Barcelone
Ont des manières qui vous étonnent . . .

On the plane the next day, he couldn't keep himself from humming "Les Cigarières de Barcelone," as he flipped through *Le Canard enchaîné* on the tray table. It didn't seem to bother anyone—there was almost no one on board. Out of nowhere, he brushed aside the paper and pulled me in close. I had the feeling I was crossing into his country hanging from the side of his crib.

Once in Marseille I shouted, "What? We're back in Dakar already?"

He didn't laugh.

He led me graciously through museums and churches. He could tell I didn't care much for them. He took me to the port ("the umbilical cord of France and its old colonies") and the Mas de Clary where Olivier de Sanderval, the founder of Conakry, had lived. He drove me to Cassis, not for Cap Canaille, but for the ghost of Trotsky. Some nights, he told me, deadpan, the calanques would let out a giant, dolorous cry, the same one the goateed revolutionary did taking that famous ice axe in the land of Frida Kahlo and Diego Rivera. A way for the city of idleness to honor its most remarkable host without the slightest effort.

"I have a surprise for you," he said the night before we left for Paris. "We're not taking the TGV. I'd rather spare you our ugliest fault for now: France's cultish love of speed. We're going to take an old train through Puy de Dôme. It's blasphemy to enter Paris at full speed. It's a treat the eyes shouldn't hurry to savor.

On the train I discovered an aspect of his personality I'd never imagined. He started singing opera. It was my first time hearing it, and it came from him. It impressed me, this music I didn't understand at all. It impressed me with its lyricism and force; more powerful than Sory Kandia Kouyaté, more vibrant, more strange! It impressed me because it came from the heart of my person.

He caught his breath and watched the landscape unfold.

"It's almost as beautiful as Fouta Djallon."

He was exaggerating a little, I suppose to flatter me. I'd already seen them, these mountain rivers, these arches, these deep valleys, this stunning mess of canyons, screes, and waterfalls, when I went to Sâré-Kali to look for Néné Biro and old crank Tierno, who was none other than my grandfather. Here I was wending the same path for other latitudes, to make other connections, other states of mind, and, again, to change my fate.

There were no more than fifty of us on this country train. In the dining car, it was like we were with family. Caught off guard, the looks started to glimmer with the same spark of admiration. When he finished singing, no one applauded, but one woman was fighting back tears.

"Make an effort, Petioute! Search, Petioute! You'll find it in Velázquez's chiaroscuros and the contraltos of Monteverdi, your jackass husband's real soul. Up to now, I've never managed to interest a single of my African friends in classical works of art or opera. Pitiful!"

He'd warned me and, stepping out into the Gare d'Austerlitz, I knew what to expect: the cold, the racial profiling, the venom of whispers, the twisting awl of a look, the stress, the delight of commotion, the misery of confinement. Still, no one could have prepared me for the biggest calamity Paris had in store: you, Madame Corre. And your spadework, your frustrated remonstrations, your obdurate rage. You, so annoying, so off-putting, so awkward with everybody! Or so I thought, until you started talking about the balafons and niâmou. I would have stayed in Agüimes if I'd known you were waiting for me on the corner to flood my ears with atrocity.

No chance of meeting people like you in Agüimes. It's a little town of a few thousand people and cubic homes, white or mauve, that circle around the San Sebastian parish temple. A peaceful town, no cars, no hobos, where even the tourists are well behaved. That's where we'd go find refuge from the hassles of Paris and winter's shenanigans. Our house is two blocks from the famous Casa de Los Camellos where caravans of traders used to take shelter.

I hesitated to go through the door when I first saw it.

"Come on! Don't be intimidated, Petioute. It's none other than your house. You'll have to get used to it. You're a countess, for God's sake! It doesn't mean anything anymore, but it has a way of dazzling idiots."

And he showed me the bedrooms and the Moorish living room, the guillotine windows, the serene, refined patio, the whitewash façade inlaid with volcanic black stone, the wooden balcony with steep awnings on the Guayadeque ravine. You read that right, Madame Corre. A countess. A real countess and a real countess's home. I'm not one to applaud myself, Madame Corre, but I'm not just any immigrant. I'm a first-class Negro. A migrant deluxe. Not a soubrette, not a babysitter, not a personal care assistant or shopkeep. I came to France through the grand entrance. With such class that I made a game out of passing back and forth by the cops so they could check my papers—ten, twenty times—so they could see for themselves that I was in perfect standing. So they could know exactly who they were dealing with. But cops have a flair for this sort of thing. They only have power over the undocumented.

I was free from all the rats of a nanny's bedroom, from a crowded home's tuberculosis, from the typhus of our Salvation Army, from the predation of slumlords. A building in Paris (we live on the first floor and rent out the others to fund Living Memories), a house in the Canary Islands, a château in Périgord—we're no Rothschilds, but to Malian garbage collectors we're in the garden of Eden. A Negro of this caliber is not easy to find. Naomi Campbell or Madame Bongo, maybe... Basically, stories in *A Thousand and One Nights* compared to Conakry! I almost couldn't believe it. I didn't know things would turn out this way: my love in a wheelchair and you on my trail, plaguing me, making me sweat, leading me to hell on foot. Merlin the Enchanter will never stop prying around in my horoscope, no question. She told me, though, old Ténin: a devil's in love with me; he won't let anyone touch me without stirring up a curse's spiteful waters. Goodbye calves, cows, pigs, Spanish and Périgord castles! This is how things will be the rest of my life: your gossipy chatter, the creaking of his wheelchair, the bewitching magnetism of his eye, and—harassing my ears—that cryptic birdsong: "Don't be stupid, Pavlov! Pavlov! Don't be stupid!"

He taught me about France, the true France, the one only found in good food, good wine, and good literature. And he insisted I know Paris from the inside—the intimate Paris, so to speak. No horse-drawn carriages, no river cruise, no Eiffel Towers or Montparnasse. For me, though, France was above all him. Long before the South's Aramon grapes and the lights of Paris. A France on its own two feet, with its big hairy chest, its strong and protective arms, its long jet-black hair and liquid blue eyes—a shimmering blue, which I bathed in with as much satisfaction as in Annecy Lake or the crystalline waters of the Cap d'Antibes. A big-hearted France, and with a heart all to myself. All that at once and for the very first time: eating well, sleeping well, museums, books, cuddling, Marais bistros, Saint-Germain cafés, Camargue rice fields, Jura's local railroads and, above all of it, the delightful feeling that, for thousands of miles in any direction, no guy named Indigo Bomber would ever stalk me again. Little by little, thanks to living with that particular France, in close intimacy, I felt its breath. I inhaled it as much as I could. But like you say, Madame Corre, happiness is a lure: you get closer to it, you see it, you get closer, you aim straight for it, but you always end up missing.

I'm through with happiness, anyway.

Our marriage almost blew up a week after we got there. The kind of stupid thing that stoked drama only in the homes of people like Philippe, people spilling over with sensitivity and poems burrowed deep in their bodies.

That day, back from my morning run, I found the apartment turned upside-down and Philippe in a state. He was roaring, enough to be heard from inside a crypt at the Panthéon. I thought he was going to burst into flames.

"For the love of God, what's going on?"

"What's going on is someone stole it. I'm going to break the guy in two."

"What'd they steal?"

"Chimalman, my Mona Lisa!"

He was making such a mess with the plates, tables, and chairs that I needed a minute to get my bearings. Right, yes... Chimalman rang some kind of a bell. He'd shown it to me in Conakry as we were packing our bags. He unveiled it under my eyes, laughing: "I present to you your one and only rival. This one here... On the day I have to choose, I wonder who'll win out." He would kiss it, gushing and squealing like a child.

You don't know who Chimalman is, do you, Madame Corre? Well me neither, I had no idea. He had to explain it to me. "Chimalman is the Aztec goddess of fertility. I bought it in Oaxaca, a lovely little city in Mexico. I'll have to take you to Oaxaca, Petioute. You'll love it there. Now, look how the hair waves, and the melancholy in her eyes. Look at that unknowable smile. Does that remind you of anything? Of course not, how stupid of me, you've never seen the Joconde. You haven't even heard of it. Sweet philistine! My goodness. I have to take you to the Louvre."

That was the first and last time I'd seen that goddess. I remember he'd dusted it very delicately, wrapped it in old newspapers, stuck it in a foam tube and placed in the middle of the suitcase so it wouldn't break. And now, my home was in shambles because of a clay goddess made by the hands of some Mexican Michelangelo.

"The magic of art, Petioute! I like to imagine that miraculous concordance: in the same second, a portrait in Florence and a statue in Oaxaca. Two versions of the same masterpiece. The contrivances of genius! You understand, Petioute? Do you understand?"

By midnight there was still no goddess, and the neighbors started to complain about the ongoing racket.

He forgot the tables and chairs. He collapsed on the carpet and started to cry. I lay down beside him and tried to calm him down. He pushed me away with such violence that I hit my forehead on a corner of the wall. My mind was made up: nothing was going to cool him down that night. I bandaged my head, drank a glass of cold water, and went to bed.

In the morning, he apologized profusely seeing my bandage.

"It wasn't me who did that. You know that wasn't me!"

He was exhausted and had lost his voice. His eyes were baggy. But the thought of his Joconde still hadn't left his head.

"You're sure you haven't seen it, Petioute? You wouldn't have put it somewhere by accident?"

"Tell me I stole—just say it!"

"I didn't say that. I couldn't say it, you know that! I know what I need to do."

"What's that?"

"Make the opposite trip: Marseille to Barcelona to Agüimes to Praia to Dakar to Conakry. Take a fine-tooth comb to every place we visited: hotels, restaurants, markets, beaches, and alleyways. I'll find it sooner or later."

"In that case, listen carefully, Philippe Claude Célestin,

Count of Monbazin. If you set off on this insane escapade, you won't find me here when you get back. Light a lamp in broad daylight and scour the planet with a fine-tooth comb and you won't see me anywhere. I'm ready to undergo every offense, but not the one where my husband cheats on me with a clay statue!"

He didn't respond, but I knew by his grumpy face and slumped posture that I'd won.

But we survived the most awful week of our existence up to now. We slept in separate rooms. I went about my days without paying him any attention. I knew he was racked with regret and I did nothing to lighten his bad conscience. When he'd join me in the living room, I'd slip away upstairs to the attic or the bathroom. If he was getting ready to come with me on my errands, I'd turn back and go put my chin on the balcony rail and fake like I was talking to passersby.

"Please, Petioute, please! I'd rather hell over this kind of life. What if we went to see a movie and take our mind off things? They're playing *Gainsbourg: A Heroic Life* right now. I love Gainsbourg, along with Giani Esposito and Boris Vian for their shit-stirring antics. Those three are the only men of this century with a sense of humor."

I said nothing. He begged me to come sit next to him. With overt reluctance, I did: my jaw locked tight, one cheek on the very edge of the sofa. So he pushed me away and got up, his face red with rage. A little later, he left and slammed the door shut behind him. On my way to the kitchen to make myself some tea, I noticed he'd left me a note: *Petioute, I'll shoot myself if tomorrow is anything like today! Philippe, the little dope who loves you.*

After the movie, he must have drunk through the bar gauntlet in Saint-Germain, because I didn't hear him come back. I found him slumped on the living room couch when I got up for breakfast—he didn't have the strength to make it to bed. He was snoring like a buzzer and radiated an odor that could make you gag.

When the clock chimed 10, the postman came to the door.

"You expecting something?" I said mechanically, knowing he wouldn't respond.

Me neither, I wasn't expecting anything. Still, I signed for it and offered as one should a decent tip.

Opening the package, I almost fainted from the shock. It was Chimalman. My rival. His own Joconde! It came with a card:

Dear Count and Countess,

A thousand million apologies for the little spat I've started between you, but I have to live as well. I gave the statuette to Don Alberto Aldavert, the great collector of Pre-Columbian art. Whatever I steal from the museums in Havana, Barranquilla, Acapulco and wherever else usually winds up with him. Overwhelmed with guilt, I'm sending it back to you. It seems to have great emotional value for you. But I'm keeping the 10,000 euro. Don't call me a criminal. I'm an honest man with a belly to feed and two gravestones to mind. Please don't ask how I managed to rob you. And the piece and the 10,000 euro—I'm not telling. You know what my mentors used to say in Karnakata? "How do you expect to learn if you don't know how to keep a secret?"

Aly Touré, your friend in Barcelona

P.S. So it is, I'll never see those godforsaken Tuamotu Islands I wanted to visit so badly. Not in God's plan. They just detected a carcinoma in me. I don't have more than three months. At the cemetery, I've already chosen my place: next to my wife. Lucky lady! Right between her husband and her lover. What lavish eternal rest!

I put all of it, the statuette and the card, in plain sight on the living room coffee table and tiptoed up to bed. I eventually dozed off after waiting in vain for the shriek of surprise to come from the human creature who'd just found his goddess.

When I woke up he was smiling, sprawled out beside me. He was stroking my hair like that very first time in the dark Boffa hotel.

"You know, Petioute, I would have shot myself if you hadn't changed your attitude today?"

"You know I wouldn't have changed my attitude if the postman hadn't rung?"

He grabbed his smartphone after we'd made love and started blasting the miserable goddess from every angle.

"That's what I should have done from the start: I wouldn't have suffered so much. The next time someone steals from me, there'll at least be a trace."

Then he grabbed a rag and rubbed it for a good half-hour before setting it back on its stand.

"Where are you going to put that thing, Philippe, Claude, Célestin, Count of Monbazin?"

"There, on the edge of the buffet. That way, she'll be visible from every angle."

"Not here!"

"Where, then?"

"At the Louvre!"

"They already have a Joconde."

"Then in the maid's room. I'm the only goddess here!"

I knew he was lying. For example, when I would disappear to the balcony with a vacuum or the end of the hallway, or when I'd leave to buy a turnip or leek at the grocer's, he'd go get it and put it on display at the end of the buffet and be secretly, intensely overjoyed. He'd rush to put it back in its place as soon as he could tell I was coming back. This childish side sometimes irritated me and sometimes awakened in me the same happiness I felt playing with Dick and Nantou under the lemon tree. But I pretended not to notice anything. It was too amusing to see that, at his age, he could still be happy as a child.

For four years of Parisian life, that was our one domestic spat. Honestly, we had no place in our diaries for squabbles, outbursts, sulking, or slammed doors. We were both lazy, messy, carefree. But our life moved on like clockwork. We weren't to blame. We just managed to live every moment with enough passion that boredom had no truck with us. Boredom, as soon as it seeps in, gives you the impression that things are turning dull, insipid, disconnected. In four years, we didn't tour the whole world but we almost did. We didn't sample every single dish, every work of art, every language, the thousand and one possible ways to live and think. But thanks to him I can say I wound up with an idea about this little blue planet. Sometimes, we'd stay long enough on the other side of the world that we'd miss Paris.

That year, when we got back, everything felt new.

"Look!" he shouted. "That's not the Gare de Lyon at all, it's the Leipzig station! Over here—Velib' bikes? Beaches along the Seine? How long till we get ski slopes down Montmartre? Holy shit! That road was about one cubit wide, look what they did to it. That's just wrong, tearing down that great little Aveyron restaurant to put in a supermarket!"

And one night we were leaving Monge plaza for a glass at the Antidote. He said to me:

"Did you notice? There was a Black man with them."

"With who?"

"The unhoused people, obviously."

"No, I didn't notice him."

"A Black tramp! It's democratizing—all the better! There's more than enough pavement, whites don't have to monopolize it!"

He was right, among the thousand and one changes Paris had in store for us was this one: a Black man mixed in with the bums on the square. He pointed him out to prove he wasn't lying, that there before me was living proof of what he was saying. I couldn't really make him out: his back was turned to me and the popped collar of his filthy fur coat kept me from guessing at his neck and the outline of his face. But his voice broke through the noise and it made me shake.

"What's wrong, Petioute?"

What's wrong? That voice, it was like I'd heard it before. But where, when, why? His tone went up a notch and sent my chill in every direction.

"Watch it, Pavlov! You say that again and it's your carotid artery."

"Carotid artery, carotid… You son of a bitch!" answered the other with a Russian accent and strong boozy voice. "For me it's just a little bath in the Seine with a fat slab of concrete on your foot. If not this!"

He took out a revolver, what looked like a Beretta.

"Does that make your gut snarl or what?"

"I'd put money on you stole that."

"This morning. But I'm not saying where. The first bullet's for you if you don't quit irritating me."

And everyone broke out laughing.

They were about ten of them and they talked in all sorts of languages. Besides French, I think I heard English, German, Arabic, and Russian. And, are you sitting down, Madame Corre? This Pavlov had a tattoo on his forehead of an ancient coin.

Meanwhile, the Black man had stood up. I saw his front half and was reassured. Because of his voice, I thought I'd recognized someone, but that was a mistake. Still, my distress must still have been legible on my face because Philippe held me tight in his arms.

"You look a little off, Petioute. You want to head home?"

"Yes. I'm afraid I might have caught a cold."

He took me by the hand and told me about Saint-Germain-des-Près, Whisky a Go Go when it was still called Le Rock'n'Roll Circus and Boris Vian, Sidney Bechet, Juliette Gréco and others would play there. It felt like someone was following us. As an act of good conscience, I turned around before walking through the front door of our building. There he was. He stayed on the sidewalk across the street with his filthy fur coat and popped collar, right in front of the bakery. A deafening worry rose up in me, but I kept myself from telling Philippe about it. "You're going to let yourself be terrorized by an everyday hobo?" I said to myself. "Come on, you're worked up for no reason. Homeless people always seem a little threatening, when in fact they're the real victims."

We ate a quick plate of charcuterie for dinner. Philippe downed a glass of Jack Daniel's and I nursed a cup of chamomile tea. He tried to coax me to bed, but I didn't have the heart for anything. Not for talking and not love.

I tossed and turned and couldn't fall asleep. I got up two or three times, pretending to go to the bathroom, and carefully pulled back the living room blinds. He was still there, kneeling down in the middle of the sidewalk this time, his dog beside him, just offset from the bakery door. The streetlights were bright enough to show everything: he was holding his liter of wine, grim face turned toward the first floor. Ours.

In the morning, stock-still with fear, I hesitated to leave. Maybe he was still there in the middle of the sidewalk, his huge shaggy dog in his arms. Who was he? How could an everyday homeless man scare the shit out of me like that? "Don't be childish, Véronique, and especially don't tell Philippe about it—you're being ridiculous."

Had he heard me? In any case, his voice pulled me suddenly out of my stupid thoughts.

"Are you waiting for anything in particular before you get croissants?"

"I'm going, I'm going!"

I went quickly to the bathroom to change.

"What an outfit! You worried someone will recognize you, Petioute?"

"I told you I was afraid of catching a cold."

He was still there, with his Doberman and his filthy coat, and the evidence leapt right out at me. Enough that I couldn't deny it anymore. True, his face had gotten puffy, wrinkled from the alcohol and drugs, the harsh weather and hardship. The scar on his left eyebrow was lost now, amid a constellation of others from fists, knives, falls, scratches, and plenty of other wounds incurred in the kind of life his had become. He hadn't completely lost his resemblance, though, to Mohamad Ali.

He spoke first, which spared me a great deal of embarrassment.

"Atou! You, in Paris! And me right here in front of you! Am I scaring you?"

I had a hard time understanding him because of his hiccups and sporadic chuckles. Then, in any event, it was his words from before that come to my ears: "No, not like this, not this wild animal here in front of you. Another me. One you've never seen, who's waited too long to clean himself up and get out of this cangue and show his true face." He had rotted away, this other man he'd promised me. All that was left was the cangue. I pinched my nose and tried in vain to get around him.

"Why are you shaking, Atou? It's just me. Yes, it's really me! And look at what life did to your Alfâdio..."

I was shaking, yes, but not with fear. With anger, sorrow, disgust.

"What do you want from me?"

"Some cash, just a little cash to straighten up this mess." He unbuttoned his coat. "I don't want to die here. I don't want my body to be here—it'll freeze."

After a minute of paralysis, I managed to open my mouth. Not to respond to him, really, more to escape his smell and the crowd of onlookers our odd meeting was beginning to attract.

"Fine! On my way out for bread at noon, I'll leave an envelope at the bakery on the condition you disappear."

"Yeah sure, Atou, I'll disappear. Soon as I get the cash."

Why him? Why now? How far was he planning to go? Should I mention it to Philippe? Back in the house, I poured myself two glasses of whisky and *no* was my conclusion. He didn't need to worry for no reason. This guy was going to take off the second that envelope was in his pocket.

But the next day, when I came down for croissants, he was standing in the same place as the night before.

"That's not enough. Ten thousand euro? Look at the state I'm in! I need a lot more to put things back together. Please, Atou. I'm begging you."

I turned on my heels without saying anything and walked back home completely distraught. I had loved that man, he gave me a daughter. Then he disappeared with a German and now out of nowhere he's in front of my door, at the end of his tether, to ask for money. How did we end up here? By what accident, what cruel fate? "Talk to Philippe about it, tell him everything, and he'll take care of it, no problem, this whole misunderstanding," I told myself.

Only when I saw him in the living room reading the paper with his cup of tea, other words left my mouth.

"Hey, what if we went to Agüimes?"

"Great idea, but not for ten days. Human Rights Watch just asked me for a big report on Myanmar, go figure."

"Myanmar?" I said back stupidly, as if that dumb question could have protected me from the disaster I could feel coming.

"You don't look too good, Petioute—not at all, actually. Do you want me to call the doctor?"

"I took some pills. It's nothing, I'm sure of it."

He went up to his office to work. I opened the buffet and swallowed to shots of whisky. That guy really fucked up my day. Putting that nightmarish image in my head wasn't enough—he also needed my money… Sensing tears on the way, I shouted to Philippe:

"I'm going for a walk! Be right back!"

"OK. Make the most of it and clear your head. Meet you at the Antidote at noon? It'll be good to eat in the open air, given the state you're in."

By lunchtime I was feeling much better. The air along the Seine and a third whisky at the Maubert-Mutualité Métro station had brought me fully back to life. When he saw me coming, Philippe didn't fail to notice.

"I love you better this way. What the hell was that yesterday? Are you sure it was the cold? He had a Guinean head on his shoulders, that homeless man, and you were looking at him in a funny way. Am I lying?"

"I almost fell for it, I admit. One minute he made me think of an old acquaintance, but I realized I was wrong once I saw his face. Now, please, let's eat. It's making me nauseous, this hobo nonsense."

After that, he suggested I go see a movie while he went back up to work.

"Start with *Gainsbourg*. It's at the UGC Odéon. Then pop over to the Champollion and see *Some Like It Hot* again—you love that movie so much. After that we can meet for a drink at the Cluny then head to Dôme for dinner."

There's always a slight delay: tragedies are born from the slightest setback. As long as things go as planned, no stone on the path, no cloud on the horizon. Sure enough, the train that crashed into a tanker somewhere in Limousin left its station either a minute too soon or a minute too late. Fate hadn't predicted it, that we devour some oysters at the Dôme and end the night at a jazz club like we did so often. Philippe, of course, changed his mind after our drink at the Cluny and, without realizing it, made a bed for the tragedy that would follow.

At the Cluny, I was watching him sip his drink and thought to myself, "He looks preoccupied, absorbed, far away, like some mysterious force was drawing him elsewhere." I grabbed my coat and purse to signal it was time to go.

"You know what we'll do, Petioute? Let's have a nice walk home and eat some steak and can of peas. This Myanmar report is a big ask. I've completely lost my appetite for oysters."

Consider, Madame Corre, that if he'd never said that, I wouldn't be behind him pushing a chair he'll never leave.

He swallowed his steak quickly, along with his peas and camembert, and, whistling, climbed up the stairs four at a time to his office after giving me a long kiss. He didn't know, I didn't know, that it was the last one of his life. I put on some music: the flutes, koras, and balafons from home. I brought him a coffee. On my way down, my attention was drawn to an unusual noise. I pulled the blinds aside: there he was, in front of the bakery, and he wasn't alone anymore. They were all there, with their dogs, their piercings, and their coats matted down with grime. I put on headphones so I wouldn't have to hear them.

Thirty or forty minutes went by. Someone knocked at the door: the Polish neighbor, probably, who'd just helped herself to a turnip or a bunch of celery. Anyway, I had the impression, slowly but surely as I moved forward, that the noise had moved from outside to invade the steps at my door.

I opened the door. It wasn't the Polish neighbor. It was

them, with their coats, their piercings, and dogs.

They shoved me back and ran straight for the kitchen. Bottles to the mouth, foodstuffs in hand, they invaded the living room stomping across the armchairs, the carpets, and sofas, and ululating like giant locusts.

"All we want is cash," Alfâdio said. "Give us the cash and we're out of here.... Come on, Atou, let's go."

Someone kissed me on the mouth, cackling.

"Alf's old lady's cute as fuck! You dumbass! I wouldn't leave those for anyone, that fine ass and pair of tits."

"Stop groping her that way," the man called Pavlov boomed with his inimitable Russian accent. "She's a countess!"

"Oh right, a countess!" the others echoed, crazed with laughter

"Hey! If she doesn't settle up, we can pay ourselves in kind: there's tons of paintings here."

Philippe didn't come down and I knew why: he would listen to opera on his headphones when he had to churn out a big project.

But after so many bottles they started walking across the tables, throwing books on the ground, and playing the pots and pans like drums. Philippe finally appeared at the top of the stairs.

"What on earth is all this ruckus! Petioute, can you explain?"

That's when Pavlov took out his revolver. Alfâdio ran after him to try and take it.

"Don't be stupid, Pavlov! Pavlov! Don't be stupid!"

I would never have thought the explosion of a bullet could make so much noise. My first reaction, despite the disaster, was amazement that the building was still standing, that the city hadn't lost any churches or bridges. Pavlov was stupid. Nothing could have stopped it. Philippe's unexpected arrival had made him panic. He shot. It was written: he had to fire. The effect of alcohol. The fatal reflex of a brain worn miserably out. The sequence of all these little chances that make the implacable rigor of fate: that plaything he'd stolen two nights before, the oysters at the Dôme that we turned our backs to, the inexplicable presence of that man—my first love, the father of my daughter—who'd left me for a sweet German woman and whom in return good luck abandoned to the putrid waters of the gutter.

"Don't be stupid, Pavlov! Pavlov! Don't be stupid!" It will ring through my head, that awful address, until my last breath. I hear it everywhere and all the time: in whining engines, a siren's wail, the din of jackhammers, hissing of percolators, birdsongs, and rolling on the timpani. "Don't be stupid Pavlov! Pavlov! Don't be stupid!"

YOU SEE, MADAME CORRE, it wasn't a stroke. It was the lethal bullet of fate, which you can never predict and which always strikes at the wrong time, in the wrong place. It's not aimed at anyone preemptively, but it's so much worse for whoever has the bad luck to wind up in its path. We'd have been off guzzling oysters at the Dôme and none of it would have happened. Although someone else would have taken our place. It's never good to change plans at the last minute. Everything is written. It always costs something to jostle God's agenda.

I'm simply repeating what I've heard, obviously not being one to understand God's affairs. If on the day your father brought to the house a Bôry Diallo you'd left, as planned, for your friend's birthday party in Roanne, your life would be completely different. You wouldn't know about the Fulani or Susu people, or balafons or the niâmou. And now, here you are up to your neck in our awful Guinean problems! You'd have marched on seamlessly with your happy little Burgundy life. Your husband wouldn't have been hanged. And your son would be there at your side with a litter of grandchildren to feed and pamper. Good God! Why did you ever come to our country? To that place where all you can count on is malaria and starvation, government sieges and public hangings! Poor Madame Corre. Ah, yes! Only I could understand you. Admit you aren't an easy case. Like the baker, like the florist, like Prospero, I thought you were at least half crazy, a pain in the ass, a murderer, the Rue de la Clef killer. Like the others, I'd have spit on your shaved head if you were ever given over to the morality mob, wouldn't think twice, wouldn't regret a thing. The whole neighborhood thinks like Prospero: "Everyone like you, Madame Corre, is a suspect." "Outsiders," they say. But where do outsiders come from? The heart of society! From that big, beautiful, marvelous social factory. Yes indeed, Madame de Beauvoir: you aren't born an outsider, you become one.

I don't see you quite the same way anymore. Oh, you still have your faults. But your green dresses, your deplorable bun, your blabbing mannerisms that exhaust me to no end—I ended up getting and giving in to all of it. You've turned into someone dear to me. I need you, and not just to furnish my solitude. Something binds us now, something strong. Something indestructible. A kind of pact that will never need to be read or signed. There is Camp B, but there isn't Camp B alone. That eighteen-year-old woman who was almost born in Da Nang, that pretty little hippy who loved René Char, Prévert, and the opera—she moves me. You were innocent, you were sincere and naïve. You thought everything was poetic: a Beaune rose or Kathmandu hemp just as much as third-world revolutions. It's true that you were from a family that never fostered hate. You weren't rich or poor, just civilized. Civilized in Cheikh Hamidou Kane's sense of the word: "the civilized man is the available man." Available to everything, available to everyone! Available: that's it, the source of your troubles. You were never cautious enough. The thing that traps the artists and poets! Be careful from now on: well-intended people are worst of all. By trying to make humankind better, we've ruined it. You'll suffer more for dreaming.

My own suffering is purely physical, I have no dream to lose. I was born in a world with no place for the ideal. I'm not complaining about it. Those big, beautiful words knock me flat: the ideal, glory, happiness… "I'm through with happiness." Well, me too, although I can't remember where—book, newspaper, graffiti?—I read that. Nothing prepared me for understanding this kind of bullshit. Just the opposite of the gentleman wriggling here, nailed down to his chair. I have no intention of changing the world, not me. No ideal, no glory, no… I'm not pursuing happiness. I'm just looking for understanding—ever and again with that voracious curiosity. I can't accept life as a burden governed by morality. For me, it's physiology, a simple functioning of things. A "brutal adventure," as Simone de Beauvoir put it. I drew a bad card. I was born into the compartment where nothing works.

Once I've made it to the misty valleys of the afterlife, here's what I'm asking God, if he exists: "Why these earthquakes and volcanoes? Why such absurd forces? Why did you give some people the right to extinguish others?"

What's better, Madame Corre, to be on the side of the executioners or the victims? Well neither! I find it too beautiful, too easy, the role of the victim. All things considered, I don't feel like a victim of anything. I've already told you that, Madame Corre—everything I've experienced concerned other people. I was only ever passing through. And then I got what I wanted: an interesting life rather than a happy life. I just find it so bland, happiness. When you've lived through what each of us has, you have no use for happiness anymore. You get enough of it in your life. You have the world right in front of your face. Raye, Yâyé Bamby, the sailor from Barcelona, Alfâdio and Philippe. It's in real life you run into them, not in comics or b-movies. Real life.

And you too, Madame Corre, you were planted in this quicksand, in this mess where instead of coddling you get slapped. Here, you sweat, bleed, drool, belch. Because here, hearts beat hard. Here, love makes sense.

The egg or the chicken, the victim or the executioner...

All things considered, I wasn't made to be cast in leading roles. I find it mawkish, dull as hell, corny. On the other hand, I'd choose death before turning over my fellow man to Gehenna or forced starvation. Could you imagine me opening the dormer window every morning not to feed the rabbits, but to see if the one I put behind bars had croaked or not? We're all executioners in some way, victims in others. What's exhausting is how we hurry back to Manichaeism the second we turn to an essential topic. But nothing can be built on Manichaeism. I too, Véronique Bangoura, daughter of Camp B, I would have spit on your shaved head if you were given over to the morality mob. All of us: Prospero, the florist, the baker. Only none of us would have dared to tell you that. Least of all, me. I am the executioner. I am the victim. It's easy to go from one side of the coin to the other: now an angel, now a demon. But if it came down to one choice, I'd prefer the side of the defeated. The strong are of little interest to me. Not an executioner and not a hero: I'd be so disappointed to end my life in the form of a granite statue. I feel better alongside the meek. "It's always weakness that bears genius," said the great pessimist Romain Gary.

And let's stop talking about executioners, victims, heroes, and granite statues. Let's talk about your son. You'll see him soon if everything comes together. For me, until you told me about him, we were killing time together, nothing more. I admit, like the others, I had my doubts about your story. You have a way about you that doesn't inspire confidence. I know now you weren't bluffing. Your son really does exist. He'd come every Friday to the Oxygène and play the prophet after his half-bottle of whisky. I swore I'd help you, Madame Corre. I owe it to you. I was wrong not to trust you. I doubted you—in all honesty, I despised you. I blame myself, Madame Corre. Now it's time for me to catch up. You're going to find Dian Charles-André again soon, I've made sure of it. My daughter, Raye, and Yâyé Bamby were able to approach that mysterious woman who's come looking for him every Friday at 11 PM for so many years. Her name is Aïssatou Barry. She's a gynecologist like him. They've been engaged for ten years—unmarried after ten years. She's agreed to have them over, but she's also warned them: her fiancé never talks about his past. He lives alone and speaks to no one.

Two days after that monologue, this is the email I received:

Dear Maman,

It wasn't easy but we did it. Aïssatou Barry set up several meeting times before one finally worked out. She started off trying to dissuade us: "His whole life is gynecology now. I don't even exist anymore. He's all but forgotten we're even engaged." But we didn't give up. At the third meeting, she eventually caved. "Well, why not throw myself into the ocean, or flames, rather. Let's see how this goes." And this morning, a miracle happened. She called Yâyé Bamby. Madame Corre is welcome.

Xoxo,

Yâyé Bamby la Petite

P.S. Know what? Mariam, the girl who told you about the notorious Indigo Bomber and who you loved so much? Well… she passed away. They found her in a bathroom stall at the Oxygène with a big needle in her arm.

On a happier note: I got my diploma! With honors. Go figure: who's daughter am I again?

After crying for my beloved Miriam, I called you on the phone.

"What if we got a chocolate at the Vésuve?"

You're going to see your son. I was shaking with the same emotion as if my uncle had hugged me in his monastery in Kindia.

At the Vésuve, I did what I'd never done before. I smiled kissing you hello. I wanted to make the moment last, though. I waited until we were parting ways to announce the good news.

"Your son's alive. He's waiting for you in Conakry. I'm paying for everything: your hotel, food, and the plane ticket."

HE WAS LIKE YOUR SON. He was like my uncle François. He was like Yâyé Bamby. Philippe was like everyone. He didn't like to bring up the past. Two or three times he told me about his dad in terse, rigid terms. I only ever had access to a single photo, and that was of his mom. A fragile, elegant woman with a perfectly round head, crowned with chestnut hair. Shimmering hazelnut eyes under beautiful, thick eyelashes. Her tender face washed with a glaring sadness. Emanating from her was the limpid, discerning soul of an artist. He was 20 years old the day he lost her, which makes me think of that famous line from Nizan hanging over our bed: "I was 20 years old, I'll never let anyone tell me it's the greatest age." She died of leukemia and, five years later, the Count of Monbazin from a fall off his horse. He inherited a love of Verlaine from his mother, and from his father—who spent his life on horseback—a phobia of riding horses. He loved handball and rugby, skiing, and high jump, which he learned from devoted, kind instructors, and resented the equine sports his strict father imposed on him, secretly hated it. Out of his upbringing as an only child came that closed-off personality—just like that repressed suffering that ate at his mother. The word Maman would soften his voice and make the corner of his eye well up, which embarrassed him. It troubled me, and my being troubled only added to his state. It happened one time in Conakry and twice in Agüimes before the Guinean sailor hummed Les Cigarières de Barcelone on the Ramblas. Maman! The slightest memory would throw him into a surge of tenderness. He'd turn juvenile and sensitive, a real kid. His ring, his bag, his nail file—he'd melt at the sight of the most trivial things. In fact, anything could make him melt, my little Périgord bear: a flower's calyx, the taste of certain meals, the idea of violence, of misery, injustice. But Maman was his sun, the life principle that connected him to the world. He still has a carnal bond with her that death hasn't managed to break.

Why waste the ink, Madame Corre? You can obviously see that Camp B natives don't have a monopoly on pain. All the world is not a stage, as one man put it. It's an immense Camp B, where one side tortures and the other side groans. We live above all else to hate each other, to dominate, to suffocate one another. "Tyranny is a habit," said Russia's most persuasive writer, Dostoyevsky.

That's the way the world works. And I, Véronique Bangoura, don't want or have the means to change it. Here's what's left for me to do: avoid the traps and weave through the punches, sweat, cheat, scramble by any means necessary to find what I'm after, to know a piece of what love is, what freedom looks like. You can keep them for yourself, your vaunted principles and grand schemes. Just give me some space to move and breathe. I'm not looking for the moon, just the pleasure of being stunned by what I see, by what reaches me. I didn't ask to be born, but I'm not upset about encountering water and air, earth and fire. Or about wailing from inside the fire of love. I don't find it particularly comfortable, my state as an earthly being, but I can live with it, feverish and attentive to everything: to people and things, smells and sounds. I insist in the belief that life is worth living out, even if it's as distressing as mine. Alas, we've taught our children to respect their masters, not to respect life. I love Philippe because he was handsome, tender, and attentive. Because he relished living and always insisted that respect for human dignity was something sacrosanct.

You often ask me why I talk about him in the past tense. He's still alive, of course, and of course I know that. Of course I feel it better than you can, better than every inhabitant in this city. Why is that? To exorcise fate—spit in its face. A few seconds earlier, he could eat. My husband could talk, paint, shake Paris with his perfect baritone voice, or chant a Verlaine poem from the top of the Eiffel Tower. Then none of it ever again because of a bullet that, clearly, had been made for someone else. "You know it's a mistake! What are you waiting for, stupid fate? Bring it all back to the present! Let it be like the movies: you let the reel run and the images start to move again." But it can't hear or see. It'll never listen to me. I could be pushing this barrel, I mean my rolling chair, for years and years to come. And fate will just make fun of me for it! I feel like sometimes I can even hear its cruel laughter shoot through all the Parisian noise.

The goose is cooked. It's time I come to my senses. The images won't move again. No good soul is going to show up and dislodge the film. The scope of the future doesn't stretch beyond les Gobelins. A big enough space to contain a half-widow pushing her half-corpse of a husband, mind you. Every day will be the same streets, the same sounds, the same internal monologue to keep nightmares and premonitions in check. But please don't tell me about monotony! As far as feelings go, and passion, the world wouldn't be enough. Between that one eye and me is a carnival of silence, a bamboula in a Küschall. *Love* is the one big word I care about, the only word that speaks to me. The others weren't made for me: too abstract, overly solemn, or a long way off. They don't speak to this world. They don't speak to life. They don't speak to me. The most beautiful of words, the only one that made me dream. Lifted up by its wings, I could break out of the house, escape my awful father and frivolous mom, Nantou's foolishness and Dick's incessant barking. Somewhere, someone was waiting for me. My little fifteen-year-old brain was firmly convinced. Then, down from the balcony, I met Raye, who already knew something about crushes, about being stood up, about swoons and sighing. All I had to do was follow suit. Correct, somewhere someone was waiting for me. A boy in a purple hat with a face like Ali. But old Ténin was there with her woeful mouth: "A genie is in love with you. He doesn't want any other man near you." I'm not superstitious, Madame Corre, and I wasn't taught to be either.

But after a while...

I already know the question burning on your lips: "Which one did you love?" Both of them! When the opportunity arises, I don't putter, I go headlong into it—my heart controls the rest of me. In each case, I believed it. In each case, the word *love* filled my ears with wonder and I threw myself into its arms with all my faith. In each case, I regret nothing. I have no sense of regret, Madame Corre. We dwell on things as they come to us, not after they're dead. Where would it lead me, anyway, collecting regrets? I loved Alfâdio. With Philippe it's forever. That's my life. And a life is yours to keep, not to trade or liquidate.

I've made my arrangements: we'll be buried side by side. It's a certainty, we'll die at the same time. Neither of us will survive the other. The same vitality flows through my brain and that eye. It's a question of circuitry, Madame Corre: soon someone will hit the switch and, like two twin lamps turning off, our love-lit hearts will stop beating.

You know what Romain Gary said? "Living is a prayer that can only be answered by the love of a woman." Sure, but will love save us from the world's fury? Maybe so, maybe not. In the meantime, everyone pushes their own barrel up the mountain, like the guy Camus talked about, that Greek condemned to his task forever. It's an untold pleasure pushing mine: not void but also not heavy to lift; invigorating and full of love. I assure you, Madame Corre, it's nothing tedious, the task of love.

I'm not asking you for anything, good people passing by. Not a helping hand or even compassion. I just want you to imagine we're happy like this.

YOUR SORROW IS COMING to an end, Madame Corre. You're going to return to Conakry, find that seven-year-old boy the world's fury tore from you on your 30th birthday, maybe the best time of life. You're going to hold him, tour the islands, stuff yourself with palm wine and bourakhé, and, maybe, once and for all, rekindle your love for the balafons and niâmou.

Seeing him will relieve you of everything else. I envy you: you have the benefit of a consolation prize. If I were bold enough, I'd get on the same plane and smash down the banco wall of that monastery, that old leper colony, and throw myself into the Abbot François' arms: "Come out from your prayers, Uncle Abbot! Be the father I never had!" But Uncle Abbot won't answer me. Uncle Abbot wants nothing to do with me. And there's nothing I can do about that. It doesn't exactly make me spring into action, being face-to-face with my past.

Over there, besides my daughter, Raye, and Yâyé Bamby, there's no one left for me to throw my arms around. I'll pass on that. You go so we can both reclaim what's ours: a memory for our breathing loved ones, a tomb for our dead. See your son, see my daughter, bless them! Let us bloom again. So our life can be a wound, a swift kick to those bastards' balls!

Let's live on, and beget more life—that's how we'll get our revenge!

I'll feel it from here when you hold your son. My vibration will be the same as if I were holding close every member of my family I never knew.

You here and him over there! How could I make that connection? I hadn't considered it when you first said his name. It took some time for him to come out of limbo, for his face to clarify in my head. Makhalé always sat him twenty-odd feet from everyone else and that woman who'd come looking for him every Friday at 11 PM would speak in a weak voice. Except one time when it looked like she was scolding him because he was slow to get up and when I thought I heard "Jean-André" or something like that. I didn't think that sometime in the future those simple words would be shrouded with the importance they have today.

To be honest, I felt guilty for turning you away that morning when, overwhelmed with tears, you planted your foot inside my door. So I sent an email to my daughter. And in the end it worked out. The miracle is about to happen. You're going to go to Conakry. You're going to see your son again. I'm picturing the scene from here... You're going to hold him close in silence. No need to shout in moments like that, no need for big gestures. In moments like that, the heart does the talking, not the mouth. It's a look that caresses, not anyone's hand. It'll be like Néné Biro and I in Sâré-Kali: involuntary sounds, mumbling, little hints, silence, long stretches of quiet joined with sighs. You'll come back whole, fully back to life. You'll come back Suzanne Farjanel. No stage makeup, no dragons. You're not the deplorable Madame Corre everyone used to laugh at anymore. The baker will stop giving you the eye, the florist won't whisper as you leave. Prospero won't call you Crotchety Anne. The opposite, he'll spoil you with his Latin-lover smile, his divine waffles, and kind words.

It's time to heal, Madame Corre, time to bloom again. Forget! Let Guinea stop being a nightmare, let it become your fountain of youth. Come back to us new, as if the time machine landed on your 18th birthday.

I'm sorry I didn't know that young and lively woman in Bôry Diallo's arms on her way to Guinea, agile and pure like a morning flower. The young woman who was always laughing, generous, a delight to live with—nothing like the one I know. Obviously, you hadn't inflicted that awful bun on yourself yet, that effacing name of "Mathilde Corre," those shapeless green dresses. You had everything to yourself: fashionable clothes, your hair in flowers, the face of an actress. I can't wait to move that neglected wife aside, that disgruntled woman, to tear off that scarecrow, so you can see exactly how you are beneath it all. A dreamer, sensitive, devilishly romantic!

Back then, you didn't just listen to Pink Floyd and race off to Kathmandu to smoke a joint. You talked about Reich and Marcuse, Foucault and Althusser, and you did it over some kir. We drive ourselves crazy to be likeable, passionate, kind. You'd think we were on earth expressly to live with others, to exchange and become more like them. Back then, all the girls seemed delirious. It was the era of long hair and short skirts. You spent your days at the movies, on café patios and at surprise parties.

A girl in the wind was a babe in that era! A completely crazy era: every season was spring. Everywhere it was party, love, and freedom. Your youth bloomed between trips with friends, concerts, and libraries. You were having a great time with your boyfriends to the rhythm of the day's music. For a change, you'd lock yourself in your room and listen to classical music. Opera aside, you melted for Brel, Montand, for Mouloudji. Like everyone, you praised the work of Kerouac, Jack London, and Boris Vian. But they never kept you from spending long hours in the barn to savor Stendhal, Chateaubriand, and Proust.

There you have it. Now you have a place in my tiny humanity between Raye and Mariam, in the warmest corner of my heart. I was careful not to hold back tears the day I found out she'd passed. She was worth those tears, they fell for a good cause. Mariam dead! My own Mariam, victim like so many others of brutal life in Conakry. I thought of you as I understood the tragedy: "Oh, my God! Please don't let that happen to Madame Corre! Please let her live on for years to come!" It's not just our lives, you see, it's our souls that have been pulled together. Sometimes you give me the shivers, positive shivers— you who are so negative.

Curious. Lately I've been comparing you to my mother. Just like that, by instinct. You're from the same generation— one age group above me. You must have listened to the same music, seen the same movies, danced the same steps. For the first time, young people were vibrating with the same feeling beyond languages and worship. Sometimes I miss the romanticism of that era I never knew. Abrasive and hurried, my own is cruelly short on melancholy.

It's actually your excessive melancholy that led you to where you are. You thought too much, loved too much, dreamed too much. Those are costly things. For a young twenty-seven-year-old in love! The "brutal adventure" brought to incandescence. But you're going to be able to breathe, you'll be able to relax. All the blows are through—you won't have any others. All you have to do is heal the ones you've taken. That's what I was thinking about the other day when we met on the square.

Right away, you'd pointed out the homeless crowd, who were perfectly performing a scene from *Ubu Roi*.

"I've never seen a Black man with them!"

You said it with a feeling of frustration—as if you'd been denied ice cream or a ball—that irritated me.

"What do you want? Should they put on the same scene for you as the day I shook hearing Alfâdio, the one where Pavlov took out his pistol?"

"Oh no, Countess, that would be an atrocity. By the way, did you ever see him again, your—?"

"No! Please, Madame Corre!"

I resumed my monologue so as not to hand you your little doughnut. It's like the stars in the sky, like the birds on the branches, water under the Pont de l'Alma: homeless folks are never the same. The ones you're talking about could already be in Rome, Aberdeen, Tulle, Honolulu. To hell with them! It's hard as hell to do right by that shrew, Madame Corre. And I moved heaven and earth to get her ready for this trip to Conakry—flights booked, hotel, food, everything.

You're talking about a beautiful eighteen-year-old from Dijon!

That afternoon, we found ourselves at the Vésuve to straighten out the details. I started by taking out a map of Paris to show you the travel agency's address.

"And don't worry, Madame Corre, everything's in order. Just enter your dates. I've got you at the Novotel. It's not the greatest hotel in the city, but it's the best location: on the beach, Loos Islands right there. It feels like every boat in the world is sailing right under your nose. You'd think you were off the coast of the Americas, a stone's throw from Barbados."

"That means I won't see my house again!"

"If you only knew, Madame Corre, how little the world over cared about your old house."

"That's because the world over never saw my old house. A blue house, a house in the form of a cruise ship. We didn't need to see the ships coming and going—we were the sailors."

"Your temper won't change my opinion. You better believe you're going to Conakry, to meet both our children and heal us forever from the demons of the past. You realize what our goal is? And you want to talk about your old house! They tear down the homes of dissenters! You're either assimilated or sold back to foreign embassies. Here, I've got your restaurant and cab vouchers. It's all paid for—don't let yourself get ripped off! And don't tell me about your old house again."

The next day, at our lunch at the Vésuve, you had the cheerful look of a kid who'd just been given an award.

"Wait, Countess, wait a minute," you said, stuffing your shaky hands in your purse. "It's in here somewhere. Here it is, Countess. Look at this: there's even a boarding pass. Leaving the 12th, next Wednesday—that's in three days—and coming back a month later. They can do that now, print boarding passes before you even get to the airport?"

I let you look at that precious thing all afternoon. Then I took you to dinner at the Bouillon Racine. We had celebrating to do.

We had no date planned for the next day. You had to go shopping. Still, I called around 1 PM.

"Come meet me on the square."

"I'm getting ready to go to Galeries Lafayette. I told you that yesterday—I have to find a suitcase, try on clothes, buy gifts."

"Meet me first. I have something for you."

I'd just gotten an email from my daughter:

Dear Maman,

A week ago now, our dear Dr. Diallo barricaded himself in a room. No matter how hard we knocked, he wouldn't open up for anyone—not even Aïssatour Barry. The four of us tried to break in night and day with no success. And this morning an odd voice came to us through the door. "I don't want to see anyone…

What does this woman from Paris want from me? What could we possibly have to say to each other?" *Then he belted two or three sentences, the ones you used to hear at the Oxygène... "You the pure ones, you the impure, no more mass, no one will be saved!"* *It went on for five or ten minutes, then there was a detonation. It's happening just this afternoon, the burial. Poor Dr. Diallo—he was only fifty years old.*

When I saw you coming, I felt the power of the bomb I held in my hands.

"Let's make this quick, Countess, I'm in a hurry. I've already got my suitcase and I'm running to get clothes and presents. Can't wait for Wednesday! I'm so anxious to see my son."

"Your son—let's take your mind off him, Madame Corre," I said, handing you the message. "Come on, I'll buy you a Sancerre at the Vésuve."

AUTHOR BIOGRAPHY

A winner of some of France's most prestigious awards, including the Prix Renaudot and the Grand Prix de la francophonie, Guinean-born author Tierno Monénembo most recently received the 2022 Baobab Prize for Best African/Diasporic Work of Literature for his novel, *Saharienne Indigo* (translation title, *The Lives and Deaths of Véronique Bangoura*). A refugee from Guinea during the regime of dictator Ahmed Sékou Touré, Monénembo migrated to France to earn a PhD in Biochemisty. Recently, his work on this novel has been recognized by Villa Albertine, and short-listed for the 2025 award for excellence in translation. Monénembo migrated to France to earn a PhD in Biochemisty. He has lived in Senegal, Morocco, Algeria, the US, and has returned to his native country where he lives in the capital, Conakry. His 14-work oeuvre centers on an enduring, often scarred sense of home in exile.

TRANSLATOR BIOGRAPHY

Holding fellowships in fiction and translation, Ryan Chamberlain earned an MFA in Creative Writing from the University of Arkansas, where he currently teaches French. Recently. ' work on this novel has been recognized by Villa Albert¹ short-listed for the 2025 award for excellence in tr⸍

PUBLISHER'S N⸍

Schaffner Press gratefully ack⸍
for their support of this v⸍
a grant to assist in its⸍